The Warrior and the Wandering Wizard

MICHAEL E. NOVAK
JOHN PAUL ADDIS

Dear Reader,

Thank you for your interest in our fantasy novel, the second of a trilogy, based on characters from the first but intended to be read on its own without need of reading The Way of the Wandering Wizard.

We would like to encourage you to take the time and post a review on the website from which you purchased the book. Your participation in this would be greatly appreciated.

We would love to hear comments and questions from you on our tale. Find us at:

thewayofthewanderingwizardseries.weebly.com

Michael E. Novak
John Paul Addis

DEDICATION

To our families and friends and all the St. Paul and St. Brendan students
who have taught us so much over the years.

Thank you.

ACKNOWLEDGMENTS

The authors would like to express appreciation for the contributions of the
many people who made this book possible. Our ex-boss Beth Burns, for her
editing input and encouragement…Aubryn Samaroo of Brown University,
for her detailed recommendations and assistance…John Kennedy Addis, for
his excellent cover design…and a very special thank you to the Reilly
family, who appear in this tale.

Prologue

Months earlier....

Late on a starless, moonless night three black-robed rogue wizards, closely followed by a small group of rat-like minions, approach a fetid swamp that conceals a hidden cemetery for one.

"Brother, beware of that plant. It will numb your senses if you touch its thorn."

"I know that. Do you take me for a fool?"

As the putrid smell of rotting vegetation assails his nostrils, he thinks frantically *why am I even here? I told them this would never work. This is mad folly that can only end in disaster. No one is looking. I could slip away and none would be the wiser.*

Sensing their brother's unease, the two stop and confront their hesitant collaborator. The taller of the two says, "Need I remind you that we must all remain resolute and put our fears of the unknown aside?" This is more of a statement than a question.

With a wild look, the other adds, "Focus on the unimaginable power that will be ours if we persevere."

Approaching the obdurate enchantment, the three raise their hands high above their heads and intone practiced, archaic words. This sixth consecutive night of ceremony is met with success. The spell shatters with the sound of broken glass.

"It-it... I don't believe it! The way has opened!"

"It was only a matter of time, brother."

The three warily approach a small mound of gnarled wood and spike-like weeds. One of the Black Robes observes, "It is as if nature itself obscures what we seek."

The leader of the grave defilers commands the rats, "Clear the tomb."

With claw and teeth the filthy beasts tear at the wood and spike-grass until a stone sarcophagus appears. The brothers approach and, with their combined strength, slide back the heavy stone lid. A thick, foul fog billows from the murky depths of the tomb. One of the Black Robes directs another, "Summon the first gift."

The tremulous Black Robe holds his quivering hands above the gaping cavity. Insects approach from all sides, slowly at first: shiny, green, spindly things, black beetles, huge clicking cockroaches, flying horrors with stingers. Their numbers increase to hundreds. Thousands. They fill the open tomb.

The wizards wait.

Small, wet, popping noises fill the night air. The writhing mound of the miniature horde collapses into itself and is absorbed by the one lying in the tomb.

"Summon the second gift."

Ancient words echo off the tombstone and mausoleum. Rats, mice, snakes of all sort appear, some carrying carrion of small fur animals in their dripping teeth and fangs. An eerie, clacking chittering fills the night air. Like lemmings of lore, the creatures fill the tomb, creating a sickening, squishing, splattering sound. The squirming heap collapses into itself and the thing inside the tomb assimilates its essence.

And stirs.

"Bring the final element."

The wizards are prepared. Four magnificent white horses are herded through the darkness, very much against their will. They are positioned around the tomb. The three dark-robed brothers slice the extraordinary beasts' shanks and blood drains into the tomb like a crimson fountain. As it flows, the terrified creatures' brilliant, white coats slowly fade to grey, then a deep, luxurious black.

The Dark Knight rises from his grotesque grave and faces the horses, ignoring the kneeling, bowing, stammering Black Wizards. The horses try desperately to escape his penetrating gaze but are held fast in demonic enchantment.

The apparition gently touches each steed's flaring nostrils and inhales the essence of the creatures. He steps before the largest stallion.

"I choose you," he rasps and kisses the horse on its glistening forehead.

One of the kneeling faints dead away.
The herald is risen.

Chapter 1

A hooded figure slips silently into a dilapidated barn. He takes stock of his surroundings and his eyes find his target. With measured steps he approaches the unsuspecting body lying on a bed of straw. He crouches, and in quick succession strikes pressure points on his victim's body, rendering it immobile. He then places one hand over the mouth of his prey, and with the other he searches and finds a dark blade. He leans very close, and whispers in the ear and the whisper enters the mind. *You are carrying this dark blade on you, Mikal Novastar from the great city of Addis, but the destiny of this blade is to be in you. Sleep, sleep…nevermore to rise.* Mikal feels the blade enter his throat just below the chin… *It is said that most dreams are not remembered, but that does not mean that they have not been dreamt.*

Mikal awakes with beads of perspiration dotting his forehead.

I cannot feel my arm. I must have slept on it.

Mikal stiffly rolls over the straw on the floor of the barn. He opens his white, swirling eyes and wonders how long he has slept.

Mikal tries to stand but instead crumbles to the ground. *My legs are numb, as well. This is not good.*

He senses Majam and links with his familiar's mind. The great white cat's senses become his own. He sees through Majam's eyes, hears with her ears, and he tastes fresh mouse.

"I do not think I will ever get used to that taste, my friend," he says on all fours facing the cat.

Majam conveys to Mikal that it is an acquired taste and would be surprised if he were to appreciate the subtle nuances of the delicacy.

Mikal finally rises fully and chuckles. He sees a ray of bright, early morning sunshine striking where his head had been. *There are advantages of being blind.*

He imagines Majam proudly displaying the recent mouse that she caught.

"Don't look so smug. With all the rodents that infest this barn, it must have been easy pickings."

Majam does not respond.

"I cannot believe I have been here over a week. This numbness in my legs and arm is most worrisome."

The door opens and Amadeus Whitestone, Mikal's current mentor in the ways of a White Wizard, enters.

"Good morning. I see you are a little unsteady on your feet. Here is your staff of light to lean upon."

Mikal thanks him and Whitestone continues, "My wife is preparing breakfast, after which there is a short journey we must undertake."

Mikal nods. "I do not know what I enjoy more: your wife's cooking or your tutoring."

Amadeus laughs lightly. "I have been truly impressed with how quickly you have adapted to your situation, but, then again, you have achieved The Effulgence, a truly remarkable accomplishment. You know also that it is a very dangerous spell and you are fortunate to be alive, even though you have lost your sight."

"Not quite all," Mikal responds. "I can still see somewhat in very bright light and I can see quite well though Majam's eyes."

"A truly remarkable creature indeed. But now, let us eat."

***

After the morning meal, they set off on their short journey.

Amadeus observes, "I see that you walk very well even when your cat Majam is not near to assist."

"You have to remember that Majam is a cat first and my familiar second. When something catches her eye, she is free to investigate, not that I could stop her. So I constantly try to anticipate what lies ahead and it becomes second nature. She seems to know when I do need her, though, and she is always but a thought away. I recognize that I am virtually blind and I cannot always rely on her as my crutch. I do have my staff of light and it also aids me with walking."

The Wizard Whitestone smiles. "I think that staff aids you in many ways."

The two continue in silence.

At length, Mikal stops and says, "Amadeus, this path we are following seems familiar to me. I know I agreed not to ask many questions, but does it not lead to the elemental ruins where field trips from the school are often held?"

"There is a field trip there today."

Mikal's heart leaps into his throat.

"My daughter…is there any chance…"

Amadeus nods slightly. "If all unfolds as planned. But, Mikal, I caution you. The visit will be brief and you must remain from view and follow my instructions explicitly. Do you understand?"

A wave of excitement and anticipation washes over Mikal.

"Oh yes, yes, certainly. And I thank you. You do not know what…"

"Do not thank me yet. Let us see how this all plays out."

Chapter 2

Before the two reach their destination, they are interrupted by the sound of trumpets. Four heavily leathered, armored riders approach. They carry long, glistening spears and are closely followed by a ruggedly constructed wagon creaking under the weight it endures. Six powerful horses strain at their task. Two more guards lead a second wagon that carries several large jars with crests blazoned upon them suggesting they contain fine wine. Two more menacing riders pass and glare contemptuously at the wizards.

Amadeus Whitestone quips, "It appears that someone will be celebrating tonight in the city of Addis. I doubt if we are invited."

Mikal responds grinning, "That is fortunate, for I am not comfortable at parties."

Amadeus chuckles. "I used to be quite the reveler, but, alas, no longer, I'm afraid. It takes far too long to recover at my age."

They eventually reach the outer wall of the element ruins. The structure had been massive and impressive at one time, but now is a crumbling ruin overrun by grass and weeds.

"Now, Mikal, follow me and watch your footing."

The two friends come across a narrow, well-traveled path and find Majam sitting patiently, licking her front paw. The great cat lifts her twitching, pink nose toward one of the many wildflowers flanking the path.

Mikal hesitates. "I smell jasmine and daffodils."

"You are correct, flowers are scattered all about. Your feline friend is here, as well."

"I know."

Amadeus and Mikal enter a small recess that is more or less intact. Amadeus closely examines the structure. He can make out flecks of worn, black and red paint. There are deep crevices in the wall, as if an ancient, powerful force had pounded the barrier over and over again in frustration. Minute fissures radiate in all directions like a barren valley's dry riverbeds.

"You must wait here, Mikal. Remain hidden, for the students would recognize you and ask awkward questions. If your presence were discovered by those who wish us ill, the school and the city itself could be threatened. I shall bring your daughter to you."

Master Whitestone weaves his way to the northern side of the ruins, followed by Majam, acting as Mikal's eyes.

He approaches a small group of students from the School of the Three Moons and catches the eye of the professor in charge. With a subtle signal the teacher acknowledges Master Whitestone.

Amadeus greets him formally and asks, "May I impose upon one of your students? I have found a worn inscription on the wall in one of the western rooms and need young eyes to read it for me."

The leader of the group nods. "I think Alison the Swift here would be happy to oblige."

Amadeus thanks his collaborator. "I'm sure this won't take long. Now, young lady, please follow me. What you are looking for is near at hand."

A bewildered Mairin, also known as Allison the Swift, responds, "And what exactly is it I'm looking for?"

***

"Father...Oh, Father!"

The young girl is nearly overcome with emotion. Her heart pounding wildly, her eyes wide with disbelief, tears of joy and relief streaming down her cheeks, she runs to and desperately embraces her parent. She buries her face deep in his chest and sobs quietly as Mikal strokes her fire-red hair and soothes her.

Finally able to speak, she reluctantly eases her embrace, afraid that he would be gone again if she were to let go completely, and manages to stutter, "I...I've missed you so much...and worried so long...and prayed so fervently that you be kept safe. There are so many rumors about you, some so fantastic I refuse to believe them."

She looks at Mikal's weathered face, much older than she

remembered.

"Oh, Father, your eyes have lost their color, they are all so white."

She raises a hand as if to touch them. "Do they hurt? Can you see at all? I have so many questions. I…"

"Hush. Hush, now. We have little time. I am fine… different… grown. I can only see in extreme bright light and even then not very well. But I do have my faithful cat Majam here, and through her eyes experience the world."

Mairin approaches the extraordinary animal, kneels, and strokes the luxurious, white fur on Majam's head.

"Father, she's beautiful."

"She thinks so, and I do, too." They laugh and Majam meows and tosses her head.

"He has written to me about you, but has not done you justice. I know you have protected him well. I thank you for that, and I am forever in your debt, oh faithful feline."

Majam bows slightly and rubs up against Mairin.

"Is anyone else with you? Talon the half-elf?"

"No…no one else," Mikal answers. "I hope he will join me in the near future, but I have no guarantee."

He reaches down and gently helps Mairin to her feet. "Now tell me how you have fared, my daughter."

"School is crazy this year, Father. We know there are wild things happening. The worst is, no one knows for sure what's real and what isn't. The rumors abound. Talk of dark assassins and impending war and some say the headmaster has gone loony. We know the school is being watched for our own protection, but we don't like it. On the more mundane side, my classes are going well. I enjoy learning new spells and am starting to master more and more of them. I am surprised, though, that they let us out on this field trip. It's the first one in some time. But father, tell me again that all is well with you."

"I miss your mother and agonize over you. I too have been learning new spells. I guess one is never too old to learn. The gentleman who led you here… I have been spending time with and learning from him. I think, he will soon ask me to do something for him in return.

"My daughter, you have grown so much in such a short time. Your mannerisms remind me of your mother, but your red hair and green eyes you received from your grandmother. You seem to represent all of the family so well. I pray for your future." Mikal's eyes begin to mist.

"Father, the white streak in your hair adds an air of mystery about you. Just think; my father...a man of mystery! Who would have ever thought it? But you must tell me more about your adventures."

A high-pitched, urgent whistling pierces the air and they both start.

Mikal asks, "What on earth is that irksome sound?"

"That's the warning signal. I must return at once to the group. I'm sorry but I have no choice. I don't want to go, but I must."

Mikal nods. "I understand. I love you. Hurry. Be careful."

The wizard kisses his daughter lightly on her forehead and watches her run from the ancient room.

He asks his cat Majam to follow at a distance and allow him the use of her senses. With his cat leading the way, Mikal discretely follows his daughter through twists and turns, almost tripping over some loose rubble on the ground. He rights himself and is about to leave the cover of the ancient ruins when Master Whitestone appears in front of him.

"I'm sorry, my friend, but you know you must not go out there. I don't believe your daughter or you are in any immediate danger, but quickly; we must return the way we came."

The two tread through the old ruins and eventually emerge into sunlight. They travel the wildflower path and descend a small hill.

Mikal longingly stares back over his shoulder, a look of unease and concern wrinkling his brow. Amadeus assures him that all is well. Shortly the two White Wizards enter a clearing hidden in a small grove. A large boulder obscures them from the road.

Exasperated, Mikal asks, "What is the purpose of all this?"

"We await our informant and master spy."

As if on cue, Mikal hears someone approaching, whistling an unusual tune. When the sound is at its peak, Amadeus joins in the melody. The whistling stops, and through Majam's eyes, Mikal watches a man dressed in light-colored clothes and a fashionable hood cautiously peer around the bolder. Satisfied, he approaches and bows slightly to Amadeus, all the while eyeing Mikal suspiciously.

The older wizard waves his hand impatiently.

"This is Melchior Brightstar, and you have my word that he can be trusted beyond reproach with anything you have to say. What have you learned?"

The informant explains, "A man who claimed he shares your last name of Whitestone was attacked and slightly wounded by a would-be assassin on the outskirts of the ruins. The inept perpetrator was quickly apprehended and is in custody. The one who calls himself Whitestone is being administered to at the Temple, and the students, who saw none of this, have returned to their school. I assure you none of them were harmed in any way."

Amadeus thanks the man and turns to Melchior. "We must be on our way."

The two wizards make quick time and talk little.

***

Eventually, they arrive at Master Whitestone's farm. Amadeus slows his gait and says, "The man who was attacked introduced himself to me months ago, claiming he was some distant relative. I had no reason to believe him and I told him I know of no family connection and that the name could prove problematic for him. Nevertheless, he introduced himself to many people using the name. I think he thought it could open doors for him or bring him prestige. Again, I warned him that this was not wise and if his name was in truth Whitestone, it would be better if he didn't declare it everywhere. He laughed at me.

"I don't think he realizes that the dark assassins associate my name with White Wizardry and have spies everywhere. Fortunately, there are many charms and protective spells about my farm and it would be extremely difficult for anyone to spy on us while we are here."

The old wizard notices a look of deep concern and consternation on Mikal's face. "My dear friend, do not worry so. Know that your daughter is safe. You are fortunate that no one saw you, or that might not be the case."

Mikal nods and says, "I thank you for allowing me to meet with my daughter."

Amadeus responds, "I'm sorry you could not have stayed longer with her. Now please come into my house. There is one last thing for us to do."

When they enter the well-built farmhouse, Mrs. Whitestone is nowhere to be found.

"Mikal, please sit and try to relax."

Amadeus places his left hand over Mikal's forehead and eyes, the other on his friend's heart. The White Wizard recites a few words, and then repeats them. Mikal feels familiar, mystical energy enter him and, with his mind's eye, he starts to see images. Like a book being opened before him, but not quite a book. He starts to make out an impression of someone. There are words written he can almost read. Then they are gone, and other images take their place. Again, Mikal is about to understand what it is he sees but that vision fades and another appears. The process speeds up as more and more images flash through his mind and are gone before Mikal can distinguish anything clearly. Then the book that is not a book closes.

Amadeus steps back. Mikal looks up at him and asks, "What is it I saw? It was too fast. I do not remember any of it plainly."

Master Whitestone smiles. "You have received secretive information about every White Wizard in the land."

Mikal shakes his head. "Something must be wrong. I saw but I can recall none of it."

Amadeus nods. "That is not entirely true. You should remember one impression."

Mikal closes his eyes. "Yes. I do remember something: your picture, information about you, your preferences of agricultural techniques, your areas of expertise. How do I know these things?"

Whitestone explains, "The truth is, the mind remembers everything it has ever experienced. The art is to bring what your mind contains to the surface. I have fixed esoteric knowledge deep in your sub-conscience. What you saw, you now know. This information will not rise to your consciousness until you are in the presence of another White Wizard. You then will know who they are as they will know who you are. The spell connects all of us. In exceptional circumstances, if one of us needs assistance, we are all joined. We are then able to share some of our magic power with our brethren. But I warn you, only use this in extreme circumstances. You can put all of us at risk. With this last spell, I have nothing further to pass along to you. Your training is complete and I welcome you fully into the ranks of the White Wizards."

Mikal stands. He places his hands upon Amadeus Whitestone's shoulders.

"I thank you and I am honored by the gifts you share with me."

"Now, Mikal, tell me what you know of the Witches of Endorr."

Chapter 3

"What do you know of the Witches of Endorr? Well, I'm waiting, you have shown promise, and you have requested more challenging tasks to prove that you are worthy of advancement. Tell me, Damien."

Somewhere in a red tower just outside the walls of the dark city of Umbra, behind a large ornate desk, sits a red-robed Grand Master Wizard. He is flanked by two impressive, scarlet cardinals. They to seem to be scrutinizing the two eager, young men.

"Master Bloodhue, I know they are a group of females that split from the Black Robes years ago. They have been looking to prove themselves. They claim to foretell the future, soothsayers and such. Oh, they are supposed to be very beautiful, and mesmerize men. I suspect there are potions and enchantments at work there. I believe they are a coven of women trying to achieve fortune and fame. Why do we concern ourselves with that ilk?"

Path Bloodhue stares at the young man. "They claim to have a crucial prophecy that will affect all the land and will…"

"And you believe them?" Damien interrupts.

Master Bloodhue stands, hands on desk. "Do not interrupt me again, boy, or you will be assigned back to an acolyte this very day." He calms a bit. "The witches would not make this bold statement if there were not some truth to it. It would be the ruin of them if it was proved false. They have sent out invitations to select groups, cities, and nobility. Exactly how significant it is, I intend to find out."

Damien bows. "I apologize. I will leave and hear their prophecy."

Path sits back down and laughs. "You would not last a minute under their alluring gaze. I'm willing to bet within an hour of their presence you would renounce yourself as a Red Wizard and join them as one of their many male subordinates. You will not enter their main tent. No, you are to escort Master Gallium. He will record everything that is said."

Damien responds, "I apologize again, but Master Gallium is very old and will need assistance."

"Then you will assist him in every way. Besides, his old age is a natural resistance to the female charms." Path chuckles. "Yes, he will do just fine. But, my eager young associate, this will be Master Gallium's last assignment. He has outlived his usefulness and his old age and arrogance have bothered me once too often. You are to make sure he has recorded everything. You may even ask him what this prophecy is, before you eliminate him."

An eager smile slowly spreads across Damien's face. "I shall burn him slowly. He will be forced to endure much pain."

Master Bloodhue shakes his head and pounds his fist emphatically on the desk top. "No! You will not. He is still a Master Red Robe. The kill should be swift and painless. Then burn his remains and leave no trace." He stands. "Wait here."

Path turns to the second young man who stands before him and takes a moment to scrutinize this candidate. He wears his long, dark hair held back with a red tie with a red feather attached to it. Master Bloodhue knows this is in style but he does not like it. The young man is clean-shaven almost to a fault and he relishes a sharp blade. Aden Ferrum's dark eyes stare down, but not quite to the floor. Path wonders *a sign of respect or insolence?*

The clean-shaven one's leather jerkin is expensive and well maintained. Its short sleeves reveal well defined muscles. His wrist braces are finely polished and made of steel with the flame symbol intricately carved upon them. On his right hand he sports a gold ring enhanced with an expensive ruby. His leather, knee-high boots are worn but well maintained and have steel shin reinforcements. What impresses Path Bloodhue the most, however, is that he carries his short flame staff just above the floor. Even though it is just over three feet long and made of iron, it weighs well over twenty pounds. This weapon is a young Red Wizard's lifeline. A talented wizard can create a myriad of weapons with this short flame staff.

"Aden Ferrum, tell me what you know about White Wizards?"

Aden's eyes lift to meet Path's. He shrugs his shoulders and scoffs,

"A colored robe, few in numbers with little power."

Master Bloodhue asks, "How do you know this?"

Aden replies, "It is what I've heard."

Path nods his head. "Yes, this is what most believe but I am not so convinced. There are no facts or evidence to back up your claim. In fact, recently there was an incident: an impressive display of power achieved by what I believe was a White Wizard. Also, how do we know they are few in number? Maybe they are many but well hidden. I do not like not knowing who my opponents are and their capabilities. This is where you come in, Aden. I have knowledge of that White Wizard. As soon as I can locate him, you are to track him and uncover everything about him."

"Then can I kill him?"

"No, not without my specific instructions. You are to join him. Gain his trust, watch and study him carefully."

"This is below my station, to work with a lesser color."

Master Bloodhue commands, "You are to follow my orders without question. You will travel with him using any guise you choose. I don't care if you become a servant or even a slave. But you will gain his trust and learn from him. I will send contacts to you so you can pass on relevant information. But you are not to harm him unless his way crosses my path. Do you understand?"

Aden Ferrum clenches his fist but bows his head. "Your will is my will. It shall be done."

"Excellent. His name is Mikal Novastar from the city of Addis. He may be traveling under the alias Melchior Brightstar. Nevertheless, my associates are searching for him as we speak and I am confident we will soon have his location. So prepare yourselves. These will be challenging tasks. Make sure that you are up to them and do not fail me. Now both of you leave."

***

"The Witches of Endorr? Well, Amadeus, if I remember my lore, a little more than ten years ago a group of female wizards, colored and non-colored robes alike, separated from their former consortia to form, oh, I don't know, a sisterhood of a sort. If I remember correctly, they felt restricted in their prior positions so they began to carve out their own separate destinies. Quite impressive really. I believe they specialize in potions and herbal remedies. I understand they can foretell the future, a claim used far too often in my opinion. Of course, there are also rumors of their beauty and, if they so desire, they can bewitch any man. A few years ago they camped at the Valley of Endorr. No one seemed to discredit their claim, so there they remain. Why do you ask?"

"Mikal, they sent out a multitude of couriers with a curious invitation. They asked that all their contacts send a representative to their Valley. Recently they received an ominous prophecy that they allege will affect the whole land. It is important for everyone to hear it."

"I wonder," Mikal asks, "What is their payment for this revelation?"

"That is also very interesting. All payments will vary and be collected upon arrival. You seem doubtful of their claim, my friend."

"Again, too often I have heard too many profess the gift of prophecy, but few have actually been blessed with it."

"I understand your hesitation but I believe we cannot ignore the summons. I would like to send you as the White Robes' representative."

Mikal questions, "Would that not divulge our identity?"

"I don't think so. There are special arrangements in place for secrecy. There is one contact for each group that wants to, how shall I say this, remain hidden. Our special password is 'Aurum'. So I'm asking you. Are you willing to go to the Valley of Endorr?"

"Are you sending me because you believe my blindness will protect me from their charms?" Mikal asks, with a twinkle in his white eyes.

"Perhaps, but I also think you will be a fine representative of our assemblage."

"But I was hoping to meet up with Talon."

"Yes, I know. If all goes well, you will be back in time to do so. Travel to the town of Ulna and leave a message there for him. I estimate it will take you four days to travel to the Valley. The revealing of the prophecy is in five, so you should have sufficient time. If you desire, upon your return, send a message from the town and I will meet you there. Is this acceptable?"

"If you ask, Master Whitestone, how can I refuse? I will leave in the morning."

Chapter 4

Mikal and his cat Majam look up to the sky. It is overcast and the clouds are moving by rapidly, but Mikal does not believe it is going to rain. He makes good time because he knows where he is going, yet remembers how tentative he was when he first walked this path.

After some time, the woods start to thicken. Late in the day, he eventually approaches the small settlement of Ulna. A resident notices Mikal and gives him a nod and a smile then continues on his way. Mikal is happy to see a light burning in the main house. He knocks and enters the building. Sitting at a heavy, wooden table are William the Blue and other residents of the town of Ulna. William looks up and smiles.

"Traveler Mikal, you are just in time for dinner! Welcome."

Mikal can smell the various foods about to be served. Majam jumps into Mikal's arms. Through her eyes, he finds a vacant seat. He thanks his host and starts to eat, realizing how hungry he has become.

He listens to conversations about daily chores and personal responsibilities and answers many questions about his travels. The main door opens and in walks Jocomund the Squirrel Master with two small rabbits that he offers to the cook. The cook accepts them but gives a questioning look of 'what am I supposed to do with these two small cottontails?'.

Jocomund sits and starts in on his meal and only then does he notice Mikal. He gives him a heartfelt greeting. After the meal, tomorrow's chores are discussed, and then more than a few residents ask Mikal for a story. He respectfully declines, claiming fatigue. Mikal is offered a bed in the main building and gladly accepts. He and Majam spend a restful night.

***

Early the next morning, most have gone their own way. Mikal, with Majam by his side, continues his journey to the Valley of Endorr. Majam meows and looks to her right. Through her eyes, Mikal sees Jocomund walking in the forest, pacing them.

"Jocomund, welcome. Come walk with us. Any news about the hermit?"

"No, I have not seen him for a number of days."

The three stop and, obscured by the woods, they glimpse a very shaggy animal walking oddly on all fours, producing peculiar noises. One moment it sounds like a bird of prey, next a small rodent. The creature suddenly stops, turns on its spine, and lays there with its four legs pointing straight to the sky. It holds this position for a surprisingly long, uncomfortable time. Then, unexpectedly, it jumps up on its hind legs and roars like a deranged bear, scattering small rodents and birds. It then returns to all fours and continues toward them with an unorthodox gait. Mikal can make out something: a piece of cloth tied around the creature's eyes.

"Jocomund, it looks like it is blindfolded."

Majam meows and runs through the woods straight at the furry creature.

Mikal asks, "Is that the hermit? The Mad Plunket?"

Not surprisingly, the hairy creature runs face-first into a tree. It raises its left hand and partially lifts up the blindfold and sneaks a peek, seeking a safer route. Majam pulls up and sits before the hermit and produces a greeting mew. The hairy creature falls to the ground and mimics the cat's meow. Mikal and Jocomund approach the two. Mikal notices at least two small birds fly into the hermit's thick, matted hair. The wizard chuckles. Unfortunately, he has seen this before.

Still blindfolded, the hermit rises, starts to sniff Jocomund, and asks, "Is that you, Squirrel Boy?"

"Yes, it is, sir. Are you okay?"

"I do not know. I have been feeling very strange, even for me. There are bizarre, precarious doin's in this land."

He turns to Mikal and removes his blindfold. His bushy eyebrows lower, attempting to blink, but his eyes are already closed. He puts his face uncomfortably close to Mikal's chest then his equally hairy nose slowly rises to Mikal's chin. Mikal feels what he hopes is a slight mystic shock.

The hermit asks, "Is that you, Mikal Novastar? Beware! The first menace has risen! Beware!" He lifts his left leg and shakes it all about.

"Know that the one you choose must lose before he has a chance to win."

A rancid burp fouls the air. "Or is that you, Melchior Brightstar?"

The hairy one waves his right arm in a large circle and emits a strange, high-pitched sound.

"The real danger is yet to awake. You cannot win against the evil, ebony one but I know you will try. Danger for all! You're from the city of Addis, are you not? If you lose, I will weep for you and for everyone. Will anyone weep for me?"

He backs away, points his head high, and howls. He suddenly stops and falls to the ground while his whole body twitches about franticly. The three can only stare in stunned amazement.

Jocomund says, "This is just how he looked just before he told me to collect my friends and wait in the tree for the sound of the pipes before helping you."

Ultimately, the Mad Plunket stops moving. He rolls over on his side and falls fast asleep.

Jocomund approaches the hermit, gently pokes him, and asks again, "Are you okay?"

"Go, leave me be," the hermit groggily grumbles.

"But, sir, you are in the middle of a forest!"

"So… can you think of a better place to take a nap?"

Jocomund whispers, "I will weep for you."

***

Mikal makes tea and waits with Jocomund. Just before noon, the hairy hermit sits up and looks around.

He asks, "What are you doing here?"

He then quickly stands and haphazardly skips off into the woods. Mikal and Jocomund cannot help but chuckle.

"Well, Jocomund, we best be on our way."

The three walk and talk for the next hour or so. At length, the Squirrel Master wishes Mikal and Majam good luck and takes a different path and fades from view.

Chapter 5

The warrior rides his well experienced mount. His leather armor is worn, but it fits well. His leather boots are not new and a dented shield is strapped to his back and a long sword to his side. His head bobbles along with the horse's stride. He looks neither to one side nor the other. A second rider, dressed in fine clothes, wears multiple rings, one with a house crest engraved in it, follows the first. Next to him an older gentleman rides, taking in the many sites of the day. The well-dressed rider spots a tall, redheaded person standing by the side of the road. This man is holding a long walking staff. As the riders pass, one notices a distinct white streak of hair, which he finds odd. The man's eyes are downcast. The expensively dressed man quips, "I see some people know their place."

The trio continues down the road.

"Well, Majam, we must be getting closer. This is the second group we have seen today. We best be moving along…is something wrong?"

The large, white cat stands at attention and looks intently into the woods. Mikal enters the familiar's mind.

"What do you see, my friend?"

There are people hiding in the forest. I think they are afraid of us.

"I find it difficult to believe that anyone would fear us. Let us investigate."

Warily Mikal moves ahead.

"Come out. We will not harm you. In fact we are here to offer support. Is there anything we can do?

Guardedly, a middle-aged women stands tall but is still partially concealed by a maple tree.

Majam conveys that there are many more hidden. Mostly young.

"My name is Melchior Brightstar. Is there anything that I can do for you?"

Mikal tentatively moves closer. The woman stares uneasily at

Mikal, unsure of what to do.

"Be not afraid. What is your name?"

"Beecher," she says weakly, avoiding Mikal's gaze.

Mikal can finally make out some of her features. She looks ragged. Heavy, deep lines are etched under her eyes, which are wide and dart everywhere. A young female child appears and hugs her just below the waist. The girl also looks anxious, and appears that she has not slept for days.

"Lady Beecher, I passed a stream a short distance from here. Let us go and drink from it. I shall share what food I have."

Mikal does not know why, but adds, "No harm will come to you or your company. Please, follow me."

Slowly, one by one, a number of people appear and warily follow Mikal. He strides purposefully toward the small stream. The group tries to keep pace. Eventually, they surround Mikal and look toward him as if awaiting further instructions.

"Please, drink."

They do not. Mikal pauses, bends down, cups his hands, and drinks from the babbling creek. Gradually, the fearful group follows Mikal's example and drinks its fill.   Mikal then picks some berries and offers them to the group, but none partake. Mikal eats the fruit and expresses how flavorsome and delicious they are. Hesitantly, they eat what is offered them. Mikal notes that none pick the berries from the tree and questions, "Are you that fearful?"

One of the older women steps into an opening in the canopy where bright sunlight shines directly upon her. Even without the help of Majam's site, Mikal can discern the woman's outline. Then a curious thing happens. The whites of Mikal's eyes start to swirl. He looks closer at the woman and perceives a dim, dusty mist inside her.

"I wonder... am I actually *seeing* fear?"

He looks over his charges. Most are hidden in shade, but when he focuses on one of them and concentrates, he can still sense the dusty cloud inside.

"Lady Beecher, what has happened here? When is the last time you have slept?"

"No one has slept for days. A few nights ago the alarm sounded in our village. We snatched up the children and hid. Then a feeling of great dread overcame us and we ran. We do not know what happened, but we fear we can never go back."

A young boy steps forth.

"I know what happened. My cousin told me. He's older than me. The men in the village felt a trouble. They were supposed to go out and face it, but only one did: Thorren, our strongest woodsman. He had his double-bladed ax with him. He stood in the main road, my cousin said. Then this large, shiny, black stallion showed up. On it, he said, a nasty, armored man sat in the saddle. The man glowed black, not white, my cousin said. Thorren never raised his ax, but fell to the ground. His chest was torn open, my cousin said. Something came out of it. He didn't know what it was. He then told me his eyes hurt and he didn't feel very good. He fell to the ground, too. I yelled at him to run, but he didn't move. I shoved him, but he didn't move. So I ran and caught up with the others." The child ends his tale with tears in his eyes in a quivering, small voice.

Mikal shakes his head and stands before them.

"We will stay here for the night. All of you must sleep. The sun is setting and I will do all I can to protect you."

Mikal starts to collect wood for a fire but only a few help and even those bring very little.

"Please, sit in a circle around the fire and watch."

They comply, but are ill at ease. Mikal steps out from the ring. He lowers his staff of light to the ground and, after uttering a few arcane words, the staff starts to glow with a soothing, white light. He begins to walk around in a circle dragging the staff, which leaves a phosphorus line behind. When he completes the circumference, the group finds itself surrounded by a soft, white luminosity. Mikal brews a seductive tea in a kettle over the fire and has everyone partake. He then tells a simple, entertaining story using a soothing, hypnotic voice. He instructs everyone to clasp each other's hands and to trust him and one another. *They must overcome their dread.* He casts a sleep spell over the group. The last thing they hear is, "Let not your hearts be troubled.

No harm will come to you this night. Sleep well."

***

Mikal and Majam stand guard. His charges all seem to be resting peacefully and breathing evenly. Somewhat late in the night, Majam becomes alert and meows quietly. Mikal easily enters her mind

"What is it, my feline friend?"

Mikal focuses on an obscure movement in the woods. Majam lets Mikal know that the whiff of odor she has detected is familiar. She had smelled it before in the city of Stonegrove.

It's a wererat. I don't like them. They are foul

The blind wizard shudders. "They are also very dangerous."

A new thought enters Mikal's mind. He stands tall and lowers his staff near the flame. For a blink of time, the light of the fire ceases, but not the flame or the heat it radiates.

Mikal, speaking to his now black cat, expounds, "I believe I have captured light from the flame. Now I will attempt to shape it into a long, jagged shard. Look to my staff. The luminosity surrounds it. Majam, be my eyes, help guide my aim."

The cat conveys to the wizard to wait until the beast's red eyes appear and to be patient. With his cat's senses, Mikal looks to where the wererat is skulking. Two crimson orbs do materialize. Mikal instantly releases the rigid, light spike from the staff. It races unerringly toward its target. A chilling scream and a brilliant burst of light assures Mikal that he has scored a hit. The lurking creature reveals its location. It is severely wounded and staggers away into the deep woods.

"We are fortunate that the sleep spell is not easily broken by sound and that all seem unaware of what just happen."

Majam hisses. *I do not sense any others, but I will stand guard for the rest of the night.*

***

Come the dawn, the villagers sluggishly awake. They appear refreshed, though somewhat confused. Mikal does not detect the gray mist of fear he sensed earlier.

One of the villagers looks to Mikal and asks, "What will become of us? Where can we go? We can't go back."

"Are any of you familiar of the city of Stonegrove?"

The old man of the group nods.

"I was there when I was young."

"Good. The city is not far from here." Pointing east, Mikal instructs, "Proceed to the Phalanges River and follow it downstream. It will lead you to the city. I shall write a letter for you to present to the Lady Lizabetha Burnshire. Here, take your fill of these berries and drink from the stream. With any luck, you might find help along the way."

Lady Beecher approaches

"We've lost so much."

"I empathize with you. I have lost my wife and I know the pain."

"You have no one, then?"

"I have a daughter."

The woman nods

"She is fortunate to have you as her father. We must take care of the children. I now believe that we can find the city. I thank you, Melchior Brightstar. We all thank you."

Majam emits a wistful meow. This time the children approach her unafraid and pet her affectionately. In doing so, they feel better as they embark upon their new journey.

Chapter 6

In time, Mikal enters the Valley of Endorr. He notices two paths to the valley below. He chooses the one less traveled. It is midmorning and riders pass him by, carrying banners and pennants of the houses to which they owe allegiance. Some are more colorful than others. Mikal approaches the main camp and starts toward a large, white tent.

It seems to me that everyone is trying to outdo everyone else. This appears to be more of a festival then a serious prophecy.

A guard strides toward Mikal.

"Get out of the road, fool. These are important people."

Mikal turns and the guard sees his white eyes.

"Are you a beggar? Turn around and leave. You don't belong here."

Mikal, holding his staff of light in his left hand, cradles his cat Majam in his right.

"I am not a beggar, but what do you have against them? I have been invited to attend the gathering."

A second guard approaches, riding a horse.

"What goes on here?"

"This man claims he has received an invitation, but look at him."

The man on horseback asks, "Sir, what is your name? Have you been given a password?"

"I am Melchior Brightstar. The word I was given is *Aurum*."

"*Aurum*, you say? You there, apologize to this man and take him as quickly as possible to the Captain of the Guard. Pass others by if necessary. Now hurry."

The soldier submissively bows and apologizes to Mikal.

"Please, sir, follow me."

The two approach the Captain of the Guard who stands in front of the grand, white tent. He has just admitted an older Red Wizard who was being assisted by a young Red Robe, who is denied entry.

"Sir, I present to you Melchior Brightstar. His credential is *Aurum*."

The Captain nods. He and Mikal enter the beautiful, spacious tent. Rows of seats spread out before them and lead to a natural-made, stone stage. Mikal notices only one or two representatives are allowed to enter behind them. Curiously, some seats have distinctive colorful fabrics shrouding them. The Captain of the Guard snaps his fingers and two young girls immediately appear.

"This is the man you have been expecting. Please escort him to his seat."

Mikal is surprised. One of the girls is holding and petting a squirrel in her arms.

"My name is Catherine and this is my friend Monica."

Monica offers a beautiful smile and asks, "What a magnificent cat...may we pet him?"

"Certainly. *She* will enjoy it. Her name is Majam."

Majam does enjoy it and purrs contentedly.

Before Mikal can ask, the girls beckon and tell him to follow. Mikal and Majam do so. They quickly walk left to a far corner of the tent, turn toward the front, pass all the seats, and walk up a few steps to where two chairs are waiting, parallel to the stage.

"We did not know how many of you would attend. Please be seated. May we get you some tea, perhaps?"

"No thank you," responds Mikal.

"If there's anything you need just let us know. We will not be far off. Goodbye, for now."

Mikal inspects the sheer fabric that he faces and is to his side; it is impressive. When he looks out toward the audience, everything is clear but looking back the other way, his seats are obscured. *A simple way to keep one's identity hidden*, he thinks.

Mikal observes, "Seeing that everyone's attention was on the stage when we entered, Majam, I believe no one in the audience is aware of our presence."

With the great cat on his lap, he senses a young girl standing off to the side. She looks like she has just entered adolescence. She gracefully walks toward Mikal. Her long, brown hair hides much of her face and her large brown eyes shine brightly.

"I knew you would come. Some questioned me but I had no doubt. It is important that you are here. I'm sorry, my name is Aurum. I thank you for coming."

Mikal responds, "My name is Melchior Brightstar and this is the cat Majam. If I remember correctly, your name means *shining dawn*."

"Of course, you are correct. It is said that when the first light of day touches the land, one sees most clearly. All my visions reveal themselves at dawn."

She absently curls a lock of dark hair with her finger.

"I believe you are known by other names as well."

Mikal only smiles.

Sensing his reluctance, she attempts a different approach.

"Sir, how long have you had this magnificent ca-"

The question is interrupted by applause from the audience. There had been a girl dancing, accompanied by enchanting music, but the dance and music has ended.

"Oh look, it's about to start! Sister Fluere has been chosen to speak for us. She is quite attractive and fluent."

Without a sound, Sister Fluere enters the stone stage. Her impossibly long, luxurious, glistening, black hair flows and moves with each step of her tall, lithe body. Her delicate, light blue dress clings to her, accentuating her female form. The shimmering fabric changes its hues and shades with every movement. Her feet lightly kiss the ground with each stride. She stops. Her exquisite, large, dark eyes catch Mikal's gaze for but a moment. She turns toward the audience and hesitates. There is utter silence. She has captured everyone's complete attention.

"I apologize, for this is neither the time nor place for enchantment or illusion."

She closes her eyes for a moment. Mikal notices that she is tall but maybe not as tall as she appeared at first glance. Her hair is very beautiful but maybe not as luxurious as it was moments ago.

"I thank you all for your presence. As you know, some of us have different talents. I believe some of your learned men have been receiving disturbing prophecies about the near future. We also have had these visions, but up to recently they have been incomplete and confusing. We have a young sister whose prescience is more detailed than any we have had before. Her first vision came months ago: three black-robed wizards found and, after six attempts, disentombed the Ebony Knight, the herald of an Ebony Wizard."

A man in a black-hooded robe stands and protests, "I don't believe this. We would never condone such a thing."

Sister Fluere nods. "I should have stated that they were rogue wizards."

"I still do not believe it! No Black Robe would take part in this seditious act."

Aurum turns to Mikal. "I am sorry. I feel like all this is happening because of me. When I was younger, my visions were rare and often pleasant but now these evil prophecies fill my waking moments. Excuse me, but I must now assist Sister Fluere."

Aurum stands and walks upon the stage and joins Fluere. The crowd is curious about this young girl.

"I am the one of whom my sister refers. Very recently I saw two of the three names of those who committed the sacrilege. There is a tall one called Judis and another named Kane. I think you know these names," she says, staring accusingly at the Black Robe Wizard.

"You still have no proof. These are but allegations from a child!"

"You would do well to believe us," insists Sister Fluere. "For the sake of all of you and all we hold dear. Our visions are authentic and accurate. The Dark Herald has risen and is spreading fear and evil across the land. His presence alone somehow feeds the sleeping Ebony Wizard. If you remember your lore, there are other signs and dire omens, like the overpopulation of rats."

There is a murmur from the crowd. Some nod their heads in agreement.

"The City of Stonegrove has experienced an overabundance of rats recently. Even more disturbing, they are led by wererats."

The whispers increase throughout the audience.

Aurum turns to Sister Fluere "It is here."

"There is another reason we have asked you here on this day, at this time."

Clamorous noise erupts from outside the great, white tent. Frantic commands can be heard. Sister Fluere attempts to reassure the crowd.

"Do not be alarmed. Recently, about this time of day, every so often a dark creature flies over our camp. I tell you, the Ebony Wizard was known to have an evil pet, no?"

There is raucous confusion as the tent's flap opens.

"Please, allow one guard to enter and give his report."

A well-armed soldier quickly strides to the front, bends to one knee, and starts to report to his masters.

He is soon interrupted. "No, tell us all what is happening."

The chagrined soldier stands and looks over the crowd,

"We saw a extremely large, raven-like, dark, foul abomination coming from the North. Sunlight was glistening off its black feathers. It circled around, an evil thing it was. We shot our arrows at it but it always soared just above them. It gave off a hideous screech, as if it were laughing at us. It sounded like, 'never, never'. More arrows we let loose, but they always fell just short. It eventually turned and flew back from whence it came. That is all I can tell you."

"We thank you. You may return to your post."

Heated discussion erupts among the assembly. One of the nobleman's scholars stands.

"If I remember correctly, this evil wizard was reputed to possess an extremely rare, ebony bird. It is said it produces foul ichor on its beak and claws and if it penetrates the skin, one becomes immobilized… then the bird and the wizard could do anything they desired to that person."

There is much discussion among the crowd. After a while a general consensus emerges. A middle-aged nobleman stands and with a strong voice quiets the audience.

"I think it's safe to say at the very least we must take these… visions seriously; they are too important to ignore. If they are true, what should we do?"

Sister Fluere explains, "The Ebony Knight must be stopped. His evil presence somehow feeds the Ebony Wizard."

Two knights stand. "We will confront this foul creature."

Sister Aurum stares at the two warriors.

"I thank you, good Sirs. The evil one's fighting ability is formidable but he also projects an aura of fear that few could stand against, let alone fight him on even terms."

Another man rises, and asks, "Why don't we get to the heart of the matter? Find the evil wizard and slay him."

Many of the audience members nod their heads in agreement.

Sister Fluere explains, "First, we do not know his location, except that it is somewhere to the North, we believe. Second, the Ebony One still slumbers. We must find this Dark Harold and slay him. Currently, he can only move at night, riding a dark and evil steed. Soon he will be able to travel during daylight, but he will not like it."

Someone yells, "Where is he now?"

"I am very sorry, we have tried to discern his location, but something is interfering with our scurrying. We can tell you where he has been, but not where he is currently or where he will be."

Again much discussion fills the audience. After some time, Sister Fluere thanks everyone again for attending.

"If there are no further questions, we have told you everything we know. Now it falls upon you to save the land. When we gather more information we will gladly pass it along. If you agree to this, please make arrangements with our contacts before you leave. May you go in peace and knowledge."

Sister Fluere stays to answer more private questions. Aurum turns and slowly walks offstage and sits next to Mikal.

"What should we do now?"

Chapter 7

Mikal watches as the multitude slowly takes its leave. Catherine, without her squirrel, and Monica approach Mikal with a tray filled with assorted food.

"Good afternoon, good wizard," Monica says shyly.

A small table is brought forth and lunch is served. Aurum and Mikal discuss the prophecy and the crowd's reaction to it. A third seat appears and Sister Fluere asks if she can join.

Mikal responds, "It would be my honor if you would. I understand that each representative or group is required to pay a fee. What is mine, may I ask?"

"No...no. We can discuss that later."

The radiant woman then explains that most of the assembled are leaving either immediately or after they have eaten.

"I should be leaving soon, as well," Mikal says.

Aurum and Sister Fluere plead with Mikal to stay.

"You may leave first thing in the morning. In fact, I will make it part of your payment. You must stay this night. Also, upon your leave, we will request a lock of your red and white hair."

Wrinkles crease Mikal's forehead and he strokes his beard meditatively. He looks quizzically at his hostess.

Sister Fluere smiles knowingly. "We promise we will not use your hair in any nefarious way. In fact, we will use it to aid you, if we can. Please, trust us. It is a small thing we ask."

Mikal lightly laughs. "I am a teacher. I know sometimes small things can lead to things unexpected. But, you have asked for my trust and I shall grant it. Trust, however, must work both ways."

The females nod in agreement. After some time, Aurum, Catherine, and Monica escort Mikal and proudly conduct a tour of their tight-knit community. The rest of the day passes quickly. They share an evening meal and afterwards entertainment is provided: a pleasant dance and enchanting songs.

An older witch starts to twitch. She croaks, "Something is not right. Something Wicca this way comes. What exactly it is eludes me. It is deeply shrouded. Tell the guards beware."

Mikal finds the nonchalant reactions to this prophecy odd.

One of the sisters waves her hands and explains, "Forgive her. In her prime, she was very talented at foreseeing the future. But now she only prattles of danger and impending doom. It never comes to pass, however, so our reaction to it is muted."

Mikal accepts this, and soon all retire for the night.

Alone in his room, he is disturbed by the old one's ranting. Sleep does eventually come upon him, but his dreams cause him a fitful night.

***

A scream awakens Mikal. Majam is fully alert; with her back arched and her fur standing straight up.

Mikal asks, "What is wrong?"

He enters the mind of his dark-haired cat.

Majam responds, I *hear wailing and screaming, and I smell rat; legions of them.*"

Mikal stands and grabs his staff of light.

"Are we forever cursed dealing with these infernal rodents?"

They move outside the tent. Through his cat's enhanced sight, Mikal can make out a large horde of rats writhing toward them. But something concerns him even more than this appalling sight: an inky, mysterious mist follows the rats. It is almost as if the vermin were pulling a malevolent blanket behind them. The camp is in an uproar. The wizard witnesses a group of guards form a defensive barrier before the oncoming mass. The soldiers slash a swath into the great host of rats, bloody swords flashing in the moonlight. The defenders seem to be standing their ground. Mikal witnesses the shadowy mist engulf the swordsmen. Chaos erupts. Some of the warriors drop their weapons and run. Others stand screaming. Still others are so confused and panicked that they slash at their own brothers-in-arms. The spectral mist is spreading out, causing great fear and paranoia. The wizard sees Aurum running toward him, frightened but not panicked. Mikal raises his staff high above the pandemonium. It flares and produces a bright, clean, white light. Mikal closes his eyes and murmurs esoteric words. The white light fans out, forming a sphere surrounding him and his cat. Sister Aurum enters the iridescent bubble.

The prophetess whispers, "What ever shall we do? Why did I not foresee this?"

"No time for questions like that. Call the others to us. There is strength in number."

Soon there are nearly a dozen people in the white sphere. It expands as more enter, including a few guards carrying torches, several guests, and Sister Aurum's associates. Most of the rats shy away from the brilliant light. If any approach, the guards lower their torches. Eerily, Majam produces loud and menacing hisses, and pounces on any that elude the flames. The blackness turns toward the huddled group and approaches as if it had a mind of its own.

Sister Aurum grabs Mikal's sleeve, "Can you prevent its effects?"

"We would have a better chance if we join against it. Sisters, I need you to sing,"

"What?" she asks, uncomprehendingly.

"Trust me. I said sing, all of you! An uplifting song, a positive song."

At first, only Sister Aurum begins to sing.

"All of you louder, stronger!"

Just before the first tendrils of the menacing mist begin to stroke the clean, white sanctuary, a sobbing Catherine and her friend Monica sprint into the protective bubble. Mikal can sense fear's unnerving caress. Instinctively, he intones a defensive spell. The singing intensifies and the light glows brighter. The black, misty blanket of fear dissipates as it comes in contact with the white sphere. At that moment, Mikal senses another's mind. Was it directing this onslaught? With his cat's senses stretched to their limits, they perceive the enemy. There seems to appear a hole in space, taking the shape of something somewhat human. Majam screams. The large, black cat leaps from the whiteness and dashes directly at the newly-revealed entity.

The cat races fearlessly toward this humanlike form. At the last moment, Majam leaps directly at her foreboding opponent. Then Mikal witnesses a strange sight. It appears that for, just a moment, his cat disappears inside the dark apparition. Relief spreads across Mikal's face when he realizes that his cat has emerged unscathed behind the fear wielder. Mikal hears not a sound from the evil presence. The inhuman creature holds its two appendages on either side of its would-be head and appears to be in great pain. Mikal forgets his charges and races protectively toward his cat. As he approaches, he feels dread emanating from the dark, human-like hole in space. The bizarre intruder senses Mikal's presence as Majam unleashes an unfamiliar, spine tingling, disconcerting cry. The vile thing takes flight and fades into the starless night.

Mikal asks Majam, "Are you harmed? Why did you do that…and, and what was that unsettling sound you made?"

I did not appreciate the way that thing smelled.

Mikal responds, "I did not smell anything."

Yes, you did. I don't expect you to be capable of identifying it.

"Do you mean the fear that shade was giving off? Majam, can you smell fear?"

Yes, of course, and I do not like it. It leaves a lingering, bad taste in my mouth.

"It seems I learn something new about you every day," Mikal chuckles. "Tell me, have you encountered one of these things before?"

Majam begins to nonchalantly lick her paw. First her right, then the other.

The two start back toward the group they were protecting. The rats are in disarray and fleeing and the malevolent mist seems to be completely dissipated. Catherine's friend Monica is holding her. She looks up and explains, "Catherine's pet squirrel Squeaky woke us up and attacked the rats. We ran and we fear the worst for her little, furry friend."

A guard hurriedly approaches Sister Aurum carrying a tattered but alive and fidgety Squeaky, and announces dire news.

"In the panic, Sister Fluere became a victim. She did not survive."
Sister Aurum cries out mournfully and collapses to the ground.

Chapter 8

After some time, the encampment comes together and takes stock of the injured and dead. As dawn fully reveals itself, the settlement realizes that little structural damage has been inflicted upon the village. There are a number of injured people, however, who need medical assistance. The Sisters begin immediately and set about their healing tasks. They learn that three guards had been killed during the melee, along with one of the Sisters whom Mikal did not know (the old witch who gave the dire prophecy), and poor Sister Fluere. Sister Aurum is beside herself with grief. Some of her associates try to provide comfort, but with little success.

Mikal hesitantly approaches the young Aurum, bends down, and looks into her soft, glistening eyes.

"I am so sorry, my child. If there is anything I can do, please but ask it of me."

She looks up and tentatively hugs Mikal.

"Thank you, you've done so much already. The white light and the confidence you provided spared most of us. You drove the rats and that evil shade from our midst."

Mikal whispers, "I wish I could have done more, and I know Sister Fluere would want you to be strong."

Aurum wipes her eyes and nods her head.

"I know, but it's so difficult."

Mikal stands straight.

"Life is not fair. Now I think the others look to you for help and guidance, even at your tender age."

The young one looks unconvinced, but some of the Sisters seem to be waiting for her directions.

"Master Mikal, I know you wish to leave soon, but I ask you to please stay for one more day. We can all use your support, especially me."

Mikal softly agrees. He and Majam spend the rest of the day doing what they can: cleaning, rebuilding, and offering encouragement to all. Early that night, the Sisters of the Valley bury their dead; a solemn ceremony indeed.

A wordless meal is served.

Sister Aurum approaches the wizard. "Mikal, I thank you again. I did not know who you were before you entered this Valley, but I did have visions of you. Curiously though, not of your cat, and I wonder why. I do know this, however: you must stop this herald of iniquity that has been summoned from the grave. But consider this: you alone cannot prevail against him. I also know you will confront a malevolent one who now sleeps, but will someday awaken, and you cannot defeat him either. I have foreseen that you will confront him, none-the-less. I cannot say how it will all end. By the way, have you ever dreamt a dream within a dream?"

Mikal tries to assimilate this disconcerting information. Sister Aurum lowers her head for a moment.

"Forgive me my digression. I am aware that you are in a hurry and I have knowledge of a secluded, little-known path out of the Valley. It should save you a few hours. I shall have Monica and her friend Catherine show you the way at first light, if it is acceptable to you. Oh, and do try to stay dry."

Mikal gives her a quizzical look, but thanks her.

"It is quite acceptable. I hope for a better night for everyone."

***

Mikal, finds himself walking the secluded path the next morning guided by the two young Sisters. Few words are exchanged between them. Mikal looks to the sky and notices ominous, heavy clouds approaching.

"I think the two of you should head back now before the rain starts."

Mikal and Majam continue their trek alone. The day darkens and the rains begin to fall. It is getting harder to see, even for Majam. Mikal almost stumbles over an odd shaped rock. He hesitates and notices that the path forks. He taps the rock for luck and chooses the path to his right. He feels the rain penetrating his traveling cloak, and the road becomes muddy.

"We must find shelter," he thinks. "Do my eyes deceive me? Is that light ahead?" Mikal approaches what appears to be an inn for travelers. It is warm and dry inside. He finds a small table and takes a seat with Majam curled at his feet.

The innkeeper approaches Mikal who asks, "May I have some hot tea and bread?"

There are only a few people in the inn, but two of them stare at him. Minutes pass, and the two men stand and stride toward Mikal. One starts to ask questions. "Who are you and where are you going?" while the other steps behind Mikal and delivers a heavy blow to the wizard's head.

The thug laughs. "Sleep well, stranger."

The wizard's mind is filled with alternating dark and bright images. When he finally awakens, he is in some sort of a jail cell. His hands are shackled and he sits on a wooden bench with his cat next to him. There are no windows and the door is made of heavy, metal bars. Hanging on the wall across the hall is his traveling robe and, leaning next to it, his staff. A lantern hangs suspended from the ceiling. The light it casts faintly touches the wizard and his cat.

"Well, Majam, these two men seem to be up to no good. I wonder what they want with us."

He looks to his cat through the dim light.

"I want to try something."

Mikal closes his eyes and relaxes. He meditates on the almost imperceptible light which reveals his form. He senses it on him and in him. Then the White Wizard slowly exhales, and ever so slightly the vague light recedes from his body. A second time he exhales, and the faint light moves still further from him. He hears the guards coming, and his cat stirs and sits on his lap.

"Now, Majam, let us see if my plan works."

One of the brutal men unlocks the cell door and opens it. The other enters but, astonishingly, he sees neither Mikal nor his cat.

"They're gone, but how can this be?"

"I told you to be careful. He was a wizard of some sort!"

The two panic and run from the cell, leaving the prison door ajar. Majam bounds off Mikal's lap and scurries across the floor. Mikal stands, *drops his shackles, crosses his cell, dons his cloak, and grabs his staff. He walks through a long corridor, opens a heavy wooden door, and steps into sunlight.*

Chapter 9

"Mikal, wake up. I thought you would want to leave early."

The White Wizard sits up disoriented.

"I must have been dreaming. It was a strange dream indeed." He hesitates. "I may have learned something useful from it though."

After a simple breakfast, the three approach the secluded path that will lead them out of the valley.

Monica asks, "Where are you going next?"

"I must report back and explain to my associate everything that has happened these past few days. I think it would be wise for you to return now, before the rains come."

The two girls look to the sky and are confused. They see what could be storm clouds, but they are at some distance.

Mikal assures the two. "The rain is coming and it will be very heavy. I believe I know where the path will take me. Thank you, you have been very kind and I hope to meet you again. It would be best if you left now."

The two girls nod, say their goodbyes, and disappear down the isolated path.

***

Mikal winces as the first touch of a cold wind surrounds him. While Majam leads the way, the wizard looks ahead and tries to memorize the path through his cat's eyes. Cool drops of rain start to kiss Mikal hands and face. The daylight dims as distant rolls of thunder foretell a powerful storm on the horizon. The wind starts to bite and Mikal leans forward to keep his balance.

"Majam, come back. I will hold you in my cloak."

With Majam's head peering out to help Mikal find his way, they make slow progress. The wizard's boots sink deeper into the mire. The sky brightens for just a moment and Mikal spies a odd-shaped rock that seems vaguely familiar. The path splits here. He gently raps the rock for luck, and takes the trail to the left this time.

"It seems like we are walking through a wall of water. We must find shelter."

A brilliant flash momentary reveals their surroundings. A tall, crude outcropping appears just off the route. Mikal huddles next to the small hill.

"At least we are somewhat protected from this awful wind and rain. What a dark and dreary night this is."

***

Not far from the soggy wizard and his cat, rides the shadow knight. The storm's full fury hits the herald as if nature itself protests the rider's very existence. A great bolt of energy crashes into a mystical, unseen net pulled by the Dark Knight and, for just a brief moment, a gash opens and a nondescript, spectral form slithers out. A deafening crack of thunder erupts, jolting the surrounding forest. Even Mikal feels its effect. The sinister warrior rides on and soon approaches Mikal's hidden position. He stops, perhaps sensing the White Wizard's presence.

Through Majam's eyes, Mikal witnesses this unnerving sight and shudders.

"I can feel the dread that this abomination is casting."

Mikal and his cat close their eyes. The White Wizard focuses and steels himself from this horror. Suddenly, Mikal opens his eyes. Another flash of blinding light fills the surroundings. The whites of Mikal's eyes start to swirl as the forest turns pitch black.

"Deep into that darkness peering, long I stood wondering, fearing what it is I am seeing. Some sort of preternatural net I spy, captured, woeful spirits cry. I must not, will not just stand by… and let this Ebony Knight drag them to perdition."

A thunderous sound rocks the very ground. The black steed is off with rider, its condemned cargo in tow. The moment has passed. Mikal waits. The storm's rage starts to ebb.

"Well, Majam, we cannot wait here forever. Let us see if we can find more suitable shelter."

With Majam's sight guiding them, the wizard slogs though the muddy path. Though the dark and rain, Majam squints and sees a dim, shivering light. A short time later, a large, nondescript man surprises Mikal by holding a lantern up to the White Wizard's startled face.

"Hold! Who are you and what are you about?" he demands forcefully.

"I am a lonely traveler looking for refuge from this storm. I am from the city of Addis," Mikal says through the droplets pouring down his face.

"Well, you and your soggy cat seem harmless enough and no one should be out in this gullywhumper. But beware; there has been a strange sighting tonight. You best go to that lighted building you see ahead."

Mikal thanks the characterless man and soon finds himself knocking on a well-made, wooden door. He opens the portal and enters. Inside, a crackling flame fills the room with warmth. Six people sit around a sizable table made of ash. A young man nods in welcome. Majam leaps from her master's robe and bounds to a cozy spot by the fire. Somewhere an old dog gives a half-hearted growl.

An aged woman responds, "Now hush, Duke. Don't mind him. Please warm yourse'f by the hearth like yer cat. Kin I get you anything?"

"Thank you. Some hot water for tea would be most welcome."

"Hey, now, why don't you take off that watersogged cloak? It be much more comfortable," a middle-aged woman with protruding ears suggests.

Mikal complies and hangs his water-laden, hooded robe on a wooden knob. From a few seats away, a small headed man with one eye stares and inquires of Mikal, "Hey you, what's wrong with yer eyes? Are you blind? You hung up that heavy cloak mighty easy."

Before the wizard can reply another man interjects, "Who are you and where are you from?"

Mikal hesitates and knows he must put these suspicious people at ease.

"I am sorry. My name is Melchior Brightstar from the city of Addis and this is my cat. You are correct. I am blind, but my cat helps me. Her name is Majam. I thank you for your warm fire and dry building. I mean you no harm."

The older women questions, "What did you do in the city of Addis?"

"I taught at the School of the Three Moons."

"Ah, a learned man!"

The door opens unexpectedly, letting in whistling rain and wind that brings with them a tall, thin man with a frantic voice.

"Martha! You must come right quick. Something's wrong with Lucy. She got caught up in the storm. I heard a scary wail, and then I found her, but she is not right! Come quick, please!"

The aged woman hurriedly dons a heavy-hooded shawl and leaves with the tall, thin man.

"I wonder what that was all about?" someone asks.

The rest shake their heads in bewilderment.

The man with one eye replies, "There are many strange happenings occurrin' o' late. I heard a two-headed goat was born on Jo Jon's farm just two days ago. Someone claimed they saw an armored knight ridin' a mighty big, black stallion."

The middle aged woman scoffs, "Why would a knight be in these parts?"

Mikal silently sips his tea. The conversation eventually changes to the more mundane affairs of the local inhabitants. Turnip greens and wheat bread are passed around. Mikal is impressed that the people of these small hamlets are so hard working and resilient and how they take everything in stride. The door opens again and the older woman enters, frantically picking up her potions and herbs. She turns, gives a quick look to Mikal, hesitates, and then leaves. A little while later, Mikal is given a mat stuffed with straw and a place to sleep close by the fire.

Chapter 10

It is well past midnight when Mikal awakens.

"I am sorry t' wake ya, but I am at my wit's end. You said you teached at the School of the Three Moons? Lemme ax you, do you know anythin' of the healin' arts?"

Mikal groggily sits up and replies, "Yes, some."

"Good, good. My name's Martha. Kin you hep me? Please come. I'll git yer belongin's and will guide you. It's just a short ways."

"Thank you, but that will not be necessary. My cat will be my eyes and I would be happy to return your hospitality. Please, show us the way."

After donning his traveling cloak and grabbing his staff of light, Mikal and his cat follow the old healing woman down a well-worn path. The wind and rain had stopped some time ago, and the drying out has begun. They approach a humble dwelling. Martha lightly knocks and enters. Though Majam's sight, Mikal takes stock of his surroundings. Across the floor his senses are drawn to a young woman lying on a bed. Her breathing is labored and she is abnormally still.

The house is modest, but sturdy. It has two small windows, one facing the east and the other the west. There is a table and a few chairs, a cupboard, and a storage chest. The woman's bed is near the fire. Mikal knows something is amiss.

The healing woman explains, "I found her thrashin' about and yellin' things I couldn't git. Even with her husbin's he'p it was difficult, but I was able to examine her. There was no dang wounds to be found. No broken bones to be set. There's no fever even. In fact, she feels cool to the touch. She was in miz'ry though. She looked like she was trying to hurt hersef so's I give her sup'tin' to calm her down. But, dang it, it dint work. I tripled the amount. She finally fell asleep, but you kin see she is in a strange way. We moved her close to the far. Tell me, Melchior Brightstar, do you know any healin' spells that might he'p her?"

Mikal approaches the prone women and recalls incantations taught to him by Amadeus Whitestone. He places one hand on her cool brow and the other on her right shoulder. The young women suddenly tenses. The White Wizard begins to intone a simple spell but suddenly stops. Somehow she is resisting it. He starts again, this time using a stronger incantation. Immediately the woman sits up, spastically throws her arms at Mikal, and emits an unearthly howl. The wizard steps back aghast but quickly gathers himself and places a potent sleep spell upon her. She falls back dead asleep, but panting as if she needed more air.

"I knew you was morein' you seemed t' be," pipes a self-satisfied Martha. "Do ya know what's wrong with her?"

Mikal shakes his head. *But I as I should*, he thinks.

The healing woman huffs, "We should all git some rest. Mebbe the mornin' will reveal what we cain't see now."

Mikal agrees and sits before the east window holding onto his staff with Majam by his feet. The old woman rests on a mat by the fire. The husband seats himself next to his wife and gently takes her hand. He does not close his eyes for quite some time.

***

Mikal stirs. He is leaning heavily on his staff which is softly vibrating. He gradually opens his eyes. To his unease, the whites in his eyes start to swirl in a disorientating way. The wizard then focuses on a polluted, malevolent apparition that appears to be *inside* the ill, young woman. The others still sleep. The sinful phantasm starts to writhe as if somehow aware of Mikal's stare. Mikal immediately closes his eyes, breaking contact. He believes he hears a muffled, distant moaning. Still, no one awakens.

"What shall I do?" he whispers to himself.

Again he becomes attuned to his staff. The light of a new day gently peers through the window, bathing the room, but it seems like a cloak of bleakness is filtering it. Mysteriously, the staff imparts to the wizard a new spell. Mikal finds himself repeating the words as if in a trance. The brightening light enters the east window and travels to the staff but not beyond. Mikal captures more and more sunlight. Majam awakens. Mikal stops his incantation, and waits. The mystical staff changes its tune. The White Wizard starts to twist his staff one way then back to the other between his palms. Slowly at first, until a single, long strand of sunlight appears. He repeats the whole process again, faster this time. Soon more sunlight strands fill the air. Mikal allows himself to become totally immersed in the spell. He now starts to weave a pattern. Majam stares mesmerized with the intricate light show above her. A design emerges.

Martha and the husband awaken. The man is about to speak but the healing woman shakes him off and softly whispers, "Don't disturb him."

The wizard's hands and voice are in perfect symphony. The hands move like an orchestra conductor's, while his voice produces a recurring melody. A cloak of sunlight starts to take shape. Again, Mikal alters the spell ever so slightly. For the final touch, a golden hood is added and the magical tune stops. The White Wizard slumps back into his chair, exhausted from the effort. The bright-hooded cloak hovers for but a moment and starts to fall.

"Please, do not let it touch the ground."

The healing-woman rushes to stop its descent. The lighted garment ever so softly falls onto Martha's outstretched arms.

She looks to Mikal. "Thar's no weight to this amazing' garmint, but I kin feel its healin' warmth."

The weary wizard asks, "Will you please place it on her and make sure it touches her skin."

The husband helps her place the young woman in a sitting position, removes her upper clothes, and places the hooded, sunlit cloak upon her shoulders. Mikal instructs them to secure the hood tightly around her head. Instantly, the young woman falls back and becomes rigid; her legs straight out with her toes pointed forward, her arms tight at her sides, her mouth gaping wide open. Disturbing, gurgling sounds come from her gasping mouth. Mikal's staff is still holding back the sunlight. The room is illuminated from the dying embers in the fireplace and from the bright cape. The White Wizard senses evil and the whites of his eyes start to swirl again. He sees one, then another, and then another dark and dusty tendril groping out of the afflicted girl's mouth. Ever so slowly this vile specter pulls itself out of its now bright, unpleasant host. It starts to twist itself around. It catches Mikal's penetrating stare and screams, but no sound is heard, though everyone feels a fleeting chill. The White Wizard lowers his staff and allows the room to be flooded with the light from the new born day. The deplorable entity cannot stand the brilliance. It slams into the back wall noiselessly, where it dissipates, leaving only a shadowy smudge.

All is quiet. Mikal's hooded, sunlight garment fades and blends into the rest the room. Then everyone becomes aware of the even breathing of the young woman and notice that her color has greatly improved. Her husband gives her a long, heartfelt embrace.

Martha looks to Mikal. "Well, I'll be a blue-nosed gopher! I don't know what t' say. That twas amazin, and we'all thanks ya. If thar's anythin' we kin do fer ya, why, you jest name it."

"Majam and I are hungry," suggests Mikal.

Martha wildly waves her arms in exasperation. "Well, shucks, darlin', I'll cook ya up more food than you and that big, sassy cat could eat in a week. Foller me."

Before they can leave, the young woman unexpectedly shouts, "I keep a clean house! How did that dirty stain on the back wall get there?"

Relieved laughter.

"I will explain later," her husband promises.

Mikal, in a matter-of-fact voice, replies, "Oh, some lamb's blood and water will remove it."

***

Soon Mikal and Majam are in the main house enjoying a feast at breakfast. The story of how the stranger healed Lucy is rapidly spreading. With each telling, the story becomes more outlandish and embellished. Mikal tries to downplay his role in the healing, but to no avail. The wizard simply sips tea while his cat laps milk. A large man with a sober look enters the cabin. Mikal believes it is the man who confronted him the previous night in the storm. He strides to Mikal.

"There is man outside who is looking for someone. He says he is a courier from the City of Stonegrove. He has a message for a Melchior Brightstar, who has red hair and may be traveling with a large cat and a half-elf. I told him nothing but that I would ask in here. Have you seen this man?" he winks.

Mikal ponders the situation.

"If he is from Stonegrove, let him in."

The man nods. "Oh, he is from the city, I can tell by the horse he rides. They are not too big, and they put markings on them. I will fetch him."

Minutes later, an official looking young man with tousled blonde hair stands before the Wizard and his cat. After a few questions, the courier hands Mikal a waxed, sealed envelope.

"I am to wait for an answer. I will be outside." After bowing slightly, he takes his leave.

Mikal notices the letter "B" imprinted in the wax. He breaks the seal and opens the letter.

Dear Melchior Brightstar,

I hope this letter finds your hands. The danger has grown. The opposition has eyes and ears everywhere and the situation is urgent. If you could possibly come to Stonegrove, I would be forever in your debt. Do not contact me directly, but go to the Baron Stannum Estate. The family can be trusted. They will contact me. Please be careful.

B.

The White Wizard strokes his beard. He rises, thanks the people, and tells them, "If a young half-elf asks for me, tell him that my cat and I went to the City of Stonegrove."

Chapter 11

Mikal sets out on the path as the locals directed. He travels uneventfully for the rest of the afternoon and at length approaches the main road that will take him to Stonegrove. The White Wizard decides to camp for the night. He chooses a secluded spot just off the main travel route. For the next few hours, Mikal and Majam are aware of travelers passing by. Luckily, no one notices their hidden camp. A rare, peaceful night passes.

The early morning light awakens the pair. They break camp and set out on the main road. Sometime near midmorning, Mikal hears what must be a wagon approaching. He steps off the road and, using his cat's sight, notices two merchants bringing their wares undoubtedly to the city. Mikal waves and the two return pleasant nods. Within minutes the wagon is out of sight. A short time later, four horsemen gallop by, dressed in impeccable uniforms. The wizard looks to his cat and comments, "This road seems safe enough."

Just after noon, Mikal steps off the road to take a short break. He heats water and brews tea. Majam looks up and meows a warning. The White Wizard hears a lone rider approach. The man is sitting tall in the saddle, looking to the right and left. His gaze catches Mikal and his cat as he rides by. He pulls up, and turns his horse toward the wizard. The equine approaches slowly. Mikal notices lather around the creature's mouth and that the steed's breathing is labored.

Looking down from his high horse, the stranger says, "Good afternoon, Mikal Novastar from the city of Addis. I have been searching for you. My name is Aden Ferrum. I am at your service."

"And what service is this?" Mikal asks.

Aden stares. "Oh, a traveling companion or your bodyguard perhaps."

"I do not require either, thank you. Who sent you?"

Aden dismounts and takes a closer look at Mikal.

"What is wrong with your eyes? Are you blind?"

The mage responds, "In some ways but not in others. Again, who has sent you?"

The wizard notices a red feather tied to Ferrum's long, dark hair and the ruby ring he wears. The stranger looks to Majam.

"My, but that is a large cat you have. I never had the need for a pet."

"She is far more than a pet."

"If you say so."

Mikal notices a short, metal staff that Aden carries on his back.

"Is that a magical rod?"

"It is, indeed."

Aden proudly displays the iron staff to Mikal. The wizard can read some of the runes etched upon it.

"You are obviously a Red Wizard. Path Bloodhue has sent you, has he not?"

Aden lowers his gazes slightly. "You are perceptive. In fact he did."

"With orders to spy on me."

"No, that's not the reason."

"Oh, really. Then tell me, why you are here?"

The Red Wizard contemplates his answer.

"I committed a serious transgression recently and my punishment is to seek you out and become your..." Aden hesitates, "... servant for a time."

"For how long, may I ask?"

"Bloodhue was vague on that matter."

Mikal laughs slightly. "It does sound like something Path would do. Go back, I neither need nor want a servant."

Aden protests, "But you must. I cannot return until I have atoned for my misdeeds."

"I am sorry," the White Wizard responds, "but I do not believe you."

The Red Wizard stands tall. "I have told you the truth. Why do you doubt me?" Mikal straightens up, holds onto his staff of light, and, with Majam's sight, looks intently at Aden.

"I believe you have mixed the truth with lies. I have no need of you. Be gone."

The two wizards hold their gaze for some time. Finally, Aden Ferrum lowers his eyes and challenges, "I will not leave. You cannot prevent me from following you."

Mikal says nothing, but gathers his few belongings and starts down the road.

***

Mikal travels at his own pace, with his cat to guide him. The Red Wizard leads his horse not far behind. This goes on for more than an hour. The path starts to dip toward a small river. Mikal is dismayed, for the bridge is washed out and the water is running high.

The White Wizard looks to his cat. "It looks as if the effects of the storm are still slowing us down. I think I can wade through with the aid of my staff."

Aden Ferrum approaches. "Well, it looks like you do need my help after all, white eyes."

Mikal does not respond but steps into the rapidly flowing river.

Aden protests, "My horse can carry us. You need not get soaking wet."

With Majam on his shoulders, Mikal wades into the river. Soon the water is waist high. Mikal is startled when Aden's horse splashes by. Just pass midstream, the rider waits and proffers his arm. The White Wizard takes no notice and continues.

The Red Wizard laughs. "Aren't you the obstinate one. I like that. But now you will be cold and wet."

Mikal almost falls but catches himself in time, to his and his cat's relief. Majam's claws dig a little deeper into the wizard's shoulders. He finally steps out of the river and removes his traveling cloak. He wrings out some of the river water. Suddenly, a piece of driftwood bursts into flame.

Mikal jumps and Aden explains, "I thought you would want to warm yourself by my fire." Immediately, the White Wizard grabs his dripping cloak and continues down the road.

Again, he hears the Red Wizard's condescending laugh.

Mikal tries to maintain a good pace but he knows the Red Wizard is not far behind. Another main road crosses their path. He is forced to step aside as a small caravan of goods heads toward the city of Stonegrove. Neither the wagon drivers nor guards pay Mikal notice. The White Wizard is surprised, though, that a few sentries give the Red Wizard long, serious looks. The last wagon eventually passes. Oddly, there is a bell hanging from it that produces a peculiar, melodious sound. Majam seems to enjoy it.

***

With the warmth of the day, Mikal's clothes start to dry.

"I believe we are not that far from our destination. With luck, we may reach it by nightfall. What do you think, Majam?"

The cat does not respond but continues down the road, sniffing different odors along the way. A lone rider hurriedly gallops by, riding a chestnut mare.

"It looks like another courier. I wonder what his destination is."

Mikal decides to take a short respite. He sits on a fallen log and unpacks some fruit given to him by Martha, the old woman healer. Majam keeps an eye on a flitting butterfly, with beautiful, identical, blood-red wings fluttering around a nearby flower. Mikal ignores Aden Ferrum even though he knows he is close by. Again Mikal is alerted by the sound of horses approaching. This time at a far more leisurely pace. Three horsemen slowly approach Mikal. The White Wizard discerns that the oldest man is a successful merchant with a guard by his side and a servant riding close behind.

The older man hails Mikal. "Good Sir, how does the road look ahead?"

On closer inspection, he notices Mikal's white eyes. "I'm sorry. I did not know you were blind."

The White Wizard chuckles softly. "Oh, think nothing of it. The road is generally fine but if you are heading south there is a bridge that is washed out."

"I thank you for the information. Here is a silver piece for it. I hope you have safe travel."

Mikal accepts the coin and nods to the merchant and his associates. The three smile and continue on their way.

"They seem nice enough, don't they, Majam?" The White Wizard rises and, with his staff in hand, continues his journey. A short time later, his cat notices two large scavenging birds circling just off the road. Majam suddenly stops and faces toward a small clump of trees.

Mikal asks, "What is it?" and easily slips into the mind of his cat.

"Yes, I do smell it. It reeks of blood and death."

With the cat's enhanced hearing, he can make out a weak moan. "Does someone need our help?"

With his cat to lead him, he cautiously leaves the road and crosses some tall grass and approaches the clump of trees. Mikal holds his hand to his nose. A putrid odor assaults his senses. Cautiously, he proceeds. The White Wizard turns his head and winces at what he sees. A lump of broken flesh lies before him. He forces himself to inspect the grotesque site. At first he believes he is looking at a short man with very thick, fleshy arms and legs. This broken creature has a heavy, long, dark, blood-drenched beard. Mikal wonders how the previous riders could have ignored such a piteous sight.

"Am I looking at a dwarf?"

The creature's left arm is crooked and broken in a distorted, misshapen manner. Most of the body is covered with black and blue welts, swelling his body to strange proportions; strange for even a dwarf. The left side of the head looks as if it has been dented. Dried blood is caked around head wound and it is leaking pus. His face looks as if it is an off-centered Cyclops', due to the fact that there is a distorted, seeping swelling just above where the left eye should be. A piece of broken wood protrudes from the right side of his stomach. Blood still leaks from it. His legs do not appear to be broken, but they are black and blue, with a multitude of tiny bites covering them. Mikal wonders if this broken creature is still alive. His cat moves closer and meows near the dwarf's right ear. The right eyelid flutters.

"By all that is holy and not, he lives."

Aden Ferrum approaches. "What have you found here? Oh, it's a dead dwarf. I can tell just by the smell," he snorts and makes a face of distaste.

Mikal quickly rebukes, "He is not dead."

Aden scoffs. "Well, he should be. He offends my senses. Look at it. It is too stubborn and stupid to know that it *should* be dead. You cannot save it. Besides the land would probably be better if you left it alone."

Mikal ignores the Red Wizard then takes out a potent healing potion he received from Amadeus Whitestone. With difficulty, he opens the wounded dwarf's swollen mouth, and pours in the healing brew.

Mikal leans back. "He is so cold to the touch. He needs warmth." The White Wizard starts to take off his traveling cloak. Unexpectedly, a flame surrounds the broken creature.

Mikal, startled, yells, "What are you doing?"

Aden explains that it is his flame and it will only produce heat, not burn the creature.

"Go ahead you may test it. I will not allow it to harm you."

Mikal suppresses his amazement and cautiously touches the flame. It does not burn. He places one hand on the dwarf's head the other over his barely-beating heart. He closes his eyes and recites his most powerful healing spell. A soft, white light emanates from the White Wizard's hands. A frail moan escapes the wounded one's mouth. Mikal sits next to his patient with Majam on his lap and waits.

"Okay, now that that's done, let's be on our way," says the Red Wizard.

The healing mage looks up and responds, "We cannot leave him. In fact, if he lives I will need your horse."

Aden responds, appalled, "Oh, so you don't need me but you need my horse. You also may thank me for my warming fire. If you want my horse you must also accept me."

Mikal begrudgingly nods his head. "I will accept your horse and you as my servant for short period of time."

The Red Wizard gives a slight bow and a sarcastic, "I am at your service, White Wizard."

"I believe he is improving; his color is better. Though I am not sure what a healthy color is for a dwarf. His breathing is definitely more even," Mikal says hopefully.

Aden concurs. "You know, you still have to take out that large splinter from his stomach. And good luck with that mangled arm."

Mikal closely inspects the stomach wound. "I hope a barbed metal piece is not attached to the wood. In any case, I intend to pull it out with my right hand. With my left, I will heal what I can. Are you capable of cauterizing the wound?"

The Red Wizard scoffs and lowers his iron staff just above the oozing gash.

"I'll show you what I'm capable of. In fact, I'm rather looking forward to burning some dwarf flesh."

Mikal gives Aden a serious look then sets himself to task. Gently at first, he moves the large spike back and forth then forcibly pulls it straight out. Luckily, there is no barbed tip to it. Without hesitation, his left hand starts to administer a localized healing. To his dismay, however, the open wound begins to bleed more profusely. The Red Wizard's iron staff flares and the smell of burning flesh fills the air. Mikal quickly pulls back his hands. The flame ceases and, to Mikal's relief, the wound is sealed.

The Red Wizard steps back. "Well, that was easy. What are you to do about that mangled left arm?"

"I am not sure. It looks like the bones are shattered. Will you try to set the arm correctly while I attempt the concentrated healing incantation again?"

Aden grips the dwarf's left arm and pulls and twists until it looks like it is in a normal position. Mikal starts his enchantment, when suddenly; the dwarf sits up and screams in agony. The healing wizard steps forward and immediately recites a sleep spell. The wounded creature falls slowly into a deep slumber. Mikal then administers the healing incantation to the arm.

"We cannot wait much longer. I want to move him before dark. The recovery is taking effect but very slowly."

Aden nods. "That is because dwarves are resistant to magic. I told you they are stubborn, even when they aren't conscious, which they are most of the time."

Mikal orders, "Give him water. I'm beginning to think he might indeed survive."

The two wizards wait a short time and, with some difficulty and protests from Aden, place the battered dwarf on the horse. They make slow progress as the sun starts to set.

"Well, Mikal, if I am to be your servant, I should know more about you. What can you tell me about being a White Robe Wizard, which I deem an inferior color?"

Mikal does not look at Aden Ferrum. "I presume you consider all other colors inferior to yours."

"Of course I do, for I know Red Wizards are the most talented and powerful wizards of them all."

Mikal responds, "And how do you know this?"

"Oh, it's common knowledge to all that have seen our power." He points ahead and asks, "Is that some sort of inn ahead?"

Within minutes they stand before a small, two-story tavern. The name *The Broken Pony* is carved into an old, wooden, weathered sign that hangs above the door.

Aden chuckles. "It seems like a appropriate name."

Mikal asks Aden to stay with the wounded dwarf and his horse.

"I will go in and make arrangements."

The White Wizard enters the old inn. He holds his staff in his right hand and cradles his cat in his left. The dining room is not crowded.

"There may be a room for us, Majam."

Within minutes, Mikal helps lower the unconscious dwarf from the horse. The two wizards carry their wounded charge into the inn. Everyone stares at the three, but especially at the battered dwarf. The innkeeper waves a wrinkled, dirty towel.

"Hey, you didn't say you had a wounded one of those. I don't want a filthy dwarf in my inn."

The White Wizard looks to the innkeeper. "I will pay you double and will leave first thing in the morning."

The proprietor looks at the two wizards. "Well, keep him quiet and be gone early."

Luckily their room is on the first floor. They place the mangled dwarf heavily on the bed. Mikal inspects the damaged creature.

Aden says, "I want to talk to the innkeeper. I'll get some food and water for us."

The Red Wizard goes behind the counter and approaches and confronts the innkeeper. "My good fellow, I may agree with your feelings toward our wounded gnome, but I must point out with whom you are dealing. When a wizard of color is kind enough to ask you for anything, you respond always with *yes, sir*. You will not question your betters."

Suddenly the Red Wizard's iron rod flares to life. An orange, hot flame surrounds it.

"See this? With a mere whim I can burn this hovel down with everyone in it in a matter of minutes. What would you do then, my good man? We will not pay double for the room. Do we understand each other?"

The flustered innkeeper stammers and nods his head.

"Now bring us food and water. Hot soup, if you have it."

***

There is a knock at the two wizards' door. A serving girl and a young boy enter, carrying food, water, and some hot soup. They set it down on a small table and leave without saying a word. Aden eagerly takes something to drink and starts eating. Mikal props up the dwarf on the bed and attempts to feed him some hot soup. The weakened dwarf's eyes slowly open and close.

The Red Wizard looks to Mikal. "It's obvious you've never seen a dwarf eat before, have you?" Aden stands, grabs the bowl of hot soup, places it on the lips of the dwarf, and aggressively pours it down wounded one's throat. It is gone in an instant.

He hands the empty bowl to Mikal. "That is how dwarves eat. Now, why don't you eat and drink, as well. You must be positively weak from hunger."

Mikal nods and takes part in the small feast.

"My good servant Aden, tell me what makes you such an expert on dwarves?"

Aden Ferrum shakes his head. "Dwarves work in the mines for us. They dig for metal and precious stones. We even let a select few forge some of our weapons. When I was younger I was a supervisor in one of the mines for almost a year. Yes, I know dwarves. Maybe too well. They are a sub race, fit only for the mines, and they should not be allowed to travel the lands like normal folk. You know, they all are cowards and cannot be trusted."

Mikal responds, "I know of that perception, but how much of it is accurate, I do not know."

Aden scoffs. "Oh, believe me it is true. For what I have seen of them, there is no doubt."

"Well, I am not sure what to believe, except that I am tired and we all need some rest. Good night."

***

Just before dawn, Mikal is awakened by his cat who is perched upon his chest. She meows once, hops over to the dwarf's bed, and sniffs his left hand.

The White Wizard rises. "What do you smell, Majam?" Mikal inspects the dwarf's left wrist. "Oh my, is that gangrene?"

Mikal slips into the cat's mind. *It smells bad, like death.*

The White Wizard also detects a noxious odor. The Red Wizard awakens from his slumber and looks over Mikal's shoulder.

"You know what that is, don't you? Alas, he does not have much time. How unfortunate for him. Only a master healer from one of the temples would have a chance to cure that poison. You know what you must do. That arm has to come off, and soon." Aden crosses his arms and shakes his head from side to side. "See, I told you so. You should've left him. He's far more trouble than he's worth."

Mikal stands. "I know what I must do, but I am not exactly sure how to do it."

The Red Wizard sighs. "I will see what the innkeeper has that may be of use."

Long minutes pass, ticking off the dwarf's life. Aden enters the room followed by a strapping man carrying a double bladed ax.

"This woodsman was having breakfast before setting out for the day. I persuaded him, with some of your coin, to do the deed. You are fortunate that I have seen this done a time or two."

They lay the dwarf on the floor. "He is still groggy. I gave him something to numb the pain," Mikal explains.

They place a block of wood under the left shoulder of the unconscious dwarf. "Woodsman, hold your ax steady, if you can."

The Red Wizard places his iron staff next to the metal axe head. A red flame appears and starts to heat the metal. Shortly, the double-bladed iron is glowing red.

"This should seal the wound instantly, I would think. Now strike!"

Without hesitation, the woodsman swings his axe above his head, staring upon the spot to strike, and brings it down and severs the dwarf's left arm just below the shoulder. After cleaning up the blood, the man receives his payment and hurriedly leaves. Mikal wraps the severed limb in a large rag that quickly is stained with blood and hands it to Aden.

"Please, get rid of this now."

The Red Wizard gives a slight bow and says unconvincingly, "I am at your service, Master."

Within the hour, Mikal is surprised at the dwarf's progress. Except for the missing arm, the dwarf is healing well. Aden returns, wiping his hands with a cloth, and Mikal tells him that the dwarf will live, only to hear a scoff from Aden.

"Well, aren't we the lucky ones? We best be off to the city of Stonegrove."

Chapter 12

"AAAAIIIIIIEEEEEEEAH! M'arm! M'arm! Ewe bass turds! Wa tave ewe dun tomb ee? Wym eye bound? Mine ite mare izreel! Ewe welp ay fourth hiss!"

The two wizards abruptly stop. Aden turns toward the dwarf with his cloak flying in the wind.

"Are you addressing us, malodorous one? I can barely understand your ranting. I presume you are inquiring about the whereabouts of your left arm and why you are restrained, no? You were unconscious; the ropes are there so you would not fall from the saddle. Your arm was filled with poison, so we severed it for your own health. You're welcome."

"You bass turd! Ewe had know rite!" protests the dwarf, "'twas m'arm!"

The Red Wizard shakes his head. "Now listen, little man. That wizard and his cat found you off the road. You were more dead than alive. Your body was broken and he healed you. Do you understand? He gave you back your pathetic life. When I first saw you I thought you were dead and there was no way anyone would waste time trying to heal a dwarf. You should thank him. He's very talented and the only reason you are here now, you ungrateful, smelly, little-" Aden trails off.

The dwarf murmurs under his breath, "If fee wuzzo talon ted, eye wooden't lost m'arm."

"I told you they are stubborn and ungrateful, not to mention stupid. He doesn't even know how to talk. Most of it is just gibberish," Aden states.

"That is not so. I have studied their language. It was necessary to read the words out loud at first to understand what was being said, but it is not gibberish. It takes practice and patience to grasp what is being written or spoken, is all."

Mikal looks to the dwarf. "I am sorry about your arm. I did all that I could to save it. My name is Melchior Brightstar, this is my cat Majam, and he is my temporary servant, Aden Ferrum."

"Yore rise look stew pit end ugh lee. Aroo wa blind whiz herd, whiz herd?" asks the dwarf.

Mikal chuckles. "Yes, you can say I am blind. But my cat helps guide me."

"Eye never knead did a pet." Mikal looks to Aden.

The dwarf asks, "Wear em eye, end wear em eye bee in tay ken?"

"We are just a short distance from the city of Stonegrove. I hope to be crossing the River Phalanges and entering the city within the hour. Is this acceptable to you?"

The dwarf leans back in Aden's saddle and does not reply.

Mikal asks, "What is your name, sir?"

The dwarf hesitates. "If few must no, mine aim iz Kairn Lanthanide Kavon.

"His name's bigger that he is." Aden smirks.

Kairn adds absently, "Stonegrove wuz smaid bie dwarves."

Mikal challenges the statement. "Dwarves may have designed the city, but giants built it."

Kairn responds defensively, "Know, knot sew. The gy rants whirr own lee annex ten shun of the dee zine ers. Weeb illtit."

They continue walking toward their destination.

"Wuddu upe plant two due tomb ee?"

Mikal hesitates, "We plan to take you to Stonegrove. Then you may go where you wish."

The dwarf nods his head and looks down at his torn and filthy rags he is wearing.

"Isle knead knew cloze."

Aden looks to Mikal. "They are greedy, also."

Mikal responds, "Yes, I know you do. I am sorry I could not purchase any at our last location. But I am sure we shall find something in the city."

Eventually, the two wizards, the dwarf, and the cat cross one of the drawbridges that protect the city and now they stand before two sentries who guard the gate.

The Red Wizard steps forward.

"I am Aden Ferrum and this is Melchior Brightstar from the city of Addis."

A stout guard holding a wooden club in his left hand gives them a cursory glance.

"And what about that one-arm dwarf?"

Mikal turns toward the guard. "He has had an unfortunate accident and he is temporarily in my care. I will vouch for him."

"What is your interest in entering my city?" the sentry asks.

"We have business at the Yellow Toad Inn," Mikal answers.

A line of people is starting to gather on the drawbridge. The guards nod and let Mikal's group pass.

Kairn questions Mikal, "Use ay this manniz yore sir vent? If that's strew, wide uzzee an ounce hiz naim firsten then hiz mass ter'z?"

The White Wizard looks to Aden. "He is correct. We are going to have to work at that."

The last time Mikal visited Stonegrove was during Festival. The streets were crowded and colorful. Now the avenues are filled with locals going about their business. The two wizards direct Aden's horse past a myriad of shops. Mikal's group is held up by a slow moving litter carries an old, obese merchant.

Kairn ask, "That bill ding to the rye tuv vus. Wha tiz zit?"

The White Wizard turns and is surprised by the question. "That is the library. It houses many books and old tomes."

"Eye wood like two vew it wye lime hear."

Aden laughs. "You have to be able to read, oh crippled, witless one. Most of the books do not have pretty pictures."

Kairn snaps back, "Ike an reeden rite. Mine aim iz Kairn; K-a-i-r-n."

Again the Red Wizard laughs. "I'm impressed that you parrot some letters but that's not reading."

The dwarf falls silent. Mikal interjects, "One needs a pass, or to know someone special, to gain entry to the library. If we have time, I will see what I can do."

As they approach the Yellow Toad Inn, Aden expounds, "I believe many of the residents are staring at us. Now I can understand them giving long looks to the one-armed dwarf out of pure curiosity and to me out of fear of the Red Robes, but many are spending their time looking and whispering about you, Melchior Brightstar. And why is that, do you suppose?"

Mikal responds, "I was here not long ago and there was an incident. I was involved. As luck would have it, everything worked out well. I did not think they would recognize me, though, since I appeared quite different then."

The Red Wizard responds, "Oh, really. Please tell me about this …incident."

They stop in front of the Yellow Toad Inn. The White Wizard asks, "Aden, please take your horse to the stable and I will escort Kairn to the innkeeper and secure us a room. Thank you."

Surprisingly, the dwarf needs only a little help dismounting from Aden's horse. The two and Majam enter the inn. Instantly, the old innkeeper welcomes Mikal and instructs his plump wife to fetch a saucer of milk for the cat. He only glances at the dwarf.

"Where's Talon?" he asks eagerly.

The White Wizard responds, "He is not with me currently but I hope to see him soon."

"Is everything alright? Your eyes and that white streak in your hair…" the innkeeper asks. He lowers his eyes. "Forgive me, it is not my business."

Mikal waves his hand. "No, no, it is perfectly acceptable to ask. Everything is... fine. I am wondering if we could rent a room."

The proprietor nods his head. "But, of course. How about the same one you had before?"

The White Wizard responds, "That would do nicely."

The Red Wizard joins the two and Mikal says, "Let me introduce you to Aden Ferrum, currently my servant. And this is Kairn, who has had a serious accident. He is temporarily in my charge. And, of course, you know my cat Majam."

"And a beautiful creature she is," responds the innkeeper's wife.

Soon the three are unpacked, and divide their room into

individual sections.

Aden asks, "So what is the plan now, oh wise one?"

"We go to the main room and order some food. You keep your eyes and ears open. I want to see if we can get a sense of what is happening here."

The Red Wizard inquires, "What do you think is happening?"

Mikal shakes his head. "I do not yet know."

Shortly, the two wizards order light repasts. The dwarf orders enough food for three and proceeds to devour it at an unbelievable rate.

Aden simply states, "Add gluttony to the list."

Mikal ignores him, and is aware of people staring and whispering about them. After dining, the three return to the room. Aden enters first and is surprised to see a woman dressed in a soft and supple black leather suit. He slips his hand around his concealed red-bladed dagger. Fortunately, Majam enters and meows pleasantly.

Mikal softly chuckles. "I am not surprised see you here, Marian Vetta."

She stands. "Do you always travel with such strange company: a one-armed dwarf and a dangerous looking man that does not belong here? Also, where is the half-elf? And what is the latest news about our thief?"

"Talon, as you can see, is not here, but I hope he will reach us soon. I am sorry, but I have no current news on our thief. If I may, this is Aden Ferrum, temporarily my servant, and this is Kairn, also temporarily under my care. Tell me, Marian, what news have you?"

The dark-clad figure shakes her head. "No news that I can share. I can only warn you to tread cautiously while you are here." Her eyes look first to the one-armed dwarf then rest on Mikal's "servant", "Strange things are about."

Mikal ponders her words. "Thank you for your words of caution. Tell me, can you give me directions to the Baron Stannum residence?"

"I can, but it may be better that you receive them from the innkeeper. Trust me. He may have someone that will escort you there."

Marian bends one knee and strokes the large, white cat. "I shall take my leave. Again, be careful."

The door closes. "Well, that was certainly cryptic," says Aden. "Now tell me about the last time you were here. You seem to have made quite an impression."

Mikal picks up his staff. "I have no time for that now." He leads the group out of the room and asks directions to the Baron's abode. As Marian foretold, the innkeeper offers a young boy to show them the way.

It is mid-afternoon once they step onto the streets of the city. They walk by the library. "Eye hav know inn trestin me ting sum know bells. Kan use ee if few can gain en tree form ee at the lie berry?" asks the dwarf.

Mikal bows his head slightly. "Yes, I think this would be a good thing for you."   They walk up the steps and a sentry bars their path. The White Wizard stands tall. "Please tell the head librarian that Mikal Novastar is here to see him." The guard stares at the White Wizard for a moment then quickly turns and enters the library.

"How menny naims dew yew hav?" asks Kairn.

Shortly, one of the two large, wooden doors opens. Out walks an eager Derek Foxhill. "Welcome, Mikal Novastar and your beautiful, white cat. Where is my friend Talon?"

"It is good to see you," the White Wizard responds. "Talon is not currently with us but I hope to see him soon. I know he would appreciate spending time with you."

"Did he find what he was seeking?"

"Yes, he did," responds Mikal.

"Oh my, I hope he will tell me all about it."

"I'm sure he will," reassures Mikal. "Now for the matter at hand. I've come to ask you a favor."

"Anything for you," the head librarian replies.

"This is Aden Ferrum, my servant." Derek nods. "And this is Kairn Lanthanide Kovan. He has recently been in a serious accident, but he wishes to see your library. I do not believe he has been in one before."

The one-armed dwarf simply states, "Eye knead nu close."

Master Foxhill looks to Kairn. "That you do. I will contact my tailor immediately. I see you speak dwarfish, can you read it as well?"

The dwarf answers, "Uv core syke an. Uv core syke an."

"Very good. I can't believe my good fortune. I've been going over some old dwarfish text and hopefully you can help with some of the translation."

A smug laugh escapes Aden. Mikal interjects hurriedly, "Thank you very much. We may not be back until late."

"That is no problem," Master Foxhill responds. "He is welcome to stay the night if necessary. As long as he promises to tell me about his travels…and what became of his arm."

The one-armed dwarf nods in agreement. "Mel key or or My kell lore watt tever yore naim iz, dew knot four git abowt mee."

The two enter the library and the door closes. The Red Wizard smiles. "Well done. We are rid of him now."

Mikal shakes his head. "I intend to return for him."

"Then you are a foolish man, Mikal Novastar of the City of Addis."

Chapter 13

With the young boy to guide them, they soon enter the Village on the Hill where the well-to-do live. All the buildings are expensively built with wood and stone. It is late afternoon when the boy turns left on a short, cobblestone path. He gives a slight bow and points to the large double doors.

"This is the House of Stannum."

Mikal places a coin in the lad's hand and thanks him. The youth skips down the cobblestone lane whistling a merry tune. Aden knocks on the large doors. One opens and a nattily attired servant appears.

Aden steps forward. "My good man, this is Mikal Novastar from the City of Addis. Tell your master he wishes an audience."

Mikal quickly adds, "Tell him we apologize for the inconvenient hour."

It is some time later that the servant reappears and tells them to follow him. They enter the estate and turn right down a hallway that leads them to a large, well-furnished sitting room. A handsome man, who fills out his tailored clothes well and has a touch of gray in his hair, stands before them. Seated next to him in a posh, red velvet chair is a well-groomed, elegant, flaxen-haired woman.

A man servant steps forward and, in a deep voice, announces, "I present Baron Reilly Stannum and the Baroness Elizabeth Stannum."

The two wizards bow formally. "Thank you for meeting with us on such short notice. I am Mikal Novastar and this is my servant Aden Ferrum."

The Baron nods, signaling the servants to take their leave. The one with the deep voice hesitates, clears his throat, and looks to Aden.

Mikal smiles. "You are dismissed. Wait for me in the lobby."

Aden scowls at Mikal for a moment, bows theatrically, and follows the servant. The Baron looks to Mikal. "Your presence here would indicate that you have received the letter from Madam Burnshire. We did not dare hope that you would arrive so soon. To be honest, we were also expecting the talented half-elf."

Mikal nods. "I was fortunate. I was nearby when your Courier found me. I expect that Talon will arrive soon."

The Baroness speaks up, "We are about to have dinner and, of course, you are invited."

Mikal apologizes, "I doubt if I shall make a good dinner guest. I had a late lunch."

The Baroness smiles. "Your presence, your wisdom, and your cat we seek, not your appetite. Madame Burnshire did mention that you are a connoisseur of teas. I have a dinner blend that you may find interesting."

Mikal responds, "Well, I do not know about the wisdom but I'm more than willing to try your tea."

The Baron moves close and in a soft voice whispers, "The moment you entered this house we sent a runner. If the Madam is free, she will meet us here later this evening. At least, that is our hope."

Mikal acknowledges with a nod.

The three exit the sitting room, walk down a different hallway, and enter the dining area. Three teenaged children stand waiting behind their dinner chairs. The proud Baroness waves her arm. "Let me introduce my children. This is my eldest daughter RaeAnne. You can see by her attire that she wears a unique style. Not only is she fashionable, she is a very skilled archer and athlete as well. I wish Talon could see her shoot." She turns to the lad. "This is my eldest son Robert Craig. He is a fine swordsman. Just ask him."

The Baron steps forward and interjects, "He fancies himself an officer already. He is not."

Ignoring him, the Baroness continues, "My youngest Margaret Carol. She has a quick wit and always wears a smile, even when her clothes are inappropriate for dinner."

The three children bow. The Baron looks to his family. "This is Mikal Novastar and his cat Majam from the City of Addis. He is a teacher at the School of the Three Moons. So I caution you, he will be watching." The Baron laughs lightly.

Surprisingly for Mikal, the dinner goes by quickly. The two young ladies are excused.

Robert Craig stands. "Father, I remind you that you are scheduled to supervise the night patrol this evening. You said I could accompany you."

The Baron looks to his wife. "Yes, I know. We will leave within the hour. Go prepare yourself."

The Baron addresses Mikal. "I'm afraid I must depart soon but I will leave you in the more than capable hands of my wife."

Mikal thanks his host for his hospitality. The Baron lightly kisses Elizabeth goodbye, turns, and goes to prepare the night patrol.

Mikal, his cat, and the Baroness Elizabeth Stannum sit in the meeting room.

Your cat is magnificent. I've heard that her fur changes color. It is now such a luxurious, raven black." The Baroness starts to gently stroke Majam.

The fastidious feline shows her appreciation by producing an almost hypnotic purr. For the next twenty minutes or so, the Baroness explains how she met Madam Burnshire and how they became such good, trusting friends. Suddenly, the Baroness stops. She raises her chin and listens closely.

"I think it's time. Master Mikal, please follow me."

The White Wizard stands with his staff in his right hand. His cat jumps and is soon cradled in his left. Silently they walk a rarely used hallway. The Baroness stops before a sizeable, finely crafted, two-door cabinet. She pulls open these doors, slides hanging clothes aside, and turns.

"Do not be alarmed. Follow me and close the doors behind you."

She opens a false back in the cabinet and walks through the hidden opening. It reveals a stone room with a marble, spiral stairway leading down into darkness. Mikal closes the doors behind him as instructed. The room becomes pitch black.

"Master Mikal, I have walked this path in the dark before, but would you please shed some light to assist me?"

"Certainly," Mikal responds. Instantly the stone room glows with a pleasant, soft blue light. They descend the circular steps that lead farther down than Mikal expected. They eventually enter a well-appointed room. It has various soft leather chairs, two torches affixed to the far wall, and three thick, lit candles set on a long, heavy, wooden table. The Baroness invites the White Wizard to sit, and then pours a red wine for herself and Mikal.

The Baroness explains, "The original occupants of this estate were accomplished smugglers. We had no idea. The head librarian and Madam Burnshire explained the history of the grounds, though neither knew of these complex passages and tunnels that we have uncovered."

Mikal notices that there is only one other exit besides the way they entered. As if reading his mind, the Baroness laughs and explains, "Along with the two you see, there are other ways to enter or leave this room. More wine?"

Before he can answer, his cat freezes and stares at the far wall. Her tail is straight up and the tip of it twitches back and forth. A secret wall panel slides open and a tall, brown-haired, stately woman appears. Majam continues to stare intently. As the woman approaches the table, the black cat arches her back, bares her teeth, and hisses.

The Baroness frantically stands. "Something is terribly wrong. That is not Madam Burnshire, in spite of how she appears."

The White Wizard holds his staff high as the would-be Madam Burnshire returns Majam's hiss with one of her own. Her fingernails grow longer, sharper. Mikal quickly recites a spell that sends a blinding, white light that engulfs the far side of the room. The creature turns away, holding her clawed hands over her eyes. A silvery dagger whistles past the White Wizard and penetrates the cringing beast's side just below the elbow. She screams an otherworldly cry. The enraged black cat leaps and starts to bite and slash at the creature's face. Mikal steps on to the table and uses it as a springboard that propels him toward the howling beast and swings his glowing staff onto the creature's back. Bones yield with sickening, crunching noises. Again, a white light fills this part of the room. The White Wizard cannot be sure, but for just a moment he thought he saw needlelike, white shards of solid light penetrate the threatening beast. The thing slumps to the ground and does not move. Majam starts to meow again. Another door made of stone noiselessly opens and out steps a second Madam Burnshire. For a moment all is silent.

"What is the problem here? That creature… why is it dressed as me?"

Unexpectedly, a large, muscular blond-haired man dressed in leather armor carrying a short sword in one hand and a silvery dagger in the other, steps past her. The headmistress introduces the warrior.

"This is Arnold, my personal bodyguard. Will you please see if that creature is dead?"

After a cursory inspection, the leather-clad warrior responds, "She is most certainly dead. She is also carrying a vial of poison like we found on the others."

He removes the silver knife from the beast's side and, out of habit, wipes it clean on his tunic.

Curiously, he sees needle sharp wounds in her back. One must have delivered the killing stroke.

Madam Burnshire looks up. "Please return the silver blade to the Baroness and remove the body from these grounds then burn it to ashes."

The bodyguard bows and sets about his tasks. "I'll be back."

The Baroness looks to the headmistress. "I must thank you for your silvery gift, but I did not think I would ever have had a chance to use it."

Madam Burnshire offers a slight smile. "Well, you used it very opportunistically, I can see."

Majam meows pleasantly. The headmistress acknowledges the sound and affectionately pets the black cat. "Master Mikal, I thank you for coming and I apologize for any inconvenience."

The White Wizard waves off the statement. She continues, "I like the white streak through your red hair. I have heard about your eyes. Tell me what they see."

Mikal lowers his head slightly. "I can see somewhat in very bright light. But recently I have become aware that I also can detect dark and shadowy things and, as you might recall, I can see through the eyes of my cat."

"Mikal, most people think they can see everything, but you see what others do not. Maybe we are the ones who are blind." She turns to Elizabeth Stannum. "The Baroness here has gifted sight. She too can see what is often hidden from others."

Mikal nods his head. "Yes, she identified your doppelganger."

"Only after your cat was so agitated it alerted me," the Baroness interjects.

Madam Burnshire asks her, "Have you any of that brandy available? I think we will all need some, for we have most important things talk about this night."

***

After her third sip, the headmistress looks to the White Wizard. "You can see our problems have gotten worse. The thing that entered here is the third one that we have encountered. They are some sort of shape-shifters. They seem to be limited only by being able to assume their own gender, and can maintain the form for but a few hours. We have also killed one wererat since you left. We captured another, but it was severely wounded and did not survive. We were, however, able to glean some information from it.

"An evil entity controls them. It stays behind the scenes, but is getting more aggressive by the day. I think something very bad may happen soon. The Baroness and I believe that even well-placed nobles and people on the City Council are either bewitched or somehow strongly influenced to do nothing. Some deny that there is a problem at all, even when we present evidence.

"I firmly believe this is all connected to the prophecy from the Witches of Endorr. Somehow, the Ebony Wizard, or something closely associated with him, is behind our current crisis. I have written letters to the heads of the School of the Three Moons requesting talented wizards to come to our aid, but to no avail. They do not refuse outright, but they have sent no one as of yet.

"As you know, our school teaches general knowledge and the art of magic is taught only in a limited fashion. I know this will make you uncomfortable, but if you would submit a letter, surely they would listen to you."

Mikal ponders the words from the headmistress. "I did not know how dire your situation was and it surprises me that my school has not sent anyone to assist." Unexpectedly, Majam leaps onto the table, her head held high, and paces back and forth. She stops to stares at her mage. Mikal asks, "What is it?"

In his mind's ear *someone is here and he has brought a friend.* Through the same secret panel that Madam Burnshire had entered earlier, walks Marion Vetta, clad in her standard tight-fitting, black leather outfit. Uncharacteristically, she smiles and bows before the three.

"I found this young archer wandering the city streets. May I present to you Talon of the Deep Woods and his cat Tamarix."

The half-elf walks past Marion as Mikal stands. The two friends hesitate for only a moment and then exchange a heartfelt embrace. The three women, however, are engrossed with the behavior of the two cats on the table. Majam sits staring intently at the Elven cat. The other is standing on all fours. His color is like golden leaves that appear in the fall. But what sets him apart from all other cats is a light green streak of fur that starts at the tip of his nose and spirals to the end of his tail. Its two, soft, emerald-green eyes stare fascinated by the splendid, black-furred Majam. Everyone laughs when Majam starts to absently lick her right paw as if nothing is happening around her.

Mikal enters his familiar's mind. *He appears to be acceptable. I like him.*

"I am pleased that he meets your approval," the wizard responds with a smile.

The Baroness looks to Mikal. "They seem to be getting along splendidly. On a more serious note, I am not sure how to say this, but I sense there is something not quite right with your servant."

Mikal nods. "You are perceptive." He addresses the group. "He is a Red Wizard."

Madam Burnshire shows little surprise. "I told you the Baroness has the ability to see beyond the surface. What do you, Mikal, know about this man?"

The White Wizard responds, "I believe Path Bloodhue has sent him to spy on me."

The Baroness ponders. "I believe I know that name."

"He is one of the key players in the Red Order. He tried to recruit me and wanted to train me in their ways, not knowing that I would become a White Wizard."

Talon interjects, "My father never liked Red Wizards very much. He said they often fall in love with power and themselves, which makes them very dangerous and unpredictable."

Mikal nods. "I agree with your father's assessment, but for now, I think I can keep him in check."

Over the next half hour, the group discusses problems and possible solutions. Marion Vetta takes her leave, but unexpectedly returns within the hour with a concerned look.

"Excuse me. I think you should know there are strange happenings and sightings in the city this night. People claim to see strange lights and even ethereal apparitions, and, would you believe, giants? I've talked to a number of reputable associates that claim this to be true. The city guard is out in force. As near as I can tell, though, these ghostly giants have not done any harm. It's the people who are frightened. I heard screams."

Madam Burnshire rises. "It is late. I think it best that we all return home and I also would like to witness some of these eerie manifestations."

All agree, and the Baroness escorts her guests up the spiral, stone staircase. She leads them through the servants' quarters and the exit. Madam Burnshire takes her leave with Arnold the bodyguard and the night prowler Marion Vetta.

Chapter 14

It is late at night in the girls' dormitory at the School of the Red Salamander, and all are asleep. A young adolescent sits up and looks to the right, then to the left, but her eyes are not open. She waits for a moment and moves her legs from under the warm blanket. She appears to stand, but her feet do not touch the ground. She moves through the long hall, but makes not a sound. She gently glides past many sleeping students.

She is aware of their memories, their current desires, and their future hopes. This does not concern her. A long, white, woolen nightgown drapes loosely all the way to her ankles. Her arms hang lightly at her side, for she does not need them.

She approaches an iron and wooden door which opens for her. She floats through the portal, and enters the streets of the city. A light breeze brushes by and goose flesh starts to form on her skin, although she does not feel it.

The young girl looks up. The stars, countless, are shining brightly in the sky. Do they guide her? She senses her direction and her dark brown hair gently flows as she moves over the streets. She sees everything, but her eyes remain closed. If anyone sees her, they look away for they know not what they see.

She becomes aware of distant shouts, screams, and she knows what is causing them. The young girl continues her quest. The moon and stars move higher in the sky. She approaches the backdoor to the Yellow Toad Inn. Without a sound, the old door opens and the young lass passes through this entry. She moves down a short hallway, stops, and turns toward her final destination. As before, this locked door slowly opens and she glides through. The room is empty. She finds a chair and lowers herself onto it. Now she waits for the one man that may be able to help her and her lover.

Chapter 15

The head servant approaches Mikal and bows slightly at the waist. "Sir, I think I should inform you that your servant was twice found in the house in rooms that he should have not entered. I just thought you should know."

Mikal nods and thanks the head servant for the unfortunate information. Sitting in a chair, separate from the rest of the help, is the Red Wizard. Next to him stands a muscular manservant, arms folded across his chest.

Mikal approaches his servant and says to his newly arrived ally, "Talon, this is my servant Aden Ferrum. Master Ferrum this is my good friend and associate Talon of the Deep Woods and his cat Tamarix."

Aden gives the half-elf a once-over. "Your associate? He doesn't look old enough to be out this late at night, and I don't care about his cat."

Talon looks to Mikal but does not respond. The White Wizard shakes his head. "It is very late and we should all return to the inn. Thank you, Baroness. Until tomorrow then?"

The three men and the two cats travel through the streets of Stonegrove. They neither observe strange lights nor hear unusual noises. They do notice more than a few people are being questioned by the night guards. They near the door to the Yellow Toad Inn and Aden comments, "Well, at least we don't have that one-armed dwarf to deal with this night." He opens the door to hear a deep, grating, unpleasant sound issue from the common room.

"Oh, no. Why can we not get rid this hairy beastie?"

Sleeping on the floor is the one-armed dwarf, snoring contentedly. An old dog, engrossed by the site, the sound, and maybe the odor from the dwarf, is unaware of the two cats. A younger man approaches the group. Mikal immediately notices that he must be related to the innkeeper.

"Excuse me, Sirs; I don't know how to fully explain this. Maybe the dwarf can."

Aden steps forward. "Spit it out, man. Why he is he sleeping on the floor and not in our room?"

"Well," the young man explains, "that's the problem. Your room, well, it is locked. It shouldn't be, but it is. I have a key but it does not work. The dwarf wanted to break the door down, but that would not do."

Aden is obviously perturbed. "This is ridiculous! It is late and I want to sleep."

He impatiently struts to the door and tries the doorknob but it does not turn. It feels oddly cool to the touch. Talon rouses the dwarf and helps him to the sealed door. The Red Wizard reveals his iron rod.

"It will only take me a moment to break in."

The dismembered dwarf is now fully awake. "Sew, ewe ar a Blud Wiz herd. Eye thot sew. Knot az imp ress sieve az eye mite hav thot." He looks to Mikal. "Wear dew yew fitt in two awl this? Noe Blud Wiz herd wood bee a sir vent four annie won butt ann other Red."

The White Wizard shakes his head. "I am sorry, but this is not the time for discussion."

Without warning, Majam walks up sits by the door as if waiting to enter, her tail slowly swinging back and forth. Mikal tentatively places his hand on the doorknob. It turns and clicks. He warily opens the door and his cat walks in.

He opens the door wider and he and Talon enter. The half-elf sees Majam sitting on the table staring at a young girl.

"Is that you, Ashling?"

The adolescent looks up to Mikal. In a not so young voice she says, "Welcome, Mikal Novastar from the City of Addis and Talon, who I see has acquired a feline friend. I have been waiting for you." The archer bows slightly to the brown-haired girl.

Aden Ferrum enters. The girl dressed in white turns and, with her eyes still closed, gives a long look to the Red Wizard. He does not say a word, but takes a step back.

Last to enter is the one-armed dwarf. Again, with her eyes still shut, she stares at the short, hairy creature who quickly succumbs to her penetrating gaze and steps back against the far wall. The teenager gently starts to pet Majam.

"Mikal Novastar, the satyr and I helped you not long ago and now we implore your assistance. As you know, evil things have entered the city. They have found one of our secret sanctuaries. They have not been able to penetrate our wards as of yet, but recently a darker evil has arrived. I believe she is a Witchraven and I fear she has the power to shatter our defenses. If she finds our secret places and defiles them, I am afraid I will never see my love again. As you know of the legend, he's not fully human and I fear the coming evil may separate us forever. I implore you. This very night, return to where I last spoke to you. Guides will appear and will show you the way. The evil thing is quartered in a nearby dank, foul cave."

The girl with the closed eyes turns toward the group. "We are desperate. I know you will accept our plea. I welcome you all as our defenders." The girl in white looks to Mikal. "I've tried to explain to this girl whose body I appropriated that when I leave she will become confused and perhaps frightened. When this is finished, please have someone escort her back to the school. She is cold. Thank her. She's been very accommodating. Hurry please. I will now return to the protection of my hideaway."

The vessel of the spirit slumps in the chair and her head slowly lowers to the table. Suddenly, she sits up, her eyes wide open, and she frantically looks about. She recognizes Mikal. "I am sorry. I thought I was dreaming. I should not be here! Help me. I am very cold and confused."

Mikal asks for a blanket and wraps it around the trembling girl. "Well, Ashling, it looks like we meet again. I am afraid I cannot stay, but I will get someone to escort you back to the school."

Aden interrupts, "You do not mean to go out this night do you?"

The White Wizard answers, "Our help has been requested. How can I refuse?"

The Red Wizard responds, "That's easy. Simply ignore the brat."

Mikal shakes his head. "This girl did not ask for help but, if she did, I would do everything in my power to comply with her wishes. No, another has requested our aid, and it is very important that we honor her desperate wish. Why do you worry, Aden? You need not participate."

The dwarf steps forward. "Isle goe."

Mikal and Talon look to the maimed dwarf. "Ike ann fite. Eye em stron gurr then nall ov yew, eve vin with won narm."

The White Wizard is surprised by the offer. "Your assistance is welcomed and appreciated. We must leave immediately. Talon, would you show us the way?"

The half-elf nods. The night innkeeper appears at the door. Mikal says, "My good man, I need someone to take this young lady back to the School of the Red Salamander. I will pay good coin."

The young man smiles. "Where did she come from? It's late and no one else is awake. I will personally show her the way."

"Very good. May I make another request? Have you an axe that we can borrow?"

"Certainly," the innkeeper's son responds. "It's out back next to the pile of wood. It's double-bladed and I sharpened it just this morning."

Aden addresses the group. "You are fools, but I will not be left behind. With me along your chances of success have greatly improved. You will need my fire."

Chapter 16

Talon informs Mikal, "Since we are in a hurry, I'll try to find the hidden door that we entered the last time we were here."

Mikal agrees. "But I do fear we may run into difficulty trying to pass through."

The group follows Talon and his cat Tamarix. They make very good time. Mikal uses Majam's senses, and, next to him is Aden, followed by Kairn carrying a double-bladed axe. After many twists and turns down long streets and back alleys they come to a small clearing. There stand two night guards brandishing long, sharp spears. Mikal steps forward with his magical, wooden staff in his right hand. One of the sentries lowers his weapon.

"Halt! Identify yourselves and state your purpose."

"I am Mikal Novastar and these are my associates. We are on a mission to assist the city."

The night watchman stares at Mikal. "I don't know. You look different, wizard. What has happened to your eyes?"

The other guard walks up to Talon. "Hey, you're that young archer who placed in our contest last month. I made ten coins off you. Well done." He pauses. "For the good of the city, you say? I think we can let them pass."

The other guard begrudgingly opens the hidden door. The would-be rescuers step through the stone portal and find themselves on the outside of the thick, stone wall.

"That went better than I thought," comments Mikal.

Talon orients himself. "This way. Follow me."

They move quickly but cautiously. The group becomes silent, listening to the sounds of the night. The two cats are in their element and nothing can surprise them. The half-elf slows, turns, and whispers, "We are getting close to the hidden grotto."

Aden is about to say something but Talon holds up his hand and silences him. He points to the two cats. Both are sitting, staring at two strange-looking fireflies. Their lights blink at the same rate. The two are soon join by many, all flickering in unison.

"These must be our guides," observes Talon.

The fireflies start to slowly move off as the group follows. Every so often the glowing insects surround large old trees. It is as if they are somehow embracing the ancient wooden sentinels. In the distance, Talon can see the outline of a large hill. A good place for a cave, he thinks. Both cats stop suddenly and look to the right in unison. Their tails point straight up and their backs arch high.

"The cats! Something Wicca this way comes, and that is not good."

The fireflies scatter and are gone in an instant. The four unlikely travelers wait. A dirty, dusty, dark, feathery cloud, ever so slowly spinning, approaches the group. The White Wizard instantly places the tip of his Staff of Light on the ground and traces a circle.

"Everyone stay in the protective sphere. I will allow nothing to harm us."

"Not even me?" comes a high-pitched, grating voice. The misty, dirty cloud coalesces into a female form. She is tall and thin. Her head and shoulders are covered in raven-colored hair with motley, dark feathers. Her skin is like alabaster, unnaturally smooth and white. Her eyes are dark and set deep. Her dress is made up of many different hues of black feathers. It appears that some grow out of her. The Red Wizard's iron staff flares defensively and he points.

"That is a Witchraven."

"What do we have here? A Red Wizard?"

Suddenly a glamour appears over the beguiling fowl. She strikes a seductive pose and becomes beautifully dangerous. "I'll wager I can make you hotter than you could ever imagine."

Aden unleashes a thin, crimson flame directly at the Witchraven. With a deft gesture, she deflects the fire harmlessly away.

"Best save your flame for later…you will need it."

Gradually she sidesteps to the left. Her image fades back to the feathery, alabaster female form. "Oh, look, a dwarf," she sneers mockingly. "You seem out of balance. I can help you with that. What happened to your arm? Did you lose it?"

She laughs hideously. A deep, guttural sound slowly escapes from Kairn. Deceptively, she continues to move to her left. "I see a young half-human. Why, you look absolutely scrumptious, I could just eat you up." Again foul laughter fills the night air. "And I just might."

Abruptly she stops. "So you are a White Wizard. I've heard there are only a few of you left. I would be careful sticking your staff into affairs about which you know little."

Mikal looks sternly at the feathery, female creature. "Then educate me. What is this is all about?"

The ungainly fowl screeches, "I am here to plant discord. But before I let my minions have their way, I must dispense with these two irritating, screeching, flea-infested felines."

Without hesitation, two ebony bolts burst forth from the witch's hands and streak toward the two magnificent animals. Instantly, Mikal raises his staff and the glowing sphere easily absorbs the deadly bolts.

"Curse you, wizard!" Furious, the deadly female raises her arms and morphs into a large, raven-like creature and takes flight. For an instant, all is dark and quiet. Mikal's eyes narrow and dart around the woods, as if they had sight. Talon's Elven ear twitches and Aden grips his heated, iron weapon and the dwarf wields his double-bladed axe.

Mikal cautions the Red Wizard, "I will not tolerate wanton destruction, no unnecessarily dangerous feats of fire."

Aden responds, "As you wish, Master, but I will not be denied my amusement."

With practiced words and gestures, ever so slowly at first, the Red Wizard evokes a thin, fiery line from the tip of his magical, iron staff. The orange, searing column continues to grow. Amazingly, every so often, red, sizzling barbs appear. The fire whip grows to almost eight feet in length. The Red Wizard holds it above his head and produces a blazing, deafening crack, leaving wisps of flame dancing in the air.

"Let come what may, for I am ready."

Talon strings his enchanted bow that the dragon Em-Le had given him. He readies an arrow and peers deeply into the night. The dwarf brandishes his axe defiantly.

Mikal explains, "As long as I maintain my concentration, the sphere should protect us. I will only allow things to pass from it."

Tamarix is the first to sense the incoming horde. He meows loudly and points with his nose the direction of the invasion. Talon can make out a large pack of shadowy wolves coming from the northwest. He readies his bow, which starts to glow blue, and lets his arrows fly. Unnatural squeals fill the air but the pack does not slow. From the east, a sizable number of wererats appear. Aden turns, lashes out with his flame whip, and scores a hit, tearing flesh and muscle from a creature's leg. A screeching howl escapes from the injured beast, and it backs away. Majam sits in front of her mage, her senses extend everywhere. Mikal is aware of all the attacks on his protective sphere, that glows white and blue. Finally, the pack of wolves slows their attack, their numbers greatly reduced. Talon continues to unleash his deadly assault, but it takes two to three strikes to fell one ravenous wolf. Dark birds crash into the protective bubble, producing eerie and unnerving, crunching sounds.

From the west, the dwarf spots a pack of grotesque figures lumbering toward the circle. A soldier, who should still be buried, carries an old, broken, rusted sword and is leading this foul pack. Without thinking, the dwarf hurls his axe. It lands squarely into warrior's head, knocking him down. Now finding himself weaponless, Kairn leaves the protective circle to retrieve his only weapon. It is not far, but before he can wrench the axe free, another undead grabs him around his shoulders. Kairn begins to panic, but with unnatural strength he starts pummeling his assailant in the head and mouth. Teeth start to fly, the skull caves in, and the undead thing mercifully collapses. Before Kairn can retrieve his axe, he hears a subtle, dangerous sound. He turns and is taken aback by an unnaturally huge, golden viper, its sinewy tongue darting in and out between two outsized, scaly lips. The serpent bares its fangs, ready to strike. A flash of fur comes between the dwarf and the summoned reptile. Tamarix hisses and moves his tail back and forth. He commands the attention of the golden viper. It strikes, but the cat evades the deadly attack. Again the feline hisses and raises his front claws. For a second time, the venomous serpent strikes and misses. From the right, a double-bladed axe strikes and severs the golden head from the snake's writhing body. The dwarf thanks the cat and they both scurry back into the protective sphere.

In a stern voice Mikal demands, "Stay in the circle! You make it difficult when you leave and return."

Aden retorts, "What do you expect? He's a stupid dwarf."

The Red Wizard snaps his flame whip again and this time it entangles a grinning wererat. Aden smiles as the fire barbs sear into the filthy creature's flesh. Suddenly, the flame erupts and instantly the scorched rat crumbles to ash.

"Did you see that? Now I'm having fun and it is for a good cause, to boot!" He laughs. Another wererat starts to claw at the protective shield.

Talon quietly declares, "I am running low on arrows. I had no idea we would be facing so many."

Unnervingly, the entire protective shield shudders for a moment. A large dire wolf slams into Mikal's protective ward. Again, from above, foul birds crash into the shield. From the west, more undead approach and pound on the white and blue bubble. Every time the dwarf impales his axe into one of undead, and it falls, another takes its place. Somehow, red-eyed rats have dug their way under the shield. Talon's Elven cat and the dwarf make short work of them.

The White Wizard feels the pressure of the attacks on all sides. The Red Wizard yells, "You know, Mikal, I have a powerful, dangerous spell that could take out most of these disgusting creatures."

"And probably burn down half the forest," Mikal mutters.

"Probably," Aden smiles.

"We must hold," Mikal demands.

The two cats turn as Talon looks southward. "Riders. At least two score approach."

The group turns, and are astounded by the sight of two ghostly giants surrounded in a preternatural, bluish light. They are running right toward the group.

Moments later, the two eerie giants disappear. Talon looks deep into the night. "It's the night watch and they will be here soon."

Mikal orders, "I have an idea. Everyone face me and tightly close your eyes."

The White Wizard holds his staff high as their surrounding shield dissipates. Then a clean, blinding white light flares. Their enemies are temporarily blinded and disoriented. Before the group can act, the Baron and his son ride up, leading the rest of the night watch.

"I do not know what happened. We were chasing those ghostly giants and they seem to have purposefully led us here."

Mikal nods his head. "Do not concern yourself with the giants."

The Baron agrees and raises his sword. "There is still work to be done this night. You've set them on the run, now we will ride them down and finish them." He continues dramatically, "Onward, men!"

The dwarf chases down slow moving undead and hacks at them.

Aden announces gleefully, "I'm going to see if I can find any more wererats. They burn so well."

Talon asks, "Mikal, are you all right?"

The mage nods his head and leans on his staff. "I am fine…a little weary is all." Talon accepts this. "I'm going to try to retrieve some of my arrows."

Mikal bends to one knee. Majam comes closer and stares at him. "I am unharmed, really," and he starts to gently pet his cat. Unexpectedly, Majam perks up and looks sharply to her left. The night becomes very still. Mikal enters her mind but sees nothing out of the ordinary, hears nothing threatening. He does smell an odor like dusty, old feathers. The White Wizard breaks contact with his cat and looks in the direction that Majam's nose is pointing. The whites of his eyes start to swirl. Mikal can make out a shadowy, spinning form coming his way.

Mikal cannot hear its approach. *I fear no one will sense her presence.* The White Wizard can see beyond her shadowy, concealing shield. The Witchraven stops and creates a mental link with Mikal.

"It's just you and me, wizard…mind and magic. Now let's see who will prevail." She hurls a powerful, dark green bolt of energy at the White Wizard. Mikal raises an invisible, mystic shield and deflects the assault with some difficulty.

"You look tired, mage. Worry not. This will be over soon."

A thick, black bolt races toward the White Wizard. With his staff he intercepts it, but the force of the blow knocks him back a step. He returns a solid white light that his opponent seems to absorb. She shudders for a moment. With great anger, she launches her third attempt. An acidic, thin, green line squirts toward Mikal. His defense seems strong but when the putrid green hits, it splits and attempts to ensnarl the White Wizard. For a moment the mage feels trapped. Somehow, ever so slightly, he expands his white light defense and it snaps the encircling, green energy, releasing him. Mikal is forced to admit that he is getting weary. The Witchraven also senses that her opponent is weakening. She starts to gather her strongest spell but before she can fully prepare it, she hears a terrifying sound. Too late, she sees a large, black cat leaping and landing, clawing and biting at her chest. An instant later, a second cat jumps on her and starts to claw at her side. The White Wizard seizes this opening and, with the last of his fading strength, lets fly a pulsating, solid, white light spear. It penetrates the relentless creature's chest and instantly explodes into a blinding brilliance. The foul thing heavily falls to the ground. The two cats are thrown free.

Warily, Mikal approaches his downed opponent. Joining him are the two cats, Talon, Aden, and Kairn. The Wizard is about to prod his prey with his staff when a dusky-hued flock of scavenger birds descend upon the group, causing much confusion.

Unbelievably, the wicked thing sits up, opens her indecent mouth, and expels a green slime that strikes Mikal on his face. Some of the filthy, thick fluid spatters into his nose and mouth, causing him to cough profusely. He tastes her sting.

"Curse you, White Wizard," but before she can finish her laugh, Talon's arrow and Aden's solid fire shaft deliver a dual, killing blow. The birds quickly scatter, producing a irritating squawking. The dwarf inspects Mikal's face.

"Thiziz knot gould. U've ben curst bye a dine wich."

Chapter 17

Mikal leans heavily on his staff. "I do not think I am injured. I feel more strange than anything."

The two cats perk up and look to the east. Talon asks, "Did anyone hear that?" Aden responds, "I heard nothing."

The White Wizard turns to the east. His white eyes begin to focus. Not far away, appears a young duchess and a handsome satyr from long ago. They are flanked by two giants and all are outlined in a shimmering, vivid gold line. The beautiful noble girl approaches.

"We thank you." All four of the apparitions bow. The dark-haired satyr lifts his woodland pipes and plays a few haunting notes. As mysteriously as they appeared, they vanish.

Talon again asks, "Surely you heard that?"

Aden shakes his head. "It was only the wind. Are you hearing things, elf?" He looks around at the carnage strewn everywhere. "I wonder what the young girl in our room thinks now that we've done what she asked of us."

Mikal answers, "She is quite satisfied, and she thanks you all."

The group looks to Mikal in puzzlement. "We best be going. I am feeling a little lightheaded."

Suddenly, all feel a slight vibration emanating from the ground. They hear many riders approaching and the Baron reins to a stop. Next to him is his son, Robert Craig, proudly brandishing a bloody sword.

"I told you to wipe that blade off and put it away," the Baron commands. "We have succeeded and have slain many this night. Only a few escaped. I am now at your service, Wizard. How may I assist?"

Talon responds, "Sir, Mikal has been cursed by an evil creature. May we have the use of one of your horses so we can immediately take him to the Temple for treatment?"

The Baron nods. "I have three horses. Take them with my blessing and appreciation. My son will escort you directly to the Temple."

The wizards mount two of the horses. The dwarf and Talon, with Tamarix in his lap, ride the third. Majam rests cozily in Mikal's cloak and they make good time. They pass the city gates and the young Baron leads them to the House of Healing.

All dismount. After walking up a long flight of granite stairs, they enter through one of the large, open doors. It is very early in the morning. The young Baron spies a lone acolyte and addresses him. "Brother, I am Robert Craig, son of Baron Stannum. I wish you to awaken the head Temple priest. This man has been poisoned."

The young priest looks to Mikal. "What was this poison?"

Aden steps forward. "This man is Mikal Novastar from the City of Addis. He's been cursed by a dying Witchraven. Do you even know what that means? Now bring your master here immediately!"

The befuddled young priest stutters, "But it's so early in the morning and he needs his sleep. I'm afraid he'll take me to task if I disturb him."

Mikal shakes his head. "Please do not make a fuss over me. I just need a good night's sleep. I'll return in the morning."

Aden insists, "We are not leaving."

Talon asks the young priest his name. "Milroy, is it? Now, Brother Milroy, Mikal and I were here just over a month ago when the festival took place."

The acolyte eyes widen. "I think I do recognize you. You are the young archer who excelled in the competition, and your errant arrow wounded that boy."

Talon nods. "We met with Patrick who served us his special blend of tea. I know it's very early, but I firmly believe he would want to participate in this healing attempt."

The young acolyte slowly nods. "I will see what I can do."

He transverses the large hall and opens the door with no handle and is gone. Surprisingly, just a few moments later, he returns, followed by the head priest Patrick who cradles a large black cat in his arms.

"I think this cat has lost her mage," he says with a chuckle. "Now, what is this all about?"

Mikal stands. "I apologize for my wayward cat. I was not aware she even left. But cats are like that."

"No need for that, my friend Mikal."

Patrick suddenly stops and stares at the White Wizard "Something is not right with you. Please, come with this way. Milroy, see to our guests' needs. I must rouse my associates. This could become quite involved and complex. Now, Mikal, tell me everything."

***

It is mid-afternoon when Talon hears a knock on the door to his room. Two temple priests enter, one carrying a tray of food and the other a pitcher of water. Talon and his cat are the first to respond. Soon, all but Mikal and Majam are partaking in a late lunch.

Without fanfare, the head priest Patrick arrives, followed by Madam Burnshire, the Baron Stannum, and his wife. The healer asks, "Did you all sleep well?"

Talon stands. "How is Mikal?"

The healing cleric pauses. "He is doing as well as could be expected under the circumstances."

Aden asks offhandedly, "Get to it, man. Were you able to remove the curse or not?"

Again Patrick seems reluctant to respond. "No, but I believe we have lessened its effects...at the very least repressed them. We would have liked to have kept him here another day or so, but he will have none of it. I ask all of you to keep a watchful eye on him and anything out of the ordinary should be reported to me at once."

"I hope I am not interrupting anything important," Mikal says, holding his cat in his arms.

The small assembly stands and Madam Burnshire proclaims, "I say again, I and the city of Stonegrove are in your debt. You are quickly becoming legends. I have already seen the difference in the city Council this very morning. Some of the members who have been acting...odd, seem to be back to their old, bickering ways."

She bows, as do Patrick, the Baron, and his wife.

Mikal's cheeks redden. "There is no need for that. I did what I believed I had to. If someone asks for assistance, should we not at least try to help?"

Aden smirks, "So, Priest, you could not remove the curse. Whom do you recommend we try next?"

Before Mikal can chastise his servant, Patrick responds, "That is a valid question and I have an answer. The person or creature that delivered the curse would be the most proficient in removing it. But seeing that the evil thing has been slain, that would be impossible. But, she was a witch, so perhaps the Witches of Endorr may be of some help." Aden nods and accepts the healer's answer. Talon interjects eagerly, "We should go there at once."

The Baroness intervenes. "May I recommend waiting until tomorrow? The Duke's youngest daughter's birthday is today and there will be merrymaking this evening. Even though the city may not yet know what you have done, Mikal Novastar, the Duke has been made aware of your ordeal and heroics." Aden rolls his eyes. "He wants to formally thank you and your group. Will you meet me at my estate just after six this evening?"

Mikal nods. "It will be our honor to see you tonight."

The group departs for the Yellow Toad Inn. They notice the streets are crowded for the festivities of the night. Upon their arrival, the innkeeper approaches Mikal. "I am sorry about your room, the door being locked and all. I have no idea how that young girl got in."

Mikal waves off the innkeeper. "There is no fault in you or your establishment. Think nothing of it. We are fortunate to be here."

After spending a short time settling in their room, they leave for the Baron's estate. The streets are now in full festival mood. "This reminds me of our last visit," Talon reminisces.

Aden chimes in, "Yes, I'm still waiting to hear what actually happened the last time you two were here."

No one responds.

The group enters a large, open square. "Melchior! Melchior Brightstar!"

Mikal turns with his cat in his arms. He sees a middle-aged woman flanked by two young children rapidly approaching. "It's me, Lady Beecher. Don't you remember?"

The White Wizard nods and speaks loudly over the revelry, "Yes, of course I do. I see you made it. How do you fare?"

"Surprisingly well. Some of us have even found work. I don't believe we ever really thanked you for what you did."

The two children give Mikal a heartfelt embrace and start to pet Majam. Lady Beecher grabs Mikal's hand and places a soft kiss upon it. In a loud voice she cries, "We all thank you. You are kind man. Tell me, have you heard anything about your daughter? How does she fare?"

Mikal shakes his head. "I have not heard anything, but you are kind to ask."

"Well, she is a lucky girl to have you for a father."

Aden steps forward. "We best be moving. We do not want to be late."

Moments later, the Red Wizard says nonchalantly, "I did not know you had a daughter. And what might her name be?"

The White Wizard abruptly stops and realizes he may have made a careless mistake.

Then he quickly moves on. The dwarf simply says, "Eye dint no hee hadda dotter."

Talon moves next to Mikal and matches his hurried pace.

Without any further delays, they arrive at the Baron's estate on time. Before they can knock, the door opens and the group is escorted into the foyer. The Baroness is waiting, and gestures to four chairs. "I hope you don't mind, but I took the liberty to help you prepare for the gala. Please be seated."

As soon as the four sit, barbers step up and start to trim and brush their guests' hair and beards. Others help the group wash their hands and face with rose water. "Not only will you look better, you will smell better," comments the Baroness.

"A futile attempt on one of use, I'll wager."

Her two daughters looking upon the scene start to giggle. The older one explains, "You do not know how often she has done this to us."

After a short time, the help is dismissed. With little fanfare, a servant enters and announces, "I proudly present Madam Burnshire."

The headmistress walks in, escorted by a young, broad-shouldered, uniformed soldier. She looks to the group. "Do not be fooled by Arnold's appearance. He is actually a very capable protector. Really."

Aden lightly coughs.

The group starts its short walk to the Duke's large, festive tent. They are escorted by half a dozen soldiers-in-arms. The Baroness explains, "My husband and my son will meet us at the pavilion."

Privately, Madam Burnshire and the Baroness detect that something is not quite right with Mikal. *Is it the curse or something more sinister*, they wonder. He is unusually quiet and is often with his cat looking over his shoulder. It is apparent he wants to be somewhere else. Surprising everyone, the Duke approaches Mikal and the group. He shakes the White Wizard's hand and quietly explains, "It seems I am in your debt for the second time, if I'm to believe what everyone has told me. I thank you all. If there is anything I can do, you need only ask."

Mikal shakes his head. "We appreciate the offer but, again, we only did what we thought was right and to protect ourselves from harm. But I would ask you for my leave, for something is weighing heavily on my mind and I need a quiet place to ponder what I should do."

The Duke stares for a moment and thoughtfully strokes his well-groomed beard. "I understand. It is often difficult to find a secluded place. Again, if I may be of assistance, please let me know. You have my leave. I will send some of my men to escort you into the city."

Mikal thanks the Duke for his offer and adds, "I do not believe that will be necessary. My associates have often demonstrated their abilities."

As the four leave the grounds, an official looking man approaches the Mage and presents him with a rather large, leather purse filled with silver coins.

"A small gesture from the Duke." The man bows and returns to the festival. Aden snatches the bag and starts to count the coins.

"There's plenty for all here."

Again the group sets out at a leisurely pace back to the Yellow Toad Inn.

***

Mikal cannot be sure, but he feels like he is being watched. He voices his concern so the travelers, upon arriving at their destination, decide to enter through the rear door.

Talon smiles. "I'm not surprised to see you here, Marian Vetta."

With her arms folded, leaning against the back wall of the inn, the dark, leather- clad female offers only a slight smile. "I need to talk to you and Mikal privately."

Aden looks to the White Wizard and Talon, hesitates, and then turns toward the dwarf. "Well, dwarf, you can buy me some ale and I will show you how to drink like a man."

The one-armed dwarf growls softly as they enter the tavern.

Mikal, Talon, and the pretty and talented young thief are seated at a table in Mikal's room. The wizard starts to stroke his cat and says, "I fear to ask, but what news do you bring us?"

The city rogue slightly shakes her head. "I know this was just happenstance, but soon everyone who wants to know will know you have a daughter."

Mikal responds, "A malicious thing happened to these people. We were in the middle of the woods and they needed to trust me. Revealing to the woman that I had a daughter at that time, I thought was a good idea. But now, I fear, I have put my daughter's life in jeopardy. I must go at once to her."

Marion Vetta shakes her head. "Do you think that is such a good idea? After all, speed is of the essence and you are, uh…velocity challenged. Besides, I hear you must see the Witches of Endorr to become completely rid of the curse."

Uncharacteristically, Mikal slams the top of the table with his open palm. "Does everyone in this city know my business?"

The female rogue shakes her head. "No, only the ones who want to know. And for many reasons, there seems to be quite a few of them.

100

Mikal, in the last month there have been many strange people entering our city. Various factions, all seeking different information. Tensions are high. I fear blood will soon be shed."

Talon stands. "I shall go to your daughter. I can borrow the Red Wizard's horse and I will not rest until I find her."

The White Wizard nods his head. "I thank you, my friend. You have only just arrived and now I send you away. I will draw you a map of the city. I shall write you a letter that should take you directly to the headmaster Aaron Cuprum. I shall include Madam Burnshire's request for assistance."

Marion looks to Talon. "I will notify the guards at the gate so you should pass freely. I must be going, too. I wish you luck and speed."

Without a sound, she stands and leaves the room. After Mikal draws the map and writes the letters, he gives Talon further information. "I think it would be best if you take my daughter to a small farm just west of the city. There lives a man name Amadeus Whitestone and he should be able to protect her. Notice I marked it on the map."

A short time later, Aden and the dwarf appear, both wearing silly smiles on their faces. Mikal tells the two that Talon will soon leave to rescue his daughter. Aden stares at Mikal with a dubious look. "I can make better time than the half-elf. I'm an excellent rider and it is my mount."

The mage shakes his head. "No, Talon will go."

Aden presses his point. "Why not me?"

The White Wizard pauses and stands tall. "Because I do not know if I can trust you."

The Red Wizard's face darkens but then he smiles. "You are wise, Mikal Novastar. It is rare to find such honesty." Then to Talon, "You best be going, elf. She is a fine horse, but I do not know if she is fond of cats."

Talon smiles. "Thank you, wizard. Come, Tamarix."

Mikal steps forward and gives his friend a heartfelt embrace. Just before Talon steps out the door, Mikal, in a strange, offhanded way, says, "Oh, Talon, my daughter likes mushrooms."

Everyone hesitates for a moment. The archer is gone.

Chapter 18

With his cat comfortably tucked in his backpack, Talon winds through the city streets. As the night rogue promised, he passes the city's gates unmolested. The horse's hooves produce a loud, wooden cadence as the half-elf crosses the Phalanges River Bridge. He turns on one of the main roads and his pace remains steady, considering the darkness of the night. He rides on until about an hour before dawn. Then Talon walks his horse, giving his mount some rest for the journey ahead.

Along the way, the cat explores the different sites, sounds, and odors of the night. When the first rays of light filter through the sky, Talon, with his cat, mount up once again and set a brisk pace. At midmorning they approach a clean, swiftly flowing stream. The horse, the cat, and the half-elf drink their fill. For a short time Talon leads his horse then, with a deft move, he is back in the saddle again, and the ride continues.

Talon is bemused at the large number of birds he sees flying in formation.

For the rest of the morning and for most of the afternoon Talon repeats the procedure with long rides and short rests. He does not slow his pace until the sun sets and the night inhibits his progress. The rider begins to recognize his surroundings and finds that he is approaching his first destination. Deep into the night, he enters the small town of Ulna, the town of his youth. Most of the inhabitants are asleep. Talon identifies himself to the town's lone guard. The man welcomes him. In a quiet voice Talon asks for some feed and water for his horse. It is granted. Soon the horse is feeding on oats and drinking.

"Is that you, Talon?" asks an old, one-eyed man.

A low-flying, dusky-feathered shape swoops over the two.

"Is that you, Eli?" asks a surprised Talon. "What are you doing up so late?"

"I don't sleeps so well. Besides, I thought I heard someone ridin'

103

up. I still can hear well enough, ya know."

"What news do you have, old friend?"

"Well, too many people are passin' through this town. I don't like it none. And too many strange rumors of undesirables passin' by the back paths. No, I predicts troubles ahead. People should stay where they belong, not travel so much. Don't stick their noses in other people's business, no 'fense to you and that redhead gent you travel with."

Talon smiles. "No offense taken, old friend. I wish I did not have to travel so far and so fast, but I must be going. Please tell William the Blue and all the town that I was here and I wish them well."

Old Eli, with his one good eye, watches the night rider swiftly fade into the forest. While he rides, Talon shares his food with his cat. He travels though woods and rides near streams, trying to take the most direct path to the city.

In a clearing, he looks up and hears a high-pitched cawing emanating from a soaring, red silhouette in the sky. Talon does not dwell upon it.

Talon experiences his second dawn. The morning sky glows red like a certain Wizard's fire. He travels through the morning, walking and riding, taking no rest for himself. He believes he is nearing his destination. He slows at an apple orchard just off the road and leads his horse to one of the trees. He chooses three apples, feeds two his horse, and shares the other with his cat. He passes by farms and later sees a tanner whose pelts emit difficult odors.

Tamarix shows his discomfort and sinks deeper into the half-elf's rucksack. Within the hour, Talon spies the outer walls of the great City of Addis. Surprisingly, he is not questioned at the gate. He dismounts and follows Mikal's map and directions. He eventually locates the School of the Three Moons.

There are two school guards lightly armed, but watchful. Talon explains that he is on an urgent mission and must see the headmaster. Both sentries are leery.

"Mikal Novastar has sent me. He is a former, well-respected teacher. I must see headmaster Aaron Cuprum. See? I have a letter."

After a brief discussion, the two guards let him pass. The half-elf asks, "Is there a stable nearby? My mount needs much care."

"We have one on school grounds," explains a tall soldier. Talon, not knowing what the proper amount should be, offers a number of silver coins if the guard would escort his horse to the school's stable. The guard does not hesitate and takes the money and the horse. The half-elf is escorted to the headmaster's office.

Talon, with his cat, enters a spacious waiting room filled with soft leather chairs. There is a table in front of a large, unlit fireplace and upon it rests an elaborate chess set made of ebony and ivory. A guard takes Talon's letter and tells him to wait. He exits through an intricately carved wooden door. Moments later, Talon, with his eleven ear, can overhear a conversation in the next room.

(*Interesting. Bring the girl here to my office, but through the back halls.*)

A kindly looking, older man enters, carrying Talon's letter.

"Good day. My name is Aaron Cuprum, headmaster of the School of the Three Moons. Please sit."

Tamarix jumps on the table that is between the two occupants. The feline stares at the older gentleman. The headmaster comments, "That is an exceptional color for a cat."

Talon nods. "Yes, it is. His name is Tamarix."

"And an interesting name it is." Cuprum sets himself in an impressive chestnut brown, leather chair that somewhat resembles a throne. "But now, the matter at hand. This is a compelling letter. It appears to have been written in haste though."

"Yes, it was," Talon explains. "By accident, it was uncovered that Mikal Novastar has a daughter. We fear that this knowledge is spreading and making its way here."

Aaron nods his head. "I see where that would be worrisome. But you must understand you are asking me to release from my charge someone that I have been protecting and firmly believe this is the safest place for her."

The half-elf looks hard at the headmaster. "Must I remind you, *I* am not asking, but her father is?"

Master Cuprum pauses and folds his hands. "Tell me, Talon, about your time with Mikal."

The half-elf looks to his cat and gently starts to pet him. "He saved my life, when I thought I did not want to be saved. I was there when he summoned his cat Majam. We traveled together, we met and had dealings with the Dragon Em-Le. I was near when he let loose much of his might and magic and greatly reduced the power of the Dark Robes. His abilities are growing, but they are attracting dangerous things. Know most of all, Mikal Novastar is a good and honest man and my friend."

The headmaster nods. "Of all the things you said, the last shows that you do know him. But…"

A knock on the door interrupts and a school guard enters. Master Cuprum stands, excuses himself, and passes through the intricately carved wooden doorway. Again, Talon can overhear the conversation.

(I'm sorry, sir, the girl is not in the school.)

[What do you mean by this?]

(Apparently she's on a field trip.)

[She was not supposed to leave the grounds.]

(I know, but supposedly she used a false name and went out with a small group gathering food for the cook.)

[Well, go get her.]

(We would, but there are two groups and we do not know which one she is with. One is southeast of here looking for special mushrooms, the other northwest to an apple orchard.)

[Have you considered sending guards to both sites?]

(Uh…)

[Send guards to both sites.]

Aaron Cuprum enters the waiting room, but to his surprise the half-elf and his cat are gone.

***

Talon, having memorized the route to the headmaster's office, quickly retraces his steps and exits the main door of the School of the Three Moons.

"Sir," he says, addressing one of the school guards, "there is supposed to be a field not far from here where one could find some tasty mushrooms. May I have directions, please?"

"Certainly. That would be Solver Field, just over a quarter mile away." He points. "Once you get close, you will see three large trees. The center one is dead or dying, people can't tell. Shall I get your horse?"

"No, no," responds the half-elf. Talon and his cat set a brisk pace and within a few minutes are standing among the large trees. It takes only a moment to notice a small group of students probing the ground, searching for what only could be the best mushrooms. Cautiously, Talon approaches. He is aware of only one teacher among them. Then he spies a tall, redheaded girl that he knows is Mikal's daughter. He sends his cat to catch her attention.

"Oh my, you are a beautiful tom."

She gently holds out her hand and the large cat gingerly sniffs it once and then again. He moves closer. She tenderly starts to pet the Elven cat. She looks up and asks, "What is your name?"

"Tamarix," responds Talon, causing Mairin to start. The half-elf bends down and talks softly, "Mairin, your father has sent me. Something disturbing has happened."

"Tell me my father is safe."

"Yes, but it is not safe for you to be here. Please believe me. He fears for your life. We must leave this place."

She stands with a freshly picked mushroom in her hand. "I don't know what to say or do."

"I understand," Talon responds. "Your father saved my life and the least I can do is to help his daughter. My name is Talon. I was with him when he summoned his beautiful cat Majam."

"Oh, Talon! I've so wished to finally meet and thank you for the faithfulness and friendship you've shown my father."

The teacher of the group approaches Mairin and Talon. "Alison, is there a problem? And excuse me, sir, what is your name and the nature of your business here?" Talon bows slightly. "Sir, my name is Talon of the Deep Woods. I have been sent by this girl's father to see her to safety."

Before the teacher can respond, Tamarix meows menacingly. The half-elf looks over his shoulder and sees two men dressed as school guards marching toward them. Mairin whispers, "I don't recognize those two."

The clothes do not fit the men well, especially the shorter one. His boots look two sizes too big for him and his tunic reaches his knees. Without hesitation, Talon moves toward the guards and delivers a swift kick to the chest of the short one who falls heavily to the ground. The other begins to draw his sword but Talon slides and takes out his legs from under him and he also falls. Before the shocked sentry knows what is happening, Talon's fist hits him in the face, knocking him unconscious.

"Mairin, come with me." Talon holds out his hand. She hesitates but for a moment, and then grasps it as they run. Surprising the half-elf, Mikal's daughter easily maintains the hurried pace that he sets.

As they enter a busy part of the city, Mairin looks over her shoulder and states, "I do not believe anyone has followed us."

Talon nods in agreement, but sets a hurried pace none-the-less. "So, Talon of the Deep Woods and his cat Tamarix, where are you taking me?"

"Not far," Talon responds. "Show me to the west gate. I have memorized the rest of the way from there. Your headmaster has your father's letter and map."

With little incident, the two and the cat make their way to the city's gate, stopping along the way to buy some food. They notice many of the city's militia are very active, looking and searching for something or someone. Mairin places her hood over her head, concealing her tell-tale red hair. As they approached the city's gate, a flock of birds also seem to be in a hurry to leave the city. The distracted guards do not notice a half-elf, a human girl, and a Elven cat leave.

The sky is dotted with dark clouds that partially obscure the setting sun. The two maintain their pace and talk about the one thing they have in common; Mikal Novastar.

"How much further?" Mairin asks, now cradling the cat in her arms.

"Soon. The man we seek is Amadeus Whitestone. He owns a farm just up the road. Your father believes he can protect you better than anyone else."

They round a bend in the road, and they see an alarming sight: a farmhouse and barn set ablaze. They stared transfixed by the glowing, pulsating inferno. The barn and then the house collapse on itself. The young people see no sign of any living thing.

Talon is reminded of a Red Wizard's flame.

Mairin asks, "What should we do now?"

Chapter 19

I feel like I am compelled to do the things I do.

A risen man sits on a snorting, black stallion. He is dressed in heavy, devoid-of-light armor. He looks down into the Valley of Endorr and waits. Soon, a significant number of shadowy birds descend around him. He raises his iron gauntlet and points to the settlement below.

"Retribution will be mine tonight."

The flock circles again and then falls into the dimming light of the Valley. The Ebony Knight follows the winding path to his destination of reckoning. The moon is high in the sky and shadows stretch everywhere.

The lone rider approaches the many colored tents that house the Witches of Endorr. His presence is sensed before seen. Three trusted guards bar the armored intruder from entry. Surprising all, the menacing warrior pulls up his dangerous steed and dismounts.

"Your fear feeds me. I have use for the three of you," he sneers.

He draws his razor-sharp, enchanted blade from its sheath made of bone and viciously attacks the three frightened sentinels. Within moments, his blade has cut and slashed the three guards severely. The Black Knight inexplicably breaks off the attack and steps back. He raises his cursed weapon and recites wicked words. Immediately, the three sentries fall to their knees and, in unison, scream eerily as their very souls are rent from them.

This continues until the sword has had its fill.

The conquering knight holds out his left gauntlet and commands the three to rise. Like puppets on strings they obey. Their eyes are glazed and their expressions are dead to the world.

"Now you will do my bidding. Go, bring death and woe to this Valley. There will be laughter and joy nevermore, for-ever-more."

The horrid one lowers himself to his knees. He bends over and delivers a obscene kiss to the valley floor. A wave of fear emanates from this malevolent mark, radiating discontent and discord that fills the valley.

"Ah, the panic and screams warn my heart and sooth my ears. This place is cursed now and forever more."

Unpleasant laughter echoes through the night.

Chapter 20

Aden turns and looks at Mikal. "I wish him luck, but he looks so young."

"I can think of no one better for this task," responds the White Wizard. "I think it is best that we try to get some sleep."

The mage, along with his cat, chooses a bed far from the door. The Red Wizard finishes a cup of grog and beds down for the night on an adjoining cot. The dwarf grabs two blankets and lies on the floor blocking the door.

Aden mutters, "Well, I guess he's good for something...a doorstop."

Shortly, the only sound in the room is the labored breathing of the dwarf.

I hear a deep, rumbling croak... first one, then many. I am floating, no flying, no soaring. There are a number of us, all with a black, bluish green luster of feathers. We dip, we soar in unison. We hear a calling. One starts a circling descent...we follow. Down we go... we see a flock of our brothers. They are feeding in a frenzy. I land but I cannot see food. I look for an opening. One unfolds. I hop in. I see, I smell, a dead carcass. It is stripped of most of its coverings. It has long red hair with a streak of white in it.

"Wizard, wake up. Are you ill? You were making peculiar sounds in your sleep and you woke me. That must've been some dream."

It is early in the morning. Birds chirp their morning songs.

Aden waits for a response. Mikal sits up and says groggily, "I am fine, I think. I had a very disturbing dream."

"You look better now." Aden excuses himself. "I'll be back soon."

Aden rudely opens the door, scattering the surprised dwarf who squeals indignantly. "Humph...you're not even a good doorstop."

In a little while, a gentle knock, and the door opens and reveals the innkeeper's wife carrying breakfast on a wooden tray. She places it on the table, wishes everyone a good morning, gently pets Majam, and turns and leaves. The dwarf closes the door, sits, and starts to gobble up the breakfast. Swiftly, Mikal snatches two biscuits and a cup of water. He brews some tea and leisurely eats the biscuits.

Majam looks up suddenly and hisses a warning. Mikal grabs his staff as the dwarf places himself in front of the White Wizard. The door slams open and a hooded man hurls a errant knife awkwardly at the dwarf. It is wide of its target and embeds in the back wall. The would-be assailant looks up for just a moment in astonishment, then falls face forward to the ground. A flame, in the shape of a dagger, protrudes from the man's upper back. Aden enters, stepping over the prone body.

"I saw two suspicious men lurking at the back of the inn. I waited until this one made his move, clumsy and unprofessional as it was."

Abruptly, the flame knife extinguishes itself. The Red Wizard searches the attacker's body. He discovers a few coins and a nondescript, black-bladed knife.

"This was probably met for you."

He holds out the blade for Mikal. "No, thank you. I already have one."

Aden looks questioningly at the White Wizard. "I have seen his type before. They are quite common in the city of Umbra. No doubt this is a dark assassin's acolyte, trying to make a name for himself."

Mikal looks to Aden. "How did you spot him again?"

"I told you he did not look right for this place. In the city of shadows he might've blended in, but not here. I will search the area for his accomplice, but I fear he will be nowhere to be found."

The innkeeper's wife, carrying a saucer of milk for the cat, is startled by the sight of the body and spills the saucer's contents..

"Oh, my! What has happened here? Ahh! Icabod!" She turns and skitters away. Majam starts to lap up some of the spilt milk.

Almost instantly the innkeeper appears, but before he can say anything, Mikal stands and addresses him. "I apologize for this inconvenience. We do not wish to bring these problems to your establishment."

The innkeeper is dumbfounded. "A criminal enters the door to your room," He sees the knife in the wall, "and tries to harm you and you apologize to me? I say to you, sir, you are free to stay here any time you desire. The fault is mine."

Soon guards appear and, after an explanation, they removed the body and leave. Aden closes the door. Kairn removes the knife from the wall, checks its balance, and places it in his belt.

"Mikal Novastar, who are you and what have you done to warrant dark assassins, though acolytes, to leave the city of Umbra and pursue you here? Surely you know there will be more to follow. And what do you mean that you have a black blade already?"

Mikal hesitates, then slowly reaches into his traveling robe and produces an item wrapped in soft leather. He hands it to the Red Wizard while the dwarf and Majam gaze fascinated at the covered item. Tentatively, Aden unwraps it and for a moment only stares. He closely inspects the metal, drawing his fingers across the blade. The dwarf steps closer, transfixed.

Aden whispers a simple spell. "There are letters etched on this blade. What do they spell?" He looks hard at the White Wizard. "This is a rare and dangerous weapon that only the Black Robes possess. It is said each one of these is crafted to slay but one person. Only their most trusted and talented assassins are awarded these. Again I ask you, what have you done to warrant their wrath? Do not misjudge me. I am impressed, but most intrigued."

Mikal sits and looks long at the Red Wizard. He leans back in the chair.

"There was a quest, retrieval, then a return. The quest took us to the city of Umbra, but, as you well know, nothing is ever simple in that city."

Aden nods his head.

The wizard continues, "Many things happened in a short period of time. I got caught up in the intrigues of the City of Shadows. That dark blade gave me entrance to the Black Robes' concave."

"So it was you?" Aden interrupts, aghast, and starts to pace. "Unbelievable! You do not know how many different rumors there are trying to explain what happened that night. It must've been some spell. Could you do that again? Could you even teach me? Oh, your eyes, this explains much. The damage you did to the Black Robes that day was joyous to us. But the things that were set in motion that same day are yet to be realized."

Mikal shakes his head. "What happened that night was not joyous. I cannot even explain what occurred. I would never teach that spell to anyone, even if I could, which I cannot. I fear what I have set motion. Are the evil tidings my fault?"

The dwarf interjects, "Eve ill wil fine da whey. It knee snow prom ting. I thaw twee whirr go een tousee the Wich iz uv End door."

The White Wizard stands. "Yes, I think we should be going. Let us gather our belongings."

***

The three, along with Majam, travel through the city. As they near the gate they notice a small assembly waiting for them. Madam Burnshire steps forward and behind her is Marion Vetta along with several others.

"Again, I find myself thanking you. You are all heroes in my eyes. We are searching for your assailant's accomplice. We have some good leads and soon we shall apprehend the scoundrel. But, Mikal, it is only a matter of time until they try again. Be ever so careful." Madam Burnshire looks to the dwarf. "I have something for you." Marion Vetta steps forward, carrying a long, wrapped item. She hands it to Kairn. He unwraps the gift; it is dwarven weapon. One side holds a bladed axe, the other a smooth hammer head.

The headmistress explains, "That has been displayed in the school's hall just outside my office long before I arrived. I did some research. Quite some time ago, a talented dwarf entered the school. I did not learn if the weapon was taken from him or if he left it. He did graduate. Oh, it said to be enchanted, though if it is, I do not know."

The dwarf self-consciously accepts the gift. "Eye em on herd. But twy?"

"Because you travel with Mikal Novastar, I wish to help you help him. With this weapon, you could bring honor to yourself and your race, Kairn."

The one-armed dwarf graciously bows to the head mistress.

The Baron Stannum steps forward.

"I would like to ask a favor, White Wizard. Could my daughter Margaret Carol join you in your travel to the Valley of Endorr? We've been in contact with the witches and they expect her. She shall visit there for a fortnight. With her is her bodyguard, Drew Foxx."

A warrior steps forward, wearing heavy, leather armor. It is worn, but well cared for. He is armed with a six foot spear, a short sword, and a hunting knife. A jagged scar mars his forehead. The bodyguard stares icily at his would-be traveling companions.

The Baron explains, "This man is a seasoned fighter and he will be a great asset in any untoward encounter. My daughter has traveled before, so she should not be a hindrance. I also instructed her to follow your directions, Master Mikal."

The White Wizard nods his head. "I am honored that you trust us with this most precious cargo."

Aden looks to the sky and rolls his eyes. "We best be going. We are losing light."

All say their goodbyes, and the group sets off for the Valley of Endorr.

Chapter 21

The flames still raging before them, Talon turns to Mairin. "You cannot go back to the school, for they know you are the daughter of a White Wizard."

"Who knows, and why should it concern me?"

"Dark assassins from the city of Umbra seek revenge upon your father. They know the name Mikal Novastar and that he has a daughter. They could use you to extract retribution."

"Oh…well, where should we go?"

The half-elf looks down the road. "I think we should find shelter for the night. Then we'll travel to the welcoming town of Ulna."

For some time, they travel near, but not on, the road. The open fields gradually transform into a forest. Talon leads Mairin toward a thick clump of trees. Tamarix searches the area. He returns and, by the cat's mannerisms, the half-elf can tell he wants them to follow. Moments later, the Elven cat stops in front of three large boulders. Among them is room for small number of people.

Talon explains, "This is a secure area. Thank you, Tamarix. We should get some rest now. My cat will take the first watch"

Mairin opens her small rucksack. It contains two apples, a slice of cheese, and some tasty mushrooms. She shares what she has. In the darkening sky, Talon can make out a few stars, even though his view is partially obscured by tall trees.

"I've told you how your father saved my life when I did not think I wanted to be saved. It was just outside the small town of our destination. I was also there when he summoned his cat Majam, a most wonderful and intelligent creature. I spent most of my life in the forest not far from here. My father was human and a talented wizard. My mother was Elven. They loved each other very much…" Talon realizes that he is rambling.

"You miss them, I can tell," Mairin whispers.

Talon nods his head. "They both died before their time." A little self-consciously he continues, "We both should get some sleep. My cat will let me know when it is my watch."

***

The warmth of the morning sun wakens Mairin. Talon is preparing a small fire between the rocks. Mairin takes out her wand and calls fire to the wood. The half-elf thanks her and places a skinned rabbit on a spit over the flame.

"The rocks should hide the fire from prying eyes. We should eat our breakfast quickly and be on our way. Tamarix did smell some dangerous odors last night. Luckily, none got close enough for him to alert me. I am concerned, however, because there are too many strange things traveling these woods."

After breakfast, they break camp and head deeper into the woods, with the cat leading.

"Talon, tell me about your special cat."

"My mother and I were attempting a summoning spell. At one time it was considered the most important spell in my mother's clan. We tried before with no success, but it was different this time. We started to lose ourselves in the spell. Because of this, goblins were able to approach our cabin undetected. Apparently, the summoning spell was working and Tamarix was finding his way to our cottage, but the spell was broken by the goblins' attack. He was not sure where to go. We did not know at the time, but he had followed us: your father, me, and Majam, that is. He finally revealed himself to my grandmother. She has a strong affinity for cats. Not until I spent time with my mother's clan did Tamarix finally reveal himself to me. But once that happened, our bond has grown strong. We understand each other. His eyes change colors. I'm learning how to read them. Also he is able to understand a certain number of signs that I do with my hands, and certain words, like: search, find, hunt, and hide. Hide he can do without prompting. Even I have trouble spotting him when he does not want to be seen. We are still learning about each other." Talon smiles and in a soft voice, "I also think it took him so long to reveal himself because he was… intimidated by Majam."

Mairin laughs, "I can understand that! I met her only once and I was intimidated." She continues her delightful laugh.

Every so often they stop, look, and listen, then continue on their way.

"Mairin, tell me about your wand. I've heard about them but I don't fully understand them."

Mairin produces her wand. "All the upper-class students have them. They help channel magic. I suppose I can do most of my spells without it. But one must be very careful; a spell can go awry if one is not. And they are fragile. Supposedly, upon graduation, it is tradition to perform a powerful spell that splinters the wand, showing that you have grown beyond it. Now, staffs and rods are a whole different thing."

"Yes, I know. You father, with what I believe was my mother's approval, unearthed a sapling growing over my father's grave. When he grasped it, it morphed back into a staff of light. He has wielded it with honor and skill ever since."

"You know, when I met my Father for that short meeting on the school field trip, I didn't even notice it. I've read about staves of light. They are incredibly unique, ancient, and very powerful."

Talon nods in agreement. "Your father has a growing affinity for the staff."

Suddenly, a large flock of birds circles above and settles in a nearby tree. Their numbers cause a rasping, irritating squawking.

"We best keep going."

The bird's cawing fades behind.

They travel for hours. Talon points out many characteristics of the forest: the trees, the birds, animals and their tracks. Mairin is fascinated with every bit of new information.

"I grew up in the city, but I did take long hikes in the woods, sometimes with my mother or father or just friends. I always felt very comfortable, but now I know how little I knew."

They stop just after noon. They have nothing to eat, but drink their fill at a crystal-clear creek.

Talon says, "I apologize. We could get to our destination quicker by a more direct route, but I believe it is safer, taking a longer, less-traveled path."

Mairin looks deep into her rucksack. "Well, I still have some mushrooms. And one moon parchment. But it will be many days before I can use it."

"Yes, I have seen Mikal's delight when he read your moon letter. We should see him sooner than you can use the parchment. In about an hour, we will be in a good hunting area, with a small river filled with fish."

They continue their trek until they reach the river. "Here, take this line and hook and bait it with a worm. Tamarix loves fish. I will see what game there is to hunt. My cat will stay with you, though he will probably only sun himself on that rock until you are successful."

Sometime later, Talon returns with a plump pheasant. Mairin proudly holds up three small fish. Tamarix is staring longingly at them.

"We shall have a feast then! Tamarix, search and guard." The cat reluctantly leaves. "We shall prepare the food and cook those mushrooms."

Soon after the pheasant and fish are placed upon the fire, the cat returns. They both laugh and they all eat their fill. Talon stands. "I'm sorry, but we must continue traveling into the night, and find a safer place to sleep."

***

Dusk approaches and the couple decide to take a short respite.

"Tamarix, search ahead, please."

While the daylight continues to fade, the two share a large rock. Minutes pass in awkward silence. Mairin notices two fireflies dancing their intricate light dance. Just as the two stand to continue their journey, they are taken aback by the sound of a soft, resonant voice.

"Excuse me. I don't mean to startle you. I'm just looking for directions. I believe I am lost."

Before them stands a short man with long, greasy, black hair. It is tied tightly back. He has a short, pointed nose and slanted, beady eyes.

"I am looking for a small town called Ulna. Have you heard of it?" The stranger studies Talon's features. "So, you are a half-elf."

Abruptly, they hear a screeching yowl. Mairin turns. "Talon, your bow! It's glowing."

The unsettling man's eyes turn red, his hair lengthens, and his fingernails sharpen and grow. The half-elf delivers a spinning kick to its chest, but the dark-haired creature ignores it. Mairin wields her wand and, with one command, a narrow stream of fire jets toward the stranger. Upon impact, the wand shatters and sends streams of fire in every direction. Tamarix hisses and leaps, landing on the face of the red-eyed intruder. Talon frantically feathers an arrow in his glowing blue bow and, in quick succession, delivers two glowing hits, one lodges in the beast's neck and the other embeds itself in its crimson eye. The creature falls to the ground dead and morphs back to human form, the cat still clawing the face.

"Mairin, are you okay? That fire went everywhere."

The girl answers, "I'm fine, but what is that that you have slain?"

Talon responds, "It's a wererat. My first encounter with them was in the City of Stonegrove. One did get away, and swore vengeance on us. Now, we believe they are in league with the Ebony Wizard."

Mairin shakes her head. "Well, I have dark assassins after me and you have wererats hunting you. Don't we make a fine couple?" A forced smile appears on the girl's face. Talon looks to Mairin's hand. "You've shattered your wand. Does that mean you graduated, or something?"

Mairin laughs. "Or something," she says mysteriously and hugs Talon impulsively. They laugh together.

"I must burn the body. You keep watch, it won't take long."

Soon the smell of flesh and fur fill the air.

"Let's be on our way. Quickly now, follow me."

The half-elf sets a brisk pace, but the young girl stays with him, even in the dim light. They travel for some time and finally Talon slows. They find themselves standing among several thick, large trees.

"Are you good at climbing trees?" asks the half-elf, looking up. "When I was seven, I slept in the branches of the tree right above us. I had a wonderful time. Now climb up to that section where the three strong branches split. Wait for me and I will set false tracks. I will be back soon."

True to his word, Talon returns and deftly climbs the tree and sits close to Mairin. "We should be safe for the night. There is plenty of room to sleep. Here is some rope if you need to secure yourself."

Marion nods and ties one end of the rope around her middle and the other around a strong branch.

"I am tired."

"As am I," Talon responds. "Sleep well and know you are safe. We shall enter the town of Ulna tomorrow."

Chapter 22

"Oh, what is all that noise? I'm tied up!" Now fully awake, Mairin realizes she has slept in the tree. "Now I remember. Where are Talon and his cat?"

Mairin hears that noise again and looks up. An acorn falls and hits her directly on her forehead. She sees two squirrels chittering excitedly on one of the branches above her.

"I'm sorry, Mr. and Mrs. Squirrel, for sleeping in your tree. I will gather our belongings and leave. Thank you."

The brown squirrels become quiet and stare at her, puzzled. She nimbly descends the tree. The half-elf and his cat return to find Mairin standing next to the giant trunk.

"I see you are all ready to go."

Mairin nods. "Yes, I had some help from a couple of squirrels."

Talon looks up quizzically. "Well, we should be on our way."

The rest of the trip passes uneventfully and by the afternoon they approach the small hamlet of Ulna. A young man carrying a pitchfork stops Talon and Mairin. The half-elf does not recognize this farmer. Talon explains to him that he grew up just outside the village in the nearby forest, and he is here to talk to William the Blue. Begrudgingly, the young farmer lets them pass. He gives the red-haired Mairin a long stare. Soon, Talon recognizes some of the town folk who nod to him while others gaze at Mairin. Finally, Talon spies William the Blue sporting a longbow made from yew on his back.

"Sir, it is good to see you. This is my friend Mairin, Mikal's daughter. How do you fare?"

William shakes Talon's hand and nods toward Mairin. "Hold on, please, let's take this conversation inside."

The leader of the village shows them the way and enters the main building.

"Please, be seated, and I will bring you some food."

William the Blue looks to Talon and then to the young girl. "It does not go well. There are too many strangers hereabouts. Some enter our village and ask way too many questions. They offer us coin. They think they can buy our information. They asked about the whereabouts of a half-elf and about a wizard with red hair. And now, just this morning, I had a dangerous looking man ask about a young girl with red hair." He looks to Mairin. "We tell them nothing, but how do they know to ask these questions?"

Talon does not respond. William continues, "There are also reports of peculiar creatures passing through our woods."

"I have no answers to your questions. I was to escort Mikal's daughter to a farm just outside the City of Addis, but we found it ablaze. She cannot return."

William the Blue looks hard at the half-elf. "She would not be safe here and neither would you. I do not know what you are involved in, but I will supply you with anything that I have. You can stay the night if you wish but, for everyone's sake, it is imperative that you leave first thing in the morning."

Talon accepts the advice. "How is Jocomund?"

William the Blue smiles. "Fine, though I have not seen him recently. I expect him back tonight, though. He will be happy to see you."

"And I, him," Talon responds.

A heavy-set woman serves dinner and everyone eats heartily. They find beds and start to relax, but still no Jocomund. The town sleeps well this night.

***

The simple hamlet awakens at dawn. There is always much to do. Talon and Mairin rise and wash themselves with cool, clean, spring water. Both of them fill their traveling packs with food and supplies. Talon turns to Mairin. "I would have liked to have seen Jocomund before we left. Maybe we should visit the hairy hermit."

Mairin responds, "He sounds interesting."

Talon nods his head. "He has many names, the Mad Plunket, for one. He's a healer and lives in a cave with many different animals and creatures. It's not far and he has aided us before. I believe sometimes the future speaks to him. I know that sounds strange."

Mairin looks Talon in the eyes. "No, that does not sound strange to me. My mother had the Sight, and she would sometimes tell me the future spoke to her. I would like to meet this hermit."

"So be it. I will show you the way."

They bid their farewells to the people they see, but most are already working in the fields. They enter the thick woods. Tamarix often runs ahead and scouts. It is a bright sunny day, but Mairin cannot help but feel a sense of foreboding. Even Talon stops often and looks in different direction as if he believes they are being watched. Abruptly, Talon stops again and turns toward Mairin. He looks up in the trees.

"I have neither seen nor heard any animals for some time. This is peculiar, but the cave is not far. Be alert."

They continue cautiously. Talon points to Tamarix. He is sitting with his chin close to the ground, staring straight ahead.

Marion asks, "Do I hear someone weeping?"

The half-elf runs ahead. He spies Jocomund lying face down, crying. Talon bends his knees and gently turns the small human over. Distressingly, he notices a number of bleeding wounds cover the diminutive body.

"What has happened here?"

Jocomund, still weeping, gasps, "I tried to stop him. But he was so big, and he was so fast. But he didn't get away though. The animals, they attacked him, the insects stung him, squirrels and badgers bit him and would not let him go. He ran, but the birds pecked at him. But then I heard it. I bet it was a big one. A huge, black bear finally got him and I heard him scream." The small human smiles weakly.

Mairin approaches. "Oh no, there is so much blood!"

Talon picks up the small human and carries him into the recluse's cave. Normally, the hermit's home is a hive of activity, but now everything is subdued. The half-elf passes one room and then another. There are many critters staring at them but none make a sound. They enter the last room. Animals are all about, but, again no sound is heard.

Lying on the floor is the hermit with a black-bladed knife protruding from his chest.

Jocomund sobs, "No, no…"

In spite of his wounds, the Squirrel Master crawls and rests his hand on his friend's leathery face. Ever so gently he closes his mentor's sightless eyes.

"I told you I would weep for you. But why did you have to die?"

The small human suddenly swoons and falls unconscious. Talon immediately picks him up and carries him into one of the earlier rooms. He lovingly lays him on a straw bed. Mairin meticulously inspects his wounds.

"I am familiar with some healing enchantments but they are for minor cuts and bruises. I do not know if they will help him."

She closes her eyes and intones a healing spell. The blood flow slows but does not cease. Talon tries to dress some of the wounds, but with little success.

Mairin stands. "I will see if I can find anything else that might help us." She looks around and leaves, only to return moments later. "Talon, I found this note on a table along with these vials. The note says, *These potions are for my friends, the Squirrel Master, Talon, and the girl with the auburn hair.*"

She shows the curious note to the half-elf. She holds in her hand three slender vials containing thick, green fluid. Talon reads the note twice.

"He must have known this was going to happen and that we would eventually show up. Amazing."

The half-elf opens the vial and spreads a small amount of the medicine on Jocomund's most critical wound. The rest he pours down his friend's throat.

"Here," he says to Mairin, "Put this in your rucksack. It is a potent, healing mixture."

Ever so softly, they hear a humming begin to vibrate throughout the cave. "Wait here." Talon reenters the room that contains the body of the dead eremite. There are two blue-jays pecking at the lethal weapon embedded in the hermit's chest. The half-elf solemnly pulls the knife from his friend's fatal wound.

Talon steps back, holding the vile blade in his hand. The creatures in the cave approach the body. Talon stares transfixed by the sight. Mice start to lick and clean the blue hands, feet, and face. Birds peck at his beard, neatly straightening the strands. Squirrels and chipmunks paw at the flowing, white hair, brushing it in their own way. A pair of badgers tugs on his matted brown robe, straightening it the best they can.

Talon decides to check on his wounded friend. Tamarix stays. He is fascinated and watches every detail. Talon finds Mairin cleansing the wounds on the tiny body and applying fresh dressing to them.

"That was an impressive elixir you gave him. See, the cuts are healing quickly. His breathing is strong and regular."

Talon shakes his head slowly. "The last time I was here it was because Jocomund had one of these in him." He displays the dark-bladed knife. "In his back. It was a mortal wound but somehow the hermit saved his life. He gave that deadly blade to your father. Sometime later, we found it had his name on it; *Novastar*. I do not know if there are any hidden runes on this one." He places the weapon on a nearby table.

Mairin looks to Talon. "I do not know what to say. So much as happened so fast."

Talon nods his head. "Your father often expressed that he could not believe all the events that he was swept up in."

The girl looks around the room. "I am surprised for a man living in a cave that everything is so well placed and clean."

A smile appears on Talon's face. "This is not how the hermit's living area normally is. Usually everything is in disarray, with all manner of creatures coming and going. Again, he must've known this was all going to happen. You would've thought that he would have tried to prevent it."

Mairin looks at the half-elf. "Maybe he knew this had to happen. It might be for the best."

Both ponder each other's words. Animals and creatures come and go and birds flutter about. Jocomund's eyes open as he weakly sits up.

"Talon, tell me it's not true… my nightmare. Is he truly dead?"

Talon gently whispers, "He is dead. Can you tell me again what transpired here?" The small human gathers his courage. "I don't know…something did not feel right. I knew I had to hurry. But as I approached the cave, I heard no animals… no forest sounds. Before I could enter I heard… a clamorous collection of sounds. I can only describe it as…all the creatures and animals in the cave screamed at once. I drew my blade… a tall, thin, bearded man was striding out. When he saw me, he laughed. I knew what he had done…I lunged at him but he easily evaded my knife. He knocked me down with his fist. Then a curious thing…he looked to his ring. It was silver and had a round, dark opal set into it. He pondered it for a moment…and said *so you have been in contact with the assassin's blade, as well.* Like I told you before, he drew his knife. I am ashamed to admit it but he… toyed with me. He danced and cut me at will and told me I would die. But then the animals came to my rescue, birds and squirrels and others. I did cut him once in the leg, as he ran…I know that big bear got him. I hoped he clawed and took large bites out of him. I wish I was bigger and stronger."

There is a sudden commotion in the cave and Tamarix enters the room with his nose and tail held high. He paces back and forth. Slowly, a solemn column of a multitude of animals marches past their room. Large and small creatures of the forest form the line. The three humans stand and stare at the inconceivable site. The prone body of the hermit is transported outside the cave. The creatures have adorned his body with flowers of all color and kind. A pleasant scent fills the air. His beard is groomed neatly. Two scores of squirrels bear the hermit's body. But the most amazing sight is the white hair. Small groups of his locks are being carried by thousands of ants, each holding and spreading out his tresses, creating a halo effect that surrounds his head. The three stare, mesmerized by the sight. Once the procession has passed, they follow, helping Jocomund along.

They enter daylight, and another spectacle to behold. Every branch of every tree is filled with all manner of animals, forming an arch. There are thousands in front of the procession, lined up, creating a pathway for the carriers of the body. A colony of honeybees swoops in and hover just above the hermit's body forming a buzzing, living shroud. A soft rain starts to fall, but the sun still shines.

Mairin looks up. "It's a sun shower...as if nature is weeping for one of its own." They continue to follow the moving hermit. Near a small stream, a large group of opossums and badgers surrounds a deep, oblong hole. At the far end of this grave is an impressive black bear. Talon takes note of its two paws. The blood-stained, long, thick claws look like two massive shovels. One side of the grave is angled for a sloping access.   Squirrels and insects lower the body to the bottom of the grave. The soft rain stops. The birds start to sing, but it is not a pleasant morning song. It is a dirge that no human has heard before. Talon is not sure, but he believes he hears a distant melody being played on woodland pipes. The squirrels and many of the creatures turn toward Jocomund the Squirrel Master. He hesitates but for a moment, steps forward, and stands tall.

"He was the smartest man I ever knew. He always treated me with kindness and respect. I think his favorite thing to do was help everyone. I know he loved everyone and showed it every day. The forest is less without him." The Squirrel Master bends down and picks up a handful of dirt and tosses it into the grave. "Let him become one with the forest." The animals are utterly silent. Then small groups of them start to fill the grave with the surrounding earth. It does not take long until it is covered over. Flocks of colorful birds descend and leave more vivid and beautiful flower petals, creating a natural mosaic.

Solemnly, the creatures start to leave, save the black bear. It lumbers toward the remaining three, with its snout held high. Mairin moves closer and holds on to Talon. Jocomund stares at the mammoth creature. Talon has his hand on his knife. Then a strange thing happens. The beast stands on its hind legs and his head starts to morph into a somewhat human shape. Marion steps back. Talon draws his blade.

In a deep, throaty voice, the monstrosity growls, "Put that puny weapon away. Show me no harm and no harm will come to you. I need to talk to the three of you."

Chapter 23

The one-armed dwarf takes point, leading a small mule hauling their supplies. Aden and Drew, the bodyguard, follow. Mikal walks with his staff in his right hand and Margaret Carol to his left. Majam, as always, walks just ahead of her mage. They make good time and encounter few travelers on the road. They find some shade and take their first respite.

Drew Foxx offers, "I apologize if this recommendation is out of line, but I'm in charge of the young lady's well-being. I have heard rumors, Mikal Novastar, that there is a bounty on your head. At the very least, there are people that wish you ill fortune. Luckily, I know this land well and I can show you less traveled paths to the Valley. It may improve our chances of escaping detection."

Aden chimes in, "Well, I don't fear detection but if there is less sun and more shade I'm all for it."

The dwarf looks to Mikal and gives a reassuring nod. "Meet, two."

Mikal says to Drew, "The Baron has given his approval of you, Captain Foxx. Show us the way."

The seasoned warrior leads them into the woods. A short time later, he finds the path he was seeking.

He turns and instructs, "Even though this is an obscure way, I ask you all to keep your eyes and ears open and talk softly."

Drew leads them through the dense, cool woods, stopping periodically to take stock of his surroundings. They find a clean stream and they fill their water containers. Margaret incessantly keeps asking Mikal questions, some about his cat, others about his training in the art of magic. The mage is patient as a teacher and tries to answer all her questions, though keeping the answers brief.

Mikal laughs softly. "You do remind me of my daughter of not too many years ago. So full of questions. Now I have one for you. What are you seeking with the Sisters of Endorr?"

The young lass pauses for a moment to gather her thoughts.

"Well, I have heard many tales about them. They're supposed to be all so beautiful, or they can make themselves look beautiful. I am not sure what I am seeking. But they are knowledgeable in some of the magic arts, are they not?" Mikal nods. "And I think it may be the word that you use to describe; sisters. I have known since I was a very young girl that it is a man's world. Only special females can rise in that world. But in the Valley, women rule. I wish to learn their ways so that I can lead wisely. As skilled as any man," she ends, a bit defiantly.

Mikal chuckles. "Maybe better." They share a laugh.

Drew Foxx decides to make camp for the night. He stands next to a rock as tall as a man.

"We can make a small fire to cook by, but we must hurry, for once the sun is fully set, the fire must be put out."

A small amount of firewood is brought forth and Aden sets the tinder to flame. A meal is quickly cooked and everyone has their fill. The fire is quickly extinguished as the last vestiges of sunlight fall over the horizon.

The bodyguard stands. "I'll take the first watch. Aden Ferrum, you take the second, and you, dwarf, shall take the third. Sleep well. We should enter the Valley on the morrow."

***

Mikal has a disturbing night. He tosses and turns and murmurs throughout. Twice Margaret Carol has to shake him to silence him, but he does not awaken. Dawn reveals heavy clouds above. Mikal rises but is silent. They share a brief breakfast.

Kairn, the dwarf, stares at the threatening clouds. "It iz go een turane."

Aden snorts, "Well, aren't you the astute observer. Let's be on our way, unless you fear that you'll melt, sweetness."

The seasoned warrior again leads the group, followed by Mikal cradling Majam, Aden, and Margaret Carol. The dwarf, still leading the mule, trails behind. The ominous clouds continue to darken, but they do not release their content. They travel most of the morning under the cover of this dim light.

"What are you doing?" asks the young girl.

The dwarf shakes his head. "Nut ting.

A short time later, again she asks, "Stop that. What are you doing to Master Mikal?"

Aden turns and confronts the one-armed one. "What is that in your hand?"

Slowly, the dwarf opens his hand. In his palm are three small, black feathers.

Margaret Carol says, "He's been grabbing these from Mikal's hair all morning."

The White Wizard runs his hand through his fire-red hair. "I have felt nothing."

Aden closely inspects the feathers and the back of Mikal's head. "I think I see feathers growing even as we speak. You feel nothing, mage?"

"No, not at all."

Aden steps between Majam and the wizard. "Mikal, give me your hand. Do you feel anything?"

"Yes, I do. Why, may I ask, are you scratching my palm? It feels as if you placed warm water there."

"No, Mikal, I took my knife and sliced your palm. You should be in pain."

"Knot a gud sine," states the dwarf.

"How insightful of you. He is becoming desensitized to the touch and is somehow growing black feathers. Tell me, wizard, you had a disturbing night. Do you remember any of it?"

The White Wizard shakes his head. "No, but I have been trying to remember. Nothing. I do not feel any worse the wear, but I am tired. I've been tired since I left the School of the Three Moons not that long ago." Mikal smiles. "This is all very odd, indeed, but we best be on our way."

Aden looking toward the dwarf and whispers, "Keep an eye on him."

The dwarf nods and the rains fall.

In the course of the next hour, Mikal stumbles twice though the road is smooth. Both times the Baroness' daughter is there to help him.

The rain is steady and is starting to muddy the path. The White Wizard places his staff in a harness on his back. Majam jumps inside her mage's traveling cloak, keeping her head exposed so Mikal can see. The drizzle lets up, and starts again. This pattern repeats itself for the entire morning. Sometime after noon, the path ends on top of a stony cliff.

The bodyguard Foxx looks into the valley. "Well, gentlemen and lady, we have made it thus far. I caution you, the way down is slow and treacherous. I believe the mule will have little difficulty, however."

In just over half an hour, they finish the descent and move across the valley's floor in search of the witches' encampment. The rain has stopped again, but the skies are still filled with brooding clouds.

"Look, I believe I can see one of the colorful tents," the Baron's daughter exclaims excitedly as she points. Suddenly, the air is filled with a dusky flock of carrion crows, all shrieking in unison an irritating sound.

Mikal covers his ears with both hands. "I cannot think with that a dreadful noise." He looks up and, with his cat's sight, he spies the foul, foreboding flock.

"Be gone!" the Mage demands. To everyone's astonishment, the dark birds fly off as if heeding the command. The group stops and stares at the White Wizard who says, "Well, at least the maddening sound is gone. Let us just keep on."

Aden nods in agreement and takes the lead. Margaret Carol softly whispers, "Something's not right."

Drew Foxx points. "Behold the tents. The canvasses are ripped to shreds."

He readies his spear and moves protectively in front of the young girl. Aden slows and raises his staff. The dwarf holds his new weapon high.

An armed warrior dressed in the encampment's colors approaches. Aden and the bodyguard cautiously lower their weapons. Majam gives off a low, throaty sound, almost like a growl.

Mikal whispers, "You are correct, Margaret Carol. Something *is* amiss. I sense danger approaches."

The colorful warrior nears, limping noticeably. He carries a broken sword and his eyes are dull and lifeless. His lower jaw hangs open and his tongue flaps obscenely in the wind. Drew Foxx steps forward and hurls his spear. His aim is true. The long, sharp weapon digs deep into the warrior's sunken chest. The hideous apparition hesitates but a moment and continues toward the group.

Aden readies his short staff. "It is a dead thing."

A fiery stream shoots toward the hellish soldier and sets it ablaze. It still does not stop. To the contrary, it charges the group, holding its sharp, broken sword above its bulbous head. The conflagration grows more intense. The dwarf launches his enchanted weapon and the blunt side crashes into the grotesque face. A shockwave propels the ghastly creature back, knocking it down. The unearthly thing tries to stand, but the magic fire has penetrated deep and the creature combusts almost instantly to ash. The bodyguard retrieves his spear and the dwarf's impressive weapon.

Majam hisses loudly and arcs her back. The Baroness' daughter follows the cat's gaze. "Look! There's someone, I think it's a girl, running. See her? The ground behind her... it's moving toward her! It's about to overtake her!"

Mikal and his cat recognize this threat. It is an incredibly large number of rats in pursuit of the hapless lass.

Margaret Carol screams, "You there! Come this way and we shall protect you." Aden stares at the Baroness' daughter.

The running girl looks up and changes her path. Her eyes dart back and forth as if trying to make a decision. Mikal waves his arms. "We can help you."

The running girl seems to recognize the mage. The bodyguard notes, "She's a fast one, is she not?"

A preteen girl approaches the group, slows, looks behind her, and then turns toward Mikal, who asks, "It is Catherine, is it not?"

"It is. I'm so glad you're here. Please don't tell Sister Aurum you saw me. We must hurry. Those rats are hungry and we must flee!"

The White Wizard addresses her. "I do not believe we are as fast as you. Aden, you have been wanting to show off your fire's power...now would be a good time."

The Red Wizard smiles. "Behold, and be amazed."

He holds his staff waist high. The filthy horde is closing. He recites arcane words, then swings his short staff toward the ground, back and forth. Gouts of flame start to spread to his right then to his left as he continues to wield his fiery weapon. A wall of flame not higher than his knees grows longer with each arc. He stops, turns, and, with sweat dripping off his face, says, "We best be moving, unless you are fond of the smell of burning rats."

The group does not hesitate and, with Majam to guide her mage, they set a swift pace while the dwarf leads the mule.

Catherine directs them away from the multitude of vermin. They eventually reach a pile of rocks that forms a rough arrow. The young girl looks around, then points across the valley toward a high cliff.

"That's the way. Let us go."

Again she runs off even more quickly. The group struggles but cannot keep up. Mikal trips and falls hard to the ground. He is helped by the dwarf. "I am sorry. Thankfully, I am unharmed. Continue."

They do, but at a reduced rate. Aden pauses. "I do not believe they are following us. I hope this girl knows where she's going. It just looked like a pile of rocks to me."

The cliff looms larger as they approach. Catherine is far ahead, but they can still see her to follow. She disappears at the base of a cliff and large boulders obscure their vision. They slow as the ground starts to slope upward. A man appears with a bow and takes aim at the group.

The young girl yells, "No, no! They're with me."

A middle-aged woman comes into view between two strangely shaped stones. "You must be the ones the Sister has foreseen. You bring both good and evil with you, but you may pass."

Catherine waits for them. "Stay close and follow me."

They traverse a hidden pass that moves up the cliff's face until they encounter another huge rock in the vague shape of a bear. The cliff side of the rock casts a deep shadow. The young girl disappears inside it. The group hesitates. Mikal, holding Majam in his arms, steps into the unsettling darkness, like going through a curtain. A welcoming light reveals a large tunnel. The others, including the mule, pass through.

The young Sister Aurum waits for them. She stares long and deep into Mikal's white eyes.

"Something is not right, but I am relieved that you are here. Please, all of you, follow me."

They travel down a natural tunnel and pass a number of intersecting, man-made paths. Sister Aurum turns and leads them into a well-furnished cavern filled with many tables and chairs. The main feature of the room is a large, natural table made of stone.

"Please, be seated. We need to talk."

Mikal introduces the men. "And this is Margaret Carol, the Baroness' daughter. She was said to have an appointment with you."

Sister Aurum nods. "I am sorry, little sister; you are not seeing us at our best. But you are most welcome here. You may decide how long you wish to stay."

Aden demands, "Witch, what has happened to your encampment?"

She hesitates. "He came... the Dark Harold. I will not describe the horrors he wrought. But I do believe it was revenge for what we have revealed about his plans. Many of us died. The fear was the worst. It would have been easy for one to lose all hope. We did not believe that we could go on, but some of us persevered. We gathered what we could and ran. We hid among the rocks below us until dawn. Monica and Catherine searched the area and they found this hidden hideaway. We are still exploring it.

"Fortuitously, we found a room, another natural cavern, nearby. The markings and the geological altar identified it as a coven. I remembered that Sister Fluorine said when we first entered the Valley, 'We have returned home.' I dismissed it at the time, but she must have known that some of our kind inhabited this cave and valley many years ago."

A middle-aged witch interrupts and approaches Mikal, holds out her arms, and rests her palms on his head. She closes her eyes. "Who has put this foul curse upon you?"

Aden stands. "It was a Witchraven. That is why we are here. We were led to believe that you could cure him. He's been sprouting dark feathers in his hair. His sense of touch is sorely lacking."

Sister Aurum looks to Mikal. "I apologize. I knew something was wrong, but I did not see. This is Sister Kali-um. She is now our eldest and most gifted healer."

Sister Kali-um carefully moves her hands toward the White Wizard's eyes. When her fingertips lightly touch the eyelids, her mouth opens wide and there is a pause. Shockingly, a loud scream escapes from her. She breaks contact and collapses to the ground. Other Sisters come and assist her.

Sister Aurum asks, "What did you see, Sister?"

The eldest witch turns and gapes at Mikal. Nothing is said. Again Sister Aurum pleads, "Are you harmed? What did you see?"

"I am sorry," Sister Kali-um responds. "Yes, there is a curse on him. A vile fluid has entered his body. Some of it remains inside...and it is festering."

The young head witch asks, "What must we do to remove this foul deed?"

The master healer stands and starts to pace. "I know the procedure but the words do not fully come to me. And they must be recited perfectly. You know what we have to do, Sister. You must retrieve our books. It is the only way. I know it is dangerous, but I have faith that we shall succeed."

Aden questions, "What books? And where are they?"

Sister Aurum explains, "When we ran, no one...I should have... but I failed to gather our artifacts. They are back at our camp surrounded by evil things."

Aden holds out his staff. "Tell me where they are and I will carve out a path to them."

Sister Aurum shakes her head. "You would not be able to find them even if I gave you explicit directions. There is an enchantment on our artifacts and if we give their location to anyone, when approached, the artifacts will not be there. Only one of our coven could find and retrieve them, but it is too dangerous."

Catherine and Monica step forward. "We could go at first light. Please allow us this honor."

The Sister frowns. "It is too dangerous, I say."

Aden strides forward. "Not for me, it isn't. I will protect them."

"I do not know. First, let us see what we can do to help Master Mikal."

For the next hour the Witches of Endorr perform healing rights on the White Wizard. At the end of that time, they all agree that they accomplished little.

"We need our books."

Sister Aurum nods. "Before anything, let us eat and then I will sleep on it and see what the morning brings."

Chapter 24

The starlight is filtered by fast flowing clouds. The White Wizard leans on his staff of light with both hands. His cat's ears are perked and her tail is held high with the tip of it twitching back and forth. He waits. He hears hooves clopping on uneven stones. He turns, and stares into the night.

A large, deep shadow of a rider on a unearthly horse moves ever closer. The fearsome shade halts and Mikal can feel its penetrating gaze. It dismounts, and strides toward the White Wizard. Mikal feels a grip on his arm.

"I am sorry I could not face him alone." Without turning, Mikal knows it is Sister Aurum standing behind him speaking. Instinctively, he taps his staff to the ground. A solid white sphere appears and protects the two of them and Majam. All becomes silent. The dark, armor-clad knight stands just outside the glowing field.

The silence is broken by the slow menacing sound of metal scraping metal until the threatening knight raises his barbed sword in his left hand. He brings it down on the bright light, sparks fly, and the White Mage holds his staff high and grips it tighter. Again and again the dark sword strikes until minute cracks start to appear in the globe.

Out of frustration, the Shadow Knight starts to pound with his right fist that wears a heavy, metal gauntlet. The assault is relentless. Mikal is rocked with each thundering blow. Minute cracks start to widen and grow longer.

Majam raises her paws, claws extended, and hisses at her opponent. This strengthens Mikal's protection, but only temporarily. The shimmering white globe finally shatters, sending shards of light everywhere. The dark creature strides forward and the White Wizard stands before him.

In a throaty rasp, the Shadow Knight commands, "Out of my way, mage, my business is with her."

"No. Am I to believe that you are a true knight?"

The armored-clad one hesitates, but does not answer. Mikal presses,

"Are you Knight or no?"

The red eyes stare from behind their metallic helm. "I am."

"Then I challenge you to a duel to avenge the abhorrent deeds of which you are guilty."

Again silence engulfs the night. "Name your champion, wizard."

"Sir Rusel Ironwood."

"I believe I know that name. I will enjoy taking his soul, if he still has one. Name the arena."

Mikal responds, "On the plains of the Valley of Endorr, the place you have cursed."

The Dark Knight nods in agreement.

"In five days then," the White Mage states.

"No, you have challenged me. I choose the day. I will not be done with my task in only five. It will be on the eighth day from this day, at dusk."

The White Wizard agrees. Again he feels the penetrating stare of his opponent. An obscene, soft laugh slowly escapes from the Shadow Knight's throat. "Do you know why we can communicate like this, mage? It is because of the curse. You are becoming one of us."

"Never," protests Mikal.

The warrior laughs brazenly. "I said the same a thing long ago."

The audacious laugher penetrates deep into the White Wizard's soul.

***

How many times have I failed at this? But desperation drives me to try again. I must find the Dark Harold. I enter my seeking meditation. I almost found you last time. I will not fail now.

Sister Aurum's body is in a restful state but her mind soars. It comes to rest on the Plains of Endorr.

I am alone. No, not so. I think he has found me."

Something dark comes her way. Suddenly, Mikal, along with his cat, materializes ahead, with his back toward her. The shaded knight reins in his stallion, and dismounts. The White Wizard raises a protective, silvery sphere. The opponent pounds on the protective shield with sword and fist. First it cracks, then it shatters and the shadowy assailant advances.

The White Mage raises his staff high and it flares with a blinding white light. The warrior steps back for a moment then continues forward. He raises his menacing barbed sword and brings it down, crashing into the White Wizard's staff of light. The staff shatters into many splinters, leaving Mikal holding a short wooden shard in his hand.

The great cat leaps onto the attacking creature but its claws cannot penetrate the armor. A scraping, maddening sound is produced by the cat's claws as they descend. The iron-clad knight seizes Majam and flings her far. Then, impossibly fast, he grasps the White Wizard's neck.

"Out of my way, mage, for you are for my master. My business is with the girl." He squeezes then tosses Mikal aside. The girl stands tall, her hands in fists, her chin held high. She glares at this huge, shadowy thing and trembles.

"I will say this only once, girl. Stay out of my mind, and do not seek me out again. My Master's cloak prevents you from ever finding me but your constant searching is irritable. Something is protecting your soul or I would possess it by now. If you do not cease, I will find the rest of your coven and kill them all, save you. You will be left alone in sorrow and misery."

The audacious laughter penetrates deep into the young girl's soul.

Chapter 25

Sometime after dawn, Sister Kali-um tells the young head witch that the White Wizard is getting worse and that the healing ritual must take place in the next twenty-four hours or the curse will be irreversible. Sister Aurum accepts the grave news. She gives the orders to waken Aden Ferrum and to bring him before her. Sometime later, the Red Wizard enters the chamber and sees Sister Aurum giving instructions to Catherine. He waits until the young head witch acknowledges his presence.

"I trust you slept well. Food will be brought forth soon." She casts her eyes to the floor and continues, "You are to escort and protect young Catherine here. I have foreseen a safe path that will get you into our encampment. But I apologize. Beyond that, all else is hidden in shade from my sight. Master Ferrum, you must understand. Catherine's life is extremely important to me. Mikal's life, as we know it, rests upon the return of our ancient texts. Are you prepared for this quest?" She does not wait for a reply. "I strongly suggest that you proceed with utmost caution and follow Catherine's recommendations. I realize this will be most difficult for you. She is familiar with the terrain, however, and has been there recently, even though she had been forbidden to do so. I hope you are in shape, for speed might be your best ally."

A young witch appears balancing a tray. "I see the food has arrived. Enjoy a light breakfast, and then we will see how a Red Wizard handles himself."

***

By midmorning the two seekers depart. Catherine points out that they are being followed by the dwarf but Aden does not respond. They cross the valley floor and arrive at the rocks that form an arrow. They wait, but the dwarf slows and then stops.

Aden asks, "Why are you following us, dwarf? You don't belong on this quest…or any other quest, for that matter."

Kairn steps forward and sits on the pile of rocks. "Isle way tier."

Catherine starts to say something but is cut off by Aden who declares, "All dwarves are stubborn and stupid. Let him sit on his rocks and wait."

Catherine has a quizzical look on her face.

"Never mind. You take point, and let's move."

The young girl walks swiftly and soon they see the outline of the ragged tents on the horizon.

Catherine whispers, "Most creatures are usually asleep this time of day. We must move quickly and quietly so as to not arouse anything unpleasant."

Aden scratches his stubbly chin and shakes his head.

They approach the corner of the outermost tent. Catherine pauses, grabs hold of one of the support posts, and starts to climb. Aden softly grumbles and follows. The young girl moves across the major beam, carefully putting one foot in front of the other. They are many feet above the ground. She encourages the Red Wizard to proceed. Fortuitously, the beam is quite wide and they move across it with relative ease.

Aden hears a low, rhythmic, bellowing sound. Catherine stops and points to the ground where Aden spies a sleeping giant, almost ten feet in length.

The young girl whispers, "He showed up recently. He's been drinking our wine by the barrelful."

Suddenly, the hairy giant belches loudly and wetly. His eyes flick open. The two stand still as gargoyles. The blurry eyes close and the rhythmic snoring resumes. Both sigh with relief, and move further along the beam. They arrive at the opposite corner of the first tent. Without hesitation, Catherine leaps onto the outsized, one-time colorful pavilion. She turns and waits for Aden.

"Oh, the follies of youth."

He gathers himself, leaps across the gap, and lands clumsily on Catherine's wooden post. She grabs and steadies him and urges him on. This beam has an upward arc to it and they move higher. The Red Wizard looks down and sees rats scurrying about. He spies another unearthly warrior, slowly swaying, deep in the shadows. Aden looks up but cannot see Catherine. He continues to the end of the thick, wooden beam. He looks down and sees she is on the ground again, inviting him to join her. He inexpertly shimmies down the wooden post, gaining splinters in his hands for his effort.

The young girl whispers, "So far, our luck holds. Now for the tricky part. We must enter the central cave. Remember, you're supposed to protect me."

Aden pulls splinters from his hands.

She lowers her carrying pack and removes four, long, ragged strips of bloodied cloth.

"Here," she whispers, "Wrap them around your feet and ankles. I took these from dead soldiers. I think they will help mask our smell."

She steps forward and cautiously turns the central cave's entry handle. She moves from sunlight into darkness. Aden follows, holding up his short, iron staff. He is about to light a flame, but the young girl grabs his arm. "No, just wait."

Minutes pass and, bit by bit, shaded images start to focus. Aden eyes adjust to the dim light that filters through minuscule cracks in the rocks. Catherine gives a light tug on Aden sleeve and steps deeper into the encampment's caves. Every step is slow and deliberate and she often stops to orientate herself. She passes doors and other pathways. The Red Mage can sense a dark, foreboding atmosphere growing. Catherine deviates from her straight path and turns left through a thick, torn curtain. Aden follows. He believes they are in a large cavern, but he cannot be sure for darkness surrounds him. Catherine quickly crosses the room and stops in front of a heavy, wooden door. She tries to open it but the handle does not budge.

"It is locked," she whispers.

Aden shakes his head. "I have a bad feeling about this, missy."

The young girl smiles and pulls out a strange looking key. She places it in the lock and presses it into the door. A soft click is heard and the door swings open.

"Wait here. I will be right back," she says.

Before Aden can protest, the girl is gone. The Red Mage feels the room getting darker. What little light there was is now gone. He allows his staff to glow softly. He can see his breath billowing before him.

Catherine returns. "I have the… oh, no." The young girl shivers. "This is the work of a Frigid Shade. It will freeze our very souls."

"No, I will not allow it." declares the Red Wizard. His staff erupts, producing a wave of blistering fire that roars across the cavern. His assessment is correct. They stand in an enormous room, the light from his flame illuminating most of the chamber. There is a darkened area in the shape of a human. The frigid entity holds up tentacle-like arms, and again the room becomes bitter cold. Aden responds a second time and narrows his flame directly at the menacing shade. Catherine darts across the room and Aden follows. They run as fast as they possibly can. They careen into things hidden by the shadows. They know the frigid shade follows.

"We're almost there!" yells the young girl. She bursts out a door into sunlight. Aden crashes into her. She explains, "It will not follow us out here."

The two take stock of their surroundings. Thousands of rats and other vermin surround them and two zombie-like warriors lumber their way, brandishing spears and axes. Without thinking, the Red Wizard encircles them with flame, keeping the nightmares at bay.

The young girl grabs Aden's cloak, but the Red Mage ignores her. He lowers his fire staff and sends out a flow of flame that hugs the ground, creating waves of heat that travel forty feet ahead of them.

Aden smiles. "Watch."

He focuses on the stream of fire and, within moments, it parts, creating a narrow pathway.

"Now you follow me, child. I will lead you from this irritating place."

They transverse the path, and before Aden reaches its end, he creates another circle of flame. The rats' and other vermin's numbers grow. Again, he throws out another stream. He splits this one as well, and they progress into another fiery circle. Catherine tugs on the Red

Mage's arm and points. A unearthly warrior lumbers toward them. Aden casts another spell and launches a hardened flame arrow which strikes the soldier in the forehead, impeding its progress.

"Keep moving." For a third time, he launches a carpet of flame ahead of them. He focuses on it and it grows wider. Even so, a burning rodent breaks through the heated barrier. The flaming creature scurries toward the two but Aden stomps and cuffs it aside with his boot. The strange warrior with the flaming arrow in its head again starts to approach them, holding its axe high. Aden concentrates and sends a stream of fire that engulfs the bellowing creature. It starts to flail its arms and staggers haphazardly away from them, igniting everything in its wake.

Catherine realizes that the fire is starting to rage out of control. The Red Wizard strains to keeps his focus as they move farther away from the inferno.

Catherine screams, "Look! The giant has awakened."

Aden turns toward this new threat. Again, a huge rat bursts through the flame, races toward the girl, and buries its pointed, disease-carrying teeth into her ankle. She panics and trips and knocks her head as she falls to the ground. Aden squashes the foul creature beneath his staff.

"My flame magic is being pushed to its limits, but my legs are still fresh," Aden thinks aloud. He picks up the young girl and, remembering what Sister Arum had said, he runs with her in his arms, dropping small fire pools behind them. He hopes the giant steps in them, burning his boots and feet. Their lead shrinks with every step. The girl starts to stir, and this clauses Aden to trip and fall. Catherine rolls free, as the Red Wizard springs back to his feet, holding his flame staff at the ready. The hairy giant has slowed, trying to stomp out his burning boots. The Red Mage takes aim and discharges a stream of fire at the huge creature, setting its thick beard and long hair ablaze. Aden picks up the girl and resumes their escape. They make good time for a short while, but his magic intensity and his legs weaken with every step. He hears a disturbing, loud bellow close behind and gently places the injured girl down.

"Run if you can!" he yells. "I shall stop him."

He propels a solid fire spear at the charging, flaming-haired giant. Astonishingly, the hairy brute knocks the hot spear out of the air. Again Aden tells the girl to run. The Red Wizard feels something closely brush by him. It flies past and impacts on the giant's knee, producing a loud, sickening, bone-crunching sound. The enraged, fiery beast tumbles heavily to the rocky ground. Kairn the dwarf runs by and quickly retrieves his enchanted weapon. The wounded, burning giant starts to rise. The axe-wielding one-armed dwarf leaps and buries his weapon deep into the massive head. The huge creature falls dead to the ground, still ablaze.

Aden looks to the dwarf. "I do not know what it is between your kind and giants but you surely do not like each other much. Not that I want to know. Oh, and by the way, my flame would have killed him soon enough."

Kairn pulls his weapon free. "My axis kwicker than yore fie er." He adds sarcastically, "O, wee doan't lie cow thay smell."

The two help Catherine continue. They approach the Endorr's cliff and a witch guard runs to assist them. Sister Aurum is waiting for them at the bear-shaped rock.

"Oh, dear. Are you injured, Catherine?"

"I think not. I was bitten by a large rat, however." She shows the red marks on her ankle. "We did retrieve a number of our books."

She hands Sister Arum a satchel that contains the sought-after texts from the hidden vault. "Aden Ferrum was unbelievably awesome!" She looks admiringly at her savior.

Aden smirks.

"I don't think there's much of our encampment left, though."

"Let us not worry about that right now. Go and have that wound treated immediately."

They enter the main cave. Aden, the dwarf, and Sister Aurum cross a threshold into a small chamber where Margaret Carol and her bodyguard wait for them. Food and water is brought forth. Aden explains how difficult the recovery was. He does not mention Kairn dealing with the giant. They are interrupted by one of the witches who explains that, with the recovered texts, they can begin the cleansing ritual on Mikal Novastar within the hour. "Everything is being prepared. Sister Catherine has been treated. There was a poison in her system. Sister Kali-um strongly recommends that she does not take part in the wizard's healing ritual. As you know, this will leave us two healers shy of the optimal number."

Headmistress Aurum nods. "Thank you for that information. Now go help with the preparation." She turns toward the Baroness' daughter. "What I am about to ask you is dangerous and difficult."

Margaret Carol holds up her hands. "Before you say anything more, I gladly volunteer to help anyway I can."

"You must understand that your participation will not be without risk. There will be ten of us where there should be eleven. We will recite the ritual words many times. Each time all of us shall attempt to draw the poisonous curse from the wizard into ourselves in the hope of absorbing a fraction of the curse. We will then expel it into a container."

Kairn stands. "Eye vol in tier two hell pew."

The head witch smiles. "Only females would have a chance of success. It is our way of life to take in things and deal with their effects. But I thank you. You may watch in silence if you care to. As long as you swear not to interfere in any way. We must take our leave and prepare. You will be notified when the time is near."

***

Later, Aden and Kairn are alerted that the ritual is about to commence and are escorted to the attempted purification of Mikal. Before they enter the largest cavern, a guard explains that they can take no weapons inside, by the order of Sister Aurum. Begrudgingly, both accept this stipulation and Aden's fire staff and Kairn's enchanted axe are left behind. They pass through the ceremonial portal, and find Mikal Novastar lying on an impressive stone table which now looks like an altar of some type. He is washed and naked, save for his clean, grey loin cloth. His eyes are closed. His red hair and beard are brushed and neatly trimmed. His white streak does not look as bright as it once did. There is no movement except for the slight rise and fall of his chest. To his right lies his staff.

If I did not know better, this looks like they're preparing him for burial, thinks the Red Mage.

Inexplicably, there is an ornate cup hanging directly above Mikal, suspended from the high, stone ceiling. Its base is made from expensive polished silver. The cup itself consists of fine crystal. The vessel's rim is covered with a thin coating of the same silver as its base. The light from surrounding fires glistens off its highly polished surface.

A string of bells softly chimes. Ten beautiful, healing witches appear, dressed in simple, white gowns. They take their assigned positions around the granite altar. As Sister Kali-um is about to give final instructions, Majam leaps on the table, approaches her master, and lies down, placing her front paws and her chin on Mikal's left arm.

"We are now eleven, Sisters. I remind you that this man's life is essential to the very survival of our land. With each round, we are to draw a small amount of this poisonous curse from him. We are to hold it in ourselves and then expel it into the glass chalice above. As we proceed, if one of us shall falter, the rest must continue at all costs. Do you understand?" A solemn nodding of heads. "Let us begin."

Next to Sister Kali-um is a short, wooded dais. On top of it lies an ancient text. With utmost reverence, she opens it. The soft sound of bells fills the room. She recites esoteric words as everyone listens intently. She holds out her arms over the prone figure and again intones the olden phrase, raising and lowering her head as she does so. The sisters mimic her movements and words. The healers hesitate, and then deeply inhale. Thus ends the first round.

Again, arms extend, heads raise and lower, and ancient words are spoken. Once again the participants inhale. This is repeated so often that Aden loses track of the number.

Without warning, one of the younger sisters suddenly bends over clutching her stomach and expels foul, brackish liquid onto the floor. She falls to her knees. The ritual continues without her.

Aden knows it is late in the day but he does not think it dusk yet. Majam, Mikal's cat, has become curiously black. The ancient healing ritual has slowed. The words are still recited, but now drone on with little enthusiasm. Arms are heavy, all are ill. Aden wonders how long the sisters can endure, but they persevere.

Sensing their weakness, Sister Kali-um raises her voice and her arms. "We must not falter, Sisters, with our task so near completion."

The ritual is repeated a number of more times. Without warning, the women fall to their knees. "We have taken all we can," declares Sister Aurum. "Now we must expel the foul curse into the vessel above."

Sister Kali-um is the first. She opens her mouth wide and produces a wretched note. Astonishingly, minute, black as onyx spheres start to escape from her gaping maw. She is joined by the group. Aden has never seen or heard anything so uncomfortable in his life. The dwarf is frustrated for he can only cover one ear with his hand. Even Majam has her mouth wide and a thick stream of black globules are being expelled from it. They travel upward in a disgusting stream. It is as if the silver crystal chalice is drawing them to it. As it fills, the nauseating sound of the healers continues. The cup becomes full but the foul spheres keep rising and overfill the vessel.

To everyone's amazement, some of the cascading, black spheres start to form the shape of a shadowy crow. Small at first, but growing. Some of the sisters have collapsed while others continue to expel the indecent curse. Mikal starts to stir. His eyes flutter open and he sees the silver chalice overflowing, creating the dark bird. His right hand finds his staff of light next to him. It flares and sends a clean, white sphere that encircles the silver chalice and the dark form.

All but two of the sisters fall unconscious. Sister Kali-um grabs a silver, ornate lid from the dais. She stands on the table and grasps the chalice in her left hand. She takes the lid in her right and captures the dark, raven image. She frantically slams the cover shut and produces a silver cord and ties the lid tightly secured. "

"This must never be opened. I believe we have been successful, Sisters."

"A men two that," says the one-armed dwarf.

Chapter 26

"Follow me," growls the huge, black bear with the face of a human. The creature lumbers on all fours and the three follow with Tamarix at their sides. They near a clump of bushes and they smell death and decay. As they move closer they hear a multitude of insects buzzing about. Lying in overgrown weeds, they see the eyeless, highly decomposed body of the Mad Plunket's attacker.

The bear creature rests on his haunches. "Nature can be soft and beautiful or ravenous and ugly, as it is here. I clawed and ripped his throat with my teeth, but the forest was not satisfied. Carrion birds plucked out his eyes and small rodents took their share. But these tiny ones are the most devastating."

They see thousands of insects and maggots working fiercely on the body. Mairin mumbles, "It's as if nature is taking its revenge on this murderer."

Jocomund points to the ring on the corpse's decomposed finger. Surprising all, Mairin steps forward, bends down, and removes the ring. A glitter catches Talon's eye as he approaches the grotesque form. He leans over and takes something shiny off the sunken chest of the foul corpse.

"What is it?" asks Mairin.

Talon shakes his head. "He was definitely a highly trained dark assassin. I saw this cat-eyed pendant before in the city of Umbra."

"I can bear this stink no longer," says the Squirrel Master, holding his nose. "Let's go back to the cave."

All agree.

They pass by the hermit's new, colorful grave. The bear-creature unexpectedly stops. "I shall wait for you here." His face morphs fully back to bear form.

Talon asks Mairin for the ring that she took from the dead body. They walk by a cool, clean, flowing stream. The half-elf bends down and rinses the pendent and ring that sparkle in the bright sunlight.

The three continue until they enter the hermit's cave. Talon quickly searches it and pockets a few items. They meet in the room where they earlier had treated the Squirrel Master.

"How are you feeling, Jocomund?" asks Mairin.

"I'm mostly okay."

She nods in understanding and asks, "What should we do now?"

Talon hesitates. "I think I should try to return you to your father. But where he is, I am not sure. It might be best to travel to the City of Stonegrove." He takes the items from his pocket and places them on the table next to the black-bladed knife. "Jocomund, do you want any of these?"

The diminutive human shakes his head. "They would only bring me bad memories. You take them."

Talon picks up the ring. "This may be enchanted. Why don't you wear it, Mairin? I would like the pendant, if there are no objections." There are none and he puts it in his pocket. "Now, what to do with the dark blade."

Mairin steps forward. "You said my father accepted one similar to this. I will take it. If nothing else, it's a better weapon than I currently have." She places the black blade in her belt inside her cloak. "I think we should talk to that bear creature now. I'm curious."

Jocomund is the last to leave. They approach the enormous, black bear.

It surprises them by saying, "Please, wait here. It would be embarrassing to change fully back to human form in front of you. There are clothes in the cave. I'll be back shortly."

The three stand in amazement as the bear-man disappears into the cave.

"Do you think we can trust him? He looks so…feral. We could run," Mairin suggests.

Talon shakes his head. "He would easily outrun us. He could have harmed us if he wanted to. I think we should trust him, but be leery. What do you think, Jocomund?"

Before Jocomund can reply, a prolonged, heart-wrenching wail emanates from the cave. They three stand in stunned bewilderment.

The creature returns in human form. The man is very tall with thick, wide shoulders. He sports long, dark hair and his face is covered in a bushy, black beard. He wears a simple cloth shirt and cotton pants. He has no shoes and his feet are also covered with thick, sable hair. His toenails come to a point. He smiles, showing white teeth.

"Now, are you more comfortable with this form?" His voice is gravelly. The man/bear looks to the newly formed grave. "He was a wonderful man. I think he understood nature better than any other human. Squirrel boy, I wonder if he knew this was going to happen. I've been spending time with him recently. Out of the blue one night, he said to me that if anything ever happens to me tell Squirrel boy everything I have is his."

Jocomund blushes and bows his head.

"Let me introduce myself. My human name is Osme. It is a simple name given to me long ago. Jocomund, will you deliver a message to the head of your village? William the Blue, is it? Tell him that if he stops hunting bears, we will help him keep watch on the village. We will do whatever we can to keep out the unwanted creatures that have been passing by. If he agrees, tell him to leave some corn and any other feed in the north field on the large, flat rock. I sometimes like to sun there. Go now."

The Squirrel Master nods goodbye to Talon and Mairin and runs into the woods in the direction of the town of Ulna.

The man continues, "If the two of you don't mind, I would like to walk with you for a while. There are things for me to tell you. Besides, I've been too long without human company."

He looks directly at Mairin. "Mairin is it? You smell nice."

***

It is mid-afternoon and the three, along with Tamarix the cat, travel through a thick, wooden area.

Mairin asks the man, "You said your name was given to you long ago? Excuse me if I'm being too bold, but how old are you?"

Osme looks up to the overhead branches. "That is a difficult question. Time seems to travel differently when I'm in bear form. And recently I've been spending far more time as an animal than a human. I remember the hermit when he was very young. He would get lost in the woods, though he didn't even know he was lost nor did he care. He was lucky I never acquired a taste for humans. Maybe a hundred years, more or less."

"That's amazing. You don't look half that old."

"Thank you, I guess. Nature has an order of things. But I learned long ago, that there are many untrustworthy and conniving humans. They do not follow anything but their own selfish desires. In my experience, most humans do not act honorably."

No one responds for some time.

They continue traveling when Osme confuses them by saying, "I heard the call, you know."

Talon queries, "I am sorry, but to what call are you referring?"

"Weeks ago, all of our ilk, and many others, heard summonses. First by a Dark Herald and then an Ebony One. Certain scavenger birds, and vermin of all types, were eager to respond. I've seen so many wererats these lasts couple of weeks. I never did like them. Like most humans, they are not to be trusted and they smell awful." He pauses. "Not you, of course, Mairin."

Talon ignores the insult. "We've had our own troubles with them. They seem to have a strong interest in both Mikal Novastar and me."

"Yes," responds Osme. "I can still smell their stink on you, though faint. The name Novastar. I have heard it before, at night. It is whispered on the wind. They hunt him. Warn him to be careful and to choose his friends with caution."

"I hardly think a White Wizard needs my advice."

"Do it anyway."

"What about wolves?" asks Talon, changing the subject..

The man ponders the question. "I believe the ones in packs will resist the call. It's the lone wolf that may answer the summons. I am different. I'd like to think stronger willed. I see nature as it should be, and strive to keep it as it is."

Mairin asks, "What do you know of dark assassins?"

"Well, they are not very tasty, I can tell you. But this is not my first encounter with them. Most people don't know that there are dark assassins outside the ranks of the Black Robes. Oh sure, they have a large number that they keep for themselves but some of the best are trained outside of their supervision. In fact, would you believe that I was recruited to be a dark assassin long ago? I was young and full of myself. I started their training and I was good but I thought I was superior. I begged for an assignment to showcase my talents. They gave me one. It was supposed to be a simple kill. Now that I think about it, I wonder if they knew I was going to fail. Well anyway, I found my target but underestimated the situation and charged without thinking. The older man easily disarmed me and knocked me unconscious. When I awoke, I was bound hand and foot.

"I was his prisoner for days. I thought he was going to kill me. But we talked and he learned about me. He told me what he was, a sorcerer, and explained that he had placed a curse on me because of the attempt on his life. He told me that if I ever attempted violence I would undergo an excruciating alteration into a bear-like creature.

"And here I am.

"The land has become more dangerous. Generally, the dark assassins are found in the city of Umbra and its surroundings. For them to venture this far is an ill-omen. Talon, please listen. I believe the danger is worse than you imagine. If the Ebony One wakes and rises he will upset the balance of nature completely. Legend has it these evil ones have the power to take the dead and use them for their own purposes. Do you understand? The order of nature is that creatures die and give back to the land for the living. As I will and as the hermit is doing as we speak. This is the way it should be. But if this Ebony Wizard comes into power, he will deny the land its due.

"Nature itself will not allow this to happen for very long. It will rise up and destroy this corruption. It will not be selective, though. It will be devastating to all. Do you understand? If you or Mikal Novastar or anyone else can stop this, you must do everything in your power."

Talon nods his head. "I thank you for this information and I will pass it on to the White Wizard. He will know what to do. He is very wise and he is my close friend."

Osme places his hand on Talon's shoulder. "Thank you for listening. It's been a long time since I've spoken. Now it is getting late, so let's build a fire and find what we have to eat."

***

Talon returns with two ducks from a nearby pond. Mairin shares some apples and dry grapes. Osme wolfs down the meal, and then curls up close to the fire.

Talon asks, "Don't you think you're a little too close to the flame?"

The man/bear laughs. "Remember, I normally have a fur coat to keep me warm. The hair on my body is a poor substitute. I feel just right about here." He paws his beard with a thoughtful look on his face. "Oh, I remember something. I'm supposed to say… goodnight." Pause. "So, goodnight."

"Uh…goodnight."

Soon the man-bear is snoring outrageously. Mairin looks to Talon. "Will he attract unwanted visitors tonight?"

Talon smiles. "With that sound, no. I believe it will repel any unwanted visitors, if anything."

Talon and Mairin continue to talk for some time, but they eventually succumb to sleep. In the morning, they discover that Osme is gone, torn clothes left behind.

Talon rises. "Well, I wish him luck wherever he may go. We should be off to the city of Stonegrove."

Chapter 27

Sister Aurum stands next to the mage's bed. Again she asks Mikal, "How are you feeling?"

The White Wizard sits up with difficulty, his cat Majam at his feet keeping vigil.

"I feel out of sorts and have a dreadful headache. I have perplexing images in my mind as well, but I believe you were successful."

The young headmistress nods. "It was a curse most foul. You have been asleep for hours. Now tell me, do you remember the dream we shared a while ago?"

"Yes, I do… it was very vivid."

Sister Aurum looks deeply into Mikal's eyes. "It was a dream, but it is also reality."

Mikal nods. "Ah, as I suspected.

"I am sorry for bringing you into my dream, but I had little choice. I told you I fear facing him alone."

The White Mage brushes the statement away with a wave of his arm. "No, no, you did the right thing. We did gather information and now events are set in motion."

Sister asks, "Who is Sir Rusel Ironwood?"

"He is a Knight Paladin from long ago."

"Will he fight for us?" asks the young headmistress.

"I believe he will, but can he win is in question. We must help prepare him for this deadly duel. I shall leave for the City of Stonegrove as soon as possible. There I will summon him."

Sister Aurum looks confused. "Summon him? I hope you know what you're doing."

Mikal gives a forced laugh. "I thank you for your trust. I will need it."

"Could you eat something?"

"Yes, I am hungry. I will eat and be on my way, for time is of the essence."

"Food and water will be provided presently and I will bring something for your head." She hesitates. "Now, Mikal, I received a... a vision or communication, I do not know which. It revealed to me that on your way back to the City of Stonegrove you should alter your path. Let me show you on this map." She unrolls a parchment and lays it on a table. "Right here, not far off the main road, is a forest. Wait there, for something or someone has information for you. I am sorry I cannot be more specific."

Again Mikal laughs. "My life's path has been unclear to me since I left the great City of Addis. I will stop and wait there, Sister, as you wish."

***

Just before dawn, the group: Kairn the dwarf, Aden Ferrum the Red Wizard, Mikal and his cat Majam gather at the cave's entrance.

Margaret Carol's bodyguard Drew Foxx steps forward toward Mikal. "Sir, the young baroness chooses to stay. Tell the baron I have elected to remain here to protect her."

He steps closer and lowers his voice. "I think sister Kali-um has taken a fancy to me." He winks and steps back.

The White Wizard, in a knowing voice, says, "Well, Master Foxx, do your duty."

They bid each other goodbye and wish each other good fortune. The three, with the cat, set out in predawn light.

They travel across the valley floor, giving the burned out encampment a wide berth. Mikal again explains that he is in a hurry and they must make good time. Before noon they find the path out of the valley. They take only a short respite, and resume their travel. They eat a light lunch while they trek. When they find the main artery to the city, Mikal directs them off the road to a nearby wooden area.

Aden is confused. "I thought we were in a hurry. We could've gone a few more hours. Pardon me, though, if you are still weary from your encounter."

"I am fatigued. You are correct, we could have gone further but I have to visit these woods."

"And why is that?" questions Aden.

The White Wizard leads the others into the woods, finds a large rock, and sits. "I am to wait. I recommend you do the same." He surveys the terrain. "We shall camp and have dinner and leave before dawn."

The dwarf gathers firewood and soon he is cooking dinner for all. "Ike kook gould."

Aden presses the issue. "We are waiting for…?"

Mikal smiles. "*I* am waiting, but for what I shall not know until it occurs."

Not long after the sun sets, fireflies surround the camp. Majam starts to pace, her tail held high.

I hear them… they are close by. They wait for us. I will show you the way.

The White Mage stands with his staff of light. "You two wait here. I shall not be long."

He follows his now black cat deeper into the woods. He hears a familiar sound which reminds him of when he visited Evalon, the Earth Princess. The White Wizard sees and then bows before three nephrons.

"You honor me with your presence."

The fairylike creatures, no bigger than dragonflies, gleefully laugh. One approaches and flutters before Mikal's nose. Her wings flicker so fast that they are only a blur.

Her oversized eyes are baby blue. Her hair has different shades of many colors. Mikal knows that if Evalon sent her, she must be very special.

In a high-pitched buzzing voice the nephron introduces herself. "My name is Hazel. My Queen has sent me and my friends." She offers Mikal a splinter of wood. "This is memory wood. Place it on your walking staff, please."

Mikal receives the splinter and does what she bids. The small piece of wood starts to softly glow. He hears the voice of Evalon, the Earth Princess, whom he met not long ago.

I am sorry for this inconvenience, Mikal, but our enemies' power is growing at an alarming rate. They have eyes and ears everywhere, I caution you. I believe they can even perceive our dreams. I must communicate with you more fully.

The splinter's glow fades and with it, her voice. Hazel flutters to one of her companions and retrieves a second piece of memory wood and presents it to Mikal. As before, he places it on the staff. It glows and continues the message.

If it is possible, please enter the top floor of the Tower of the Dragonfly in the City of Stonegrove one night hence. I will send a special messenger.

The glow dims and the missive ends.

Hazel is surprised to find her third companion flitting playfully around Majam the cat. She catches the attention of the little sprite who blushes deeply and hands over the third piece of wood.

Please, White Wizard, if you would exchange some of your red hair with these nephrons, I will be able to locate you in the future. Your name is not safe, so please use caution.

The final splinter of memory wood ceases to glow. Mikal ponders the message. He plucks a few strands of his red hair and offers them to Hazel. She quickly snatches them and then places some of her hair in the White Mage's hand. He puts them in his pocket. Then a strange sight; the third sprite plucks some of Majam's fur and tries to replace it with some of her hair. The cat is nonplussed but takes it in stride and looks toward her master.

"I thank you all and may your way home be without incident."

The nephrons bow and are gone in an instant. "Majam, show me the way back, if you would."

Before they reach the camp, they spy Aden sitting on a rock waiting for them. Mikal asks the Red Wizard, "Well, did you find anything interesting?"

"Whatever are you talking about?"

***

Later that day, not far from the main road, Talon and Mairin walk toward Stonegrove.

"It sounds like you admire this Brian Quickhands character,

Talon."

"Not at first, but he does have his talents, and when he sacrificed a year and a day of his life to help us escape from the City of Umbra, I could not help but admire him. I admit I did not trust him when we first met."

"I just can't believe my father is involved in all this. It's remarkable that all of what you've told me took place in such a short period of time."

Talon's cat Tamarix perks up and stares intently ahead. Talon points. "We must be near the main road. People are gathered ahead. There are mounted guards. By their colors, I can tell they're from the City of Stonegrove."

Talon and Mairin approach the group. They see two wagons pulled by tired mules. The half-elf can hear one of the guards giving directions to the little caravan. "Yes, if you turn here you'll be heading toward the Valley of Endorr. If you continue to go straight, you should reach Stonegrove by this afternoon."

Mairin notices a fair-skinned, tall man with long, white hair standing near the lead wagon. One of the guards rides his horse closer to Talon. "Are you the archer who placed in the festival not long ago?"

Talon blushes. "Yes, I'm the one."

The mounted guard smiles. "I won ten gold pieces because of you. Thank you very much. Is there anything I can do for you?"

Mairin steps forward. "Yes, can you tell me if a blind wizard carrying a staff and traveling with his cat came this way?"

The soldier leans back in the saddle. "Why, yes, yes I can. He left here just a few days ago. I recall that he was traveling with another man and a one-armed dwarf. They were going to the Valley of Endorr, if I remember correctly."

Surprising Mairin and Talon, they find that the tall man with white hair is standing near them. On closer inspection, his nose comes to a point and he looks far younger than his white hair would indicate. His most distinctive feature is his deep-set, dark eyes.

With a slight bow, he says, "Excuse me, if I may be so bold. Did I hear you are going to the Valley of Endorr? How fortunate."

Talon responds, "I did not say where were we are going."

"Oh, forgive me. It is just that I'm looking for someone to accompany me to see the Witches of Endorr. I have business with them, and knowing the roads are not safe, three is better than two. You have to agree to that." He hesitates. "But where are my manners? Let me introduce myself. My name is Sebastian Wolfram, at your service."

The man driving the first wagon asks, "Mr. Wolfram, are you going to continue traveling with us or no?"

Sebastian turns and bows. "No, sir. I hope to travel with this couple for now, if they'll have me. I thank you for your company though, and safe travel to all."

The tall, white-haired man looks back to Talon and Mairin. "Well, should we be on our way?"

The half-elf holds his hand up. "Mr. Wolfram, will you please give us a moment?"

"Most certainly." Sebastian steps a few paces away and inspects a nearby butterfly fluttering about.

"I don't trust him," Talon whispers to Mairin.

"I don't know if I do either, but what can we do?"

"If we deny his company, he will probably follow us and that is a worst case scenario. If we agree to his offer, we should tell him nothing except our names. And, Mairin, never mention your last name."

She nods and they step forward. "Well, Sebastian, we accept your offer. Can I ask you what your business is at the Valley of Endorr?"

Sebastian hesitates. "I have a client who has paid me good money to purchase some special brews that the witches conjure up. He's an older, wealthy merchant and he would prefer that his name be kept secret, if you know what I mean."

Talon and Mairin both nod, but neither is sure what he means. The tall white-haired man steps back. "I know you don't trust me, but I hope to earn your confidence. I usually do succeed at this."

Sebastian pulls open his traveling cloak. "See? I carry a short sword, a hunting knife, and a throwing knife. These are the only weapons I have, and I pray that I do not have need of them."

The half-elf accepts Sebastian's words. "Let me introduce us. I am

Talon and I am escorting this young lady Mairin. This is my cat Tamarix."

The cat holds his nose high and he looks as if he is trying to judge the scent of this new human. His tail is held straight and sways back and forth. The cat keeps his distance from this white-haired man.

"Mr. Wolfram, I beg one favor. Do not ask us what our business is in the Valley of Endorr, for it is ours alone."

Sebastian Wolfram bows. "I accept. I know the wisdom of keeping secrets from strangers. Let us be on our way, for the light of day will not last forever."

He winks at Mairin.

Chapter 28

Majam takes point and the group sets off for the City of Stonegrove. Their travel is uneventful. They happen upon only a few travelers and they see no city guards. Late in the day, Mikal abruptly stops and pulls out a long narrow piece of cloth from his traveling cloak. "Funny. I have held onto this for some time now."

He surprises the group by blindfolding himself. Aden asks, "What's this all about?"

"It is a simple disguise. I now look like I am totally blind. I caution you, we are going to have to go slowly. Before, I could make out images, like rocks and trees and even people, though I could not identify them. But now everything is blind to me. My cat will assist me, but I will have to accustom myself to this."

The Red Wizard scoffs, "This disguise may work on non-clever people. But, come to think of it, most people in this land are not very clever, are they? Oh, Kairn, in case you're confused by his disguise, this remains Mikal Novastar. But I caution you, Mikal, the most dangerous ones will see right through this ruse."

"Well, then I guess I will have to rely on you to protect me," Mikal says with a grin. He holds out his staff in front of him and searches for anything before him. "We must reach the city by nightfall."

***

Just before sundown, they stand before two soldiers who guard the main gate to the city. They question everyone trying to enter. A heavy-set guard scrutinizes Mikal, Aden, and Kairn the one-armed dwarf.

He directs his inquiry to Aden. "What are your names and what is your business here?"

"I am Aden Ferrum and this is…"

Mikal interrupts, "I am Timothy. I am here to see, so to speak, Madam Burnshire at the School of the Red Salamander. She is expecting me shortly and I do not wish to disappoint her. This is Kairn my servant."

The thickset guard looks distastefully at the dwarf. "Well, don't let him wander alone in the city. We don't take kindly to that." The sentry waves them on. "You may pass."

They move deliberately into the city, Mikal tapping the ground before him. Majam looks up at the many looming towers scattered about. Mikal says, "We must find which one is called the Dragonfly."

Aden shakes his head. "There are many. We should ask someone."

After questioning some local townspeople and vendors on the street, the Red Wizard amends his statement. "We should ask someone with knowledge about this tower."

The dwarf speaks. "Week udd goat two the lie barry. Miss tier Focks hill wood no."

Mikal nods. "I was thinking the same thing."

"It worries me greatly that that the two of you are beginning to think alike," quips Aden.

"I believe the library lies this way."

The three wind their way through the city streets and soon stand before Stonegrove's impressive library. It is late, and the double doors are closed. The dwarf knocks loudly with his strong right arm. They wait, and he knocks again. One of the massive double doors opens slightly.

A young boy looks up at the three strangers. "I am sorry, but we are closed."

Mikal bends slightly and softly says, "Tell Master Foxhill that Mikal Novastar has an important question to ask of him."

The boy's eyes brighten. "Weren't you with Talon at the archery contest weeks ago?"

Mikal nods. "I was indeed. You were the boy who was wounded, or should I say chosen."

"Yes, I am he. Where is Talon?"

Mikal shakes his head. "He is not with us at this time but I hope to see him soon. Go now and give your master my message."

The boy runs off, leaving the door ajar. The three and the cat step into the vestibule and close the door behind them. Shortly, the head librarian and the young boy approach the group.

"Oh, Mikal, are you injured?" asks Foxhill earnestly.

"Forgive me." The White Wizard removes his blindfold, revealing his milky, swirling eyes. "I was wearing this blindfold for a different reason." Foxhill accepts this without explanation.

"You know Kairn,"

Mr. Foxhill responds, "Of course. It is nice to see you again and thank you for your interpretations."

"Eye inge joid dit. Enny tyme."

"And this is Aden Ferrum and, of course, my cat Majam."

The young boy kneels down and pets the large, dark pet. "Our time is short, my friend. May I ask you which of the many towers is called the Dragonfly?"

Derrick hesitates. "That is a rare question. I dare say, only a few people in the city would know."

Mikal smiles. "That is why we came to you."

"If I remember my lore correctly, when one of the first towers was built, the Duke's daughter chose it for her quarters. And every night at sundown, dragonflies of all sorts would flit about. Thus the dragonfly tower. Again, few people would know this. You say your time is short?"

Mikal nods. "I have a special meeting tonight at the top of that tower if I can gain access to it."

"A special meeting, you say?" Derrick gives a quizzical look.

"I am sorry that I am being so cryptic, but it is necessary."

The head librarian looks to the White Mage. "You would have to go through a number of important people to gain entry to that tower. Mikal, my best estimate would be two to three days…or you can follow me tonight," he says with a sparkle in his eye. "I would ask one favor. If I get you there on time, may I witness this special meeting? I will not interfere in any way. If not, promise to relate to me what transpires. Life can be so dull in this town."

Mikal responds, "I can make no promise at this time, but I indeed need your help."

Derrick addresses the boy. "Hurry, young Robert, and fetch my cloak. It is coolish out this night. I recommend that Aden and Kairn remain here. You should make yourselves comfortable. We have plenty of food and drink and, of course, books to read. The boy knows where everything is."

"As if a dwarf is going to read."

Aden continues, "I recommend that I accompany you. The city is not safe and I can offer my protection."

The librarian shakes his head. "I disagree. I know the city, and I tell you Mikal has nothing to fear. From what I know of him, he can protect both of us. Why don't you try some of my wine? It is quite good, you know."

Mikal grabs his staff. "I agree with Derrick. You stay here and try some of his wine."

"Just what I need - to spend the night with a drunken dwarf."

Chapter 29

"Derrick, it may be best that I use the name Timothy, at least for tonight. I will wear my hood up, as well."

The re-blindfolded White Wizard holds on to Derrick's arm. With his cat just ahead of them, they set out for the Dragonfly Tower. Mikal, using Majam's senses, can notice people as they pass by. Most move aside and some look away.

A few start the strange, familiar mantra: *None shall bar his path and all will prevent him from leaving.* Mikal still does not understand its origin or meaning.

They move without incident through the streets until they come upon a young woman drawing water from a well. The head librarian presents himself. "Good evening, young lady. I am Derrick Foxhill and this is my friend Timothy and his lucky, black cat. I am wondering if you could spare water?"

The woman looks to Derrick then to Mikal. It is as if she knows that she should recognize them, but she does not. "Yes, sirs, drink."

She offers a brimming ladle and the head librarian and "Timothy" have their fill. Majam does not partake. Upon returning the ladle, Derrick tells her, "Here are some silver coins for your kindness."

The young woman eyes grow wide and her mouth opens in a smile. "What are you about, sirs?"

"A private affair. We must be on our way," Derrick replies.

They enter the upscale, noble part of the city. The head librarian surprises Mikal by turning toward the main gate of the Duke's estate. Two neatly uniformed guards stand before iron wrought bars.

Before they can question Derrick Foxhill, he stands tall and with a distinct voice intones, "I am the head librarian and I am on a mission of great import. I must enter the estate without delay."

The guards hesitate, and Foxhill threatens, "Do not dare bar my way." The two relent and open the gates.

"Well, we passed the first obstacle," Derrick whispers.

They travel across the grounds until they arrive at the main doors. An impeccably attired sentry blocks their path. "The Duke has retired for the evening and he will see no one."

Derrick waves his hand. "That is acceptable for we are not here to see him. I am here with my friend Timothy to gain access to the Dragonfly Tower."

The guard's forehead wrinkles in puzzlement. The head librarian laughs and points upward. "That one."

The guard follows his gaze and protests, "But some of the Duke's court live in that tower, and it is very late."

Derrick shakes his head. "I give you my word we shall not disturb anything. And I know that no one lives on the top floor and that is our destination. We must go there. Get out of my way. If you are not sure what you should do, go ask the Duke. I am sure that he would not mind, and you would only lose your head if I am mistaken."

The librarian grabs Mikal's arm and moves past the perplexed guard. "Luckily, I have been a guest in this Hold quite often. Also, it is most helpful that I have memorized all of the blueprints of the older buildings in the city."

He easily finds the door to the winding staircase that leads to the top of the tower. Mikal fears he might be too late.

As they wend their way up the spiral staircase, they arrive at a trap door. Derrick stops and says, "You know, Mikal, the dwarf Kairn finds you most puzzling. He holds no grudge against you, for he knows your actions saved his life but he wonders why you did such a selfless act on one such as he. Kindness is something he has seldom encountered. He has grown quite fond of you, and that also confuses him."

The White Wizard does not know how to respond.

They find the door unlocked and enter the top floor of the Dragonfly Tower, high above the city. A lit torch casts its weak light on a circular room no more than twenty feet across. In its center is a small, round table with two plain chairs. There are unlit braziers at the four cardinal points and next to them four carved dragonfly tiles set into the circular wall. The spacious windows are covered with wooden shutters.

Mikal removes his blindfold and, with the help of Derrick Foxhill, opens the shutters wide. The head librarian asks, "What should we do now? No one is here."

The White Wizard laughs. "I am going to sit and wait."

Majam jumps and sits on the table just in front of her master. Mikal allows his staff to produce a soft, bluish-white light. The night continues as the stars rise higher in the sky.

Something catches the eye of the cat. She stiffens. A flying creature of some sort rapidly approaches the tower and begins to circle.

Mikal mumbles, "That is a raven, curse them."

A knowing voice from behind corrects him. "I believe it is a Blackhawk, not a Raven."

The large, flying thing circles a second time, and then plunges from sight. Mikal waits, and sees it returning from the north, slower than before. It enters the tower through one of the newly-opened windows. The Blackhawk lands on the back of the chair across from Mikal. No one moves. The hawk twitches its head first to the right than to the left. It spreads its glistening wings wide and grows larger and changes before their eyes. When the metamorphosis is complete, a striking female with impossibly long, smooth, onyx hair stands before them.

"My name is Mira. I come with great haste in the name of Evalon, the Earth Mother, Mikal Novastar, White Wizard from the great City of Addis…" Mira lowers her gaze. "And his beautiful, black cat Majam. Greetings."

Mikal rises from his chair and bows slightly.

She continues, "Who else is here among us?"

Mikal responds, "This is Derrick Foxhill, the head librarian of the City of Stonegrove. He is my guide and I trust him completely."

The mysterious lady/hawk nods and positions her hands on the table, palms up. "Mikal, you are to place your hands on mine and, soon after, my lady will speak through me. You will hear her voice and you can speak to her through me. If you break contact, the enchantment will vanish."

The White Mage sits and places his hands in hers. He senses a mystical energy traveling between them. Mira's head starts to droop, causing her glistening hair to fall, obscuring her face. Unpredictably, her head snaps forward and her dark eyes open wide.

She smiles. "Good fortune is with us this night. It is good to see you again, White Wizard. Wear your new title well."

Mikal's eyes start to swirl and he becomes aware of an aura surrounding the lady/hawk. It is the same one that surrounded Evalon when he first met her.

Evalon: *I know you have had contact with the Dark Harold. What has transpired between the two of you?*

"It was but a dream, but I was told it was real. I challenged him to combat in seven days at the Valley of Endorr. He asked me who would be my Champion and I responded 'Sir Rusel Ironwood'. Have I chosen poorly?"

"*The champion is acceptable. Is he aware of your choice?*"

"He is not, but I hope to summon him before dawn. I pray he will accept."

"*In that there can be no doubt,* Lady Evalon's voice declares.

"My concern, good lady, is that the Dark Knight casts a dreadful aura of fear that few can resist. Also, the Paladin's light armor is old and worn. The tip of his sword is broken, as you might know. He lacks a horse."

Mikal waits for a response. "*I know the location of enchanted armor. It will serve our purpose well, but it is dangerous to acquire and far more so to wear. Listen closely. There is a small lake east of the city. In its center area, there is an eternal mist. No sailor or fisherman will take you there, but you may rent a small boat. A tiny island lies in the mist and on it stands an ancient tower. When you enter, you will feel compelled to take the stairs to the top floor. Resist. If you follow, you will forget why you are there. Instead, on the ground floor you must seek a trapdoor and traveled down below the lake. There will be obstacles and tests along your path. You must defend yourself, but do not harm any creature. Tell the last Guardian that your champion fights in my name and with my colors. I will get them to you somehow. Sir Rusel should have the means to capture a war horse.*"

Now, as for the sword…"

Majam instantly stands, her ears perked, and meows menacingly. A shadowy raven swoops into the tower. Majam leaps and knocks it from the air. Instantly, more dusty colored ravens fill the tower. Chaos erupts. Mikal abruptly stands and grabs his staff. The communication enchantment with Evalon is broken.

The White Wizard yells, "Close your eyes!" A blinding white light overflows the room, blinding and disorientating the dark flock of birds. Mira steps back and morphs into the huge Blackhawk. She takes flight, tearing into two ravens with her razor-sharp talons. She darts away, outdistancing any pursuers. The tower, though, is still filled with the carrion birds. Mikal is startled by a high-pitched sound and the four braziers flare to life. The foul birds immediately flee. The White Mage spies the head librarian standing by one of the lit braziers with a torch.

Derrick says offhandedly, "I thought it was common knowledge that birds don't like fire and loud sounds."

Mikal can only smile.

Derrick gushes, "That was amazing! Where did all those birds come from? And that Hawk, it turned into a woman. And you spoke to someone else who I have a feeling is far away. Tell me, Mikal, does this is happened to you often?"

The White Wizard grins and shakes his head. "I must admit, yes. At least of late. Master Foxhill, the night is almost gone. Please give me directions to the old building that I believe is now a barracks."

The head librarian nods. "There is one east of here. It is rumored to have been built before the city even existed."

"I believe that is the one," Mikal eagerly responds.

"Forget the directions. It is quicker if I personally show you the way."

"Yes, but it is late."

"I know. I have not been out this late since… I have never been out this late, ever. It is quite exhilarating." He then adds theatrically, "Follow me."

They clamor down the steps and, with the White Mage's cat guiding him, they transverse across the Duke's estate. They ignore questions from the guards.

"This way, I believe."

It is a few hours before dawn, but there are still people in the streets. Some Mikal believes are up to no good. They all move aside when they recognize the head librarian. In less than half an hour they find themselves outside the doors of the ancient barracks.

Mikal holds his staff high. "Should we knock?"

Derrick shakes his head, opens the door, and enters. Dim light, bad odors, and loud snoring greets them, but no one is awake to question them.

The White Mage takes the lead. "Follow me, sir."

Mikal stops at the back wall and allows his staff to glow. He finds the hidden handle and, as before, opens the secret portal. He hears a gasp from Mr. Foxhill. As they enter a large circular room with a cobblestone floor, Mikal's staff glows brighter and illuminates the entire area.

The head librarian takes a moment to interpret the murals on the wall. "This looks like a room for meditation. Paladins, the ancient knights of the Wizard Wars, would have met here."

The White Wizard nods. "Please, wait over there by the unlit sconce."

Mikal takes his position at the first mural and repeats the pattern he did weeks earlier. When he has concluded the circuit, he evokes the name of Sir Rusel Ironwood.

Derrick breathes in sharply, for he sees in the center of the room a thin, wavering, luminous, green line. It is approximately six feet tall. The column thickens and assumes a human form. The aura fades, and before them stands a knight clad in chain mail and a shield, but no helmet. He wears heavy, leather boots and his hair is almost shoulder length and fair. On the left side of his clean-shaven face is a scar that travels from his eye to his chin. Whatever had been on the shield long ago has been obliterated. The Paladin is awake.

He places his hand on his sword. "Your need is great and I am here." His eyes focus in the gloom. "Oh, it is you Mikal Novastar. How long since I was last summoned?"

"Not long. Just a few weeks."

"That is good. I see your lucky black cat is with you still, but where are the others and who is this?"

"This is Derrick Foxhill, the head librarian of the City of Stonegrove. He is my guide this night."

The ancient knight looks long at the older man. "Well met, Derrick Foxhill, head librarian."

Master Foxhill stares, slack-jawed.

Mikal says, "I will fill you in on the affairs of the others later."

"Mikal, I somehow know you have chosen me for your champion."

"Yes, I have, with all humility. The reason is that the Dark Harold has risen and he is seizing souls and spreading fear and terror throughout the land. Will you fight him for me and for a noble cause?"

"Why, I would be honored. Name the place and the time."

"In six days at the Valley of Endorr. I believe I can procure an enchanted suit of armor for you and I was told you might be able to capture your own war steed."

The Paladin ponders a moment. "I believe I may be able to, but it has been so long. I hope the way is still open for me." Mikal sighs with relief. "Forgive me, Mikal, but you look exhausted."

"That is an understatement. It has been a long and trying night."

"Let us go then and find a bed for you to rest. Bring your friend along"

The three, with the black cat leading them, leave the sleeping barracks and enter the main streets. Derrick points ahead. "The library is this way. There are beds for us all." He pulls Mikal closer and whispers, "Is that really Sir Rusel Ironwood from the Wizard Wars?"

"There is no doubt."

"Oh, my."

Just before dawn they enter the double doors of the library. They find the boy and the snoring dwarf fast asleep. Aden Ferrum is nowhere to be found. Derrick nudges the young servant awake. "Tell me, boy, where is Aden Ferrum?"

The lad rubs his eyes and looks around. "I do not know, sir. He was here when I fell asleep."

"No matter. Bring us something to drink and some water to cleanse ourselves."

The one-armed dwarf continues to bellow away. The boy returns, carrying two pitchers on a tray. Majam turns and stares intently at the front door. Aden appears, and it is evident by the look on his face that he is surprised to see everyone gathered there. He straightens and strides into the room.

Mikal stands. "Sir Rusel, allow me to introduce my current company. This is young Robert, Derrick's servant. The snoring one over there is Kairn, the dwarf. And this gentleman, returning from where I do not know, is Aden Ferrum, a Red Wizard. Aden, this is Rusel Ironwood, a Paladin."

"A Paladin, you say? Wherever did you unearth him? It looks like he has seen one battle too many."

Sir Rusel stares hard and long at Aden. "Red Wizard, I say to you, in my time even the Red Mages I fought beside left fiery death and destruction in their wake." Sir Rusel raises his right hand and points to the Red Wizard. "Do not play us false, or I will hunt you down and exact vengeance in this life or the next."

Aden lifts his fire staff.

Chapter 30

Sebastian asks, "Mairin, have you been to the Valley of Endorr? I can tell by that look that you have not. Neither have I, but I have heard rumors. Supposedly, the witches are talented healers and they are quite noted for herb and potion lore. Some say a few can even foretell the future. I do not know about that. They are all supposedly beautiful, and it is said that they can bewitch any man and make him their servant. What do you believe, Mairin?"

"I have heard the same, but let me ask you this; do you not fear the witches if they can make you their servant?"

Sebastian laughs. "I am no man's servant, but a beautiful witch, that is another matter. Let me think upon it."

Talon interrupts, "If I remember the map I saw in the Stonegrove library, we should be getting close to the valley wall. The way down is said to be slow and difficult."

Late in the afternoon, the three, along with the cat Tamarix, stand on the edge of a cliff. A switchback trail leads to the valley floor. The half-elf surveys the descent. "The question is, we can either camp here for the night and take the trail down at first light, or start down now and camp at the end of the path."

Sebastian says nothing, but looks to Mairin. The young lass is anxious to see her father. "I would prefer to start immediately and camp later."

With the cat taking point, they start their descent. The way is difficult and the light is fading but eventually they arrive at the valley floor. Talon finds a secluded spot just off the path.

"Search, Tamarix." Immediately the cat is gone.

Sebastian inquires, "That is an impressive cat. For what did you tell him to search?"

The half-elf shrugs. "He will look for any danger in the immediate area. It will not take long. We should gather firewood for the night."

They soon share an evening meal. Talon looks to the moon that is rising over the horizon. "We should leave at first light, so I recommend we get our sleep now. Tamarix will take the first watch and I will take the next."

Sebastian speaks. "I shall gladly take the third. Just please wake me when it is my time." Talon hesitates, but nods reluctantly.

***

With the first rays of the new day, Talon awakens and prepares a small breakfast of cheese, dates, and water. The white-haired man joins the group and looks surprisingly refreshed for standing the third watch.

Mairin stands. "Well, let's be off."

Talon extinguishes the fire. "We should follow this path and soon we will be on open ground. The witches' encampment should be but a few hours travel."

The way is uneventful. Sebastian does point out the seemingly inordinate number of birds in the air, most with dark feathers. Talon does spy some with red and yellow plumage.

Mr. Wolfram makes the observation, "Usually when I see this many birds, I am traveling through a forest of trees. We are surrounded by open plains and rocks. I find that curious."

A few hours pass, when something catches Talon's eye. He moves to the front of the little procession and stops and looks intently across the valley floor. The white-haired man holds his pointed nose high. "I do believe I smell something burning."

Tamarix sniffs the air as well. Mairin asks, "Talon, what do you see?"

"I believe it is the witches' encampment, but I cannot be sure. It looks like a great fire has taken place, but I see movement. Wait. There are men mounting horses. They are galloping this way."

"What should we do?" questions Mairin. Talon reveals his bow and readies an arrow.

Sebastian Wolfram raises his arm. "Elf, lower that bow. There are too many and they are approaching fast. If you do not stop them all, they will hunt us down. Look around. Open ground surrounds us and we are short on supplies. I can talk our way out of this. Trust me."

Chapter 31

They feel the vibrations of the hooves as the riders close in. The white-haired man turns his back to the approaching marauders. "Mairin, give me your ring and anything else of value. I shall attempt to hide them."

"I really do not have anything of value."

Sebastian repeats, "Give me that ring or it will surely be lost."

Both Talon and Mairin witness Sebastian uncover a medallion that hangs from his neck. His eyes grow wide when Talon offers the cat pendant he had taken from the hermit's murderer. Wolfram takes the ring, the pendant, and his medallion and hides them in a hidden compartment in his left boot.

Talon bends down. "Tamarix, hide."

The cat is out of sight immediately. The white-haired man straightaway turns, stands, holds up his arms, and addresses the rapidly approaching riders. "Please, hold! We are mere pilgrims en route to see the Witches of Endorr."

The five unkempt riders brandish weapons and surround the three. Talon can tell that the horses have been pushed to their limit and are not well cared for. A short, stocky, smelly man spurs his horse and moves closer. Talon notices flies buzzing around him. He lowers a short spear in front of Sebastian's pointy nose.

In a calm voice the white-haired man introduces himself. "I am Sebastian Wolfram, this is Talon, and this is Mairin, a Witch of Endorr," he lies.

The short, dirty man stares at the girl. "A witch, you say?"

Sebastian nods. "Yes, she was on a leave of absence. We are helping her return." He points in the distance. "What has happened to the encampment? You must be powerful warriors to overcome the Witches of Endorr." He pats his robe. "By the way, I am sorry but we have nothing of value."

The malodorous marauder looks to Talon. "Boy, handover that

bow and any other weapons you have. That goes for the rest of you." He spits.

The half-elf hesitates. Sebastian Wolfram offers his sword and hunting knife. He addresses the half-elf. "Talon, please do as he says and things will be all right."

Reluctantly, Talon gives up his enchanted bow and short sword. The pudgy, fly-ridden rider is satisfied. "Now, back to our camp."

The walk to the encampment is filled with jibes and laughter directed at Talon and Mairin. Once the captors determine that Talon is a "half-breed", he becomes their primary target. The three remain silent. Shortly they enter the burnt campsite. Sebastian can tell that this was an impressive array at one time, but wonders what occurred here. He knows whatever has happened is beyond the capabilities of these marauders.

The captives are brought to a burly man with wild, blonde hair. "So, what do we have here, eh? Three little lost lambs, to be sheared or slaughtered?" The man laughs at his own joke. The stocky, smelly man lays the weapons before his leader. The straw-haired man inspects them haphazardly.

"So, fine weapons for sheep slaughtering, no?" guffaws the stocky man.

"We found them on the open plains. They claim they were coming to see the Witches of Endorr. That white-haired... sheep says the girl here is one of the witches."

"So, she claims she's a witch? She does not look like a beautiful, young witch."

Sebastian steps forward. "Sir, may I have the honor to know your name?"

The beefy man with the wild hair studies Sebastian. "So, you want my name? Why not? My name is Brent Plumbum."

Sebastian bows. "Master Plumbum, may I introduce my company? The young half-elf is a talented archer. His name is Talon. You can see how appropriate his name is. The beautiful young lass is named Mairin and she is in her traveling guise. And I am Sebastian Wolfram, at your service." He bows from the waist.

The wild-haired man is impressed with Sebastian. "So, you still claim she's a witch?"

The marauder leader's gaze rests on the young female. "So, tell me, girl, are you really a Witch of Endorr?"

Mairin lowers her eyes. "Yes, I am."

"So, how old are you?"

Sebastian starts to cough and catches the young female's eyes. He interrupts, "She's older than she looks."

The leader steps forward. "So, you like to talk? Well, stop wagging your tongue or I'll cut it out, you white-haired lamb."

Some of the underlings laugh lustily. "So, girl, what is your age?"

Mairin looks directly at the bandit leader. "I am twenty and eight years."

A low murmur spreads throughout the marauders' camp. "So, twenty-eight, eh? You will get a chance to prove that you are one of the Witches."

Brent asks the smelly man, "So, they did not have any coin on them?"

The short, stocky one attempts to swat away the flies from his face and lowers his chin. "Well, they gave us their weapons."

The bandit leader's backhand slaps his underling in the face, leaving a welt.

Master Plumbum points to one of the younger plunderers. "So, I suggest you search them now."

A man with long, greasy hair strides up to Talon. The half-elf holds open his cloak. The young bandit removes a knife and a small bag of coins. He tosses the bag to his superior. He continues to inspect Talon, checking for hidden pockets and offhandedly probes both boots. He starts the same procedure with Sebastian, finding the fine throwing knife, but, unexpectedly, no coins. As he searches the right boot, a long, unnerving, distant howl fills the camp.

The short, stocky man declares, "I told you, Plumbum, there are wolves out there!"

Brent again backhands the smelly man, sending flies everywhere. "So, you're afraid of wolves? Wolves do not concern me. And call me

Master Plumbum. I kind of like that. Hey, Greasy, check the girl."

Mairin removes her cloak and hands it to the young bandit. "Nothing to be found here, sir."

The girl gives him her rucksack which he opens and inspects. "Some food and clothes is all." He feels something. "Wait... something is wrapped up." He unfolds the cloth. "Look at this! It's a black-bladed knife."

"So, something of value after all, eh? Here, give me that," Brent commands.

He inspects the blade closely and turns it over in his hand. "Perfectly balanced. This blade is for killing, not healing. So, how did you come by it?"

Talon interrupts, "A large, hairy man gave it to her. It was taken from someone's back."

Brent chuckles. "I bet it was. So, the question is how did it get there?"

His question is met with silence.

He addresses Wolfram. "I like you but I don't trust you." He looks to the stinking one. "So, bind the hands behind the elf and the white-haired sheep," he commands, and to Mairin he says, "We have an injured man in the back. So, girl, if you want to live, you do your best to heal him. You two show them where he is and keep an eye on them."

On the way, they find themselves stepping on small bones that make irritating, crunching sounds beneath their feet.

"Those are rat bones," one of the captors informs them. "There are pockets of skeletons spewed about everywhere."

Mairin, Wolfram, and Talon are lead to a small canopy that looks like it was made from shreds of a larger tent. The injured man lies inside. He has suffered many lesions and a severe, gaping stomach wound. Mairin kneels and closely inspects the life-threatening injury. Both Talon and Sebastian kneel next to the young girl.

The white-haired man whispers, "Cleanse the wounds and look like you know what you're doing." Sebastian stands and speaks to one of the guards. "She needs clean water and cloth. Fetch some." Sebastian looks to the other. "This man has a fever and may have a disease of some sort." The guard pales and takes a few steps backward. Sebastian returns to his knees and is surprised to find Mairin moving her hands over the more serious cuts and healing them with spells.

"This is good," Sebastian says. "But what of the stomach?"

"I have a vial in my pack that should readily cure him."

Sebastian looks up. "You there, retrieve her rucksack."

"I have been ordered not to leave you," the guard protests.

"Yes, she, however, is supposed to cure this man and she needs her potions. If he dies, Master Plumbum will blame you."

The unhappy, suddenly concerned guard turns and begrudgingly exits the tent.

Sebastian shakes his head. "My, but these men are not very bright. Plumbum is remarkably dense, if you know what I mean. I also believe they are but scavengers and have not been here long. They are, however, dangerous."

The first guard returns with water and clean cloth and Mairin cleanses the many lacerations. The second guard appears and gives the young girl her rucksack. She rummages through it and produces a vial of green fluid.

Talon explains to a quizzical Wolfram, "That is a powerful healing brew."

Sebastian nods. "Give him only a bit."

Mairin looks at him puzzled. "Am I not supposed to cure him?"

"Yes, certainly…only not too quickly. As long as the man is healing but not cured, they will let us live…or you at least."

The teenager applies a small amount of the thick, green liquid to the gaping stomach wound. She then feeds a small amount to the critically injured man.

The short, smelly, stocky man and another bandit enter the tent and approach the three captives. Mairin informs the stinking one, "I have done all that I can do for now. We can only wait and see."

"He'd better live, witch." He roughly grasps Mairin's upper arm and rudely pulls her to her feet. "All of you…come with me now."

They are ushered to a burned-out, tattered tent. Inside, two wooden stakes have been driven into the ground. Talon and Sebastian are tied to the stakes, with their hands behind them.

The fly-infested scavenger looks to the girl. "We will leave you unbound for now. But if you run off or try to release your friends, we will split all your throats." The smelly one laughs sardonically.

Wolfram asks, "Excuse me, sir, but do you have any notion of what befell this encampment?"

"Huh?"

"What happened here?"

One of the scavengers looks about. "We don't know. It was like this when we found it this morning."

The short, smelly bandit slaps his collaborator hard across the face. "Shut up, fool. Tell them nothing."

Not far from where the three are held, a commotion of whistling and cheering erupts. The sound soon subsides and the three captives are left wondering what it was all about. Sometime later, they hear the crunching of rat bones.

The young bandit with the greasy hair strolls in. "I'm here to relieve you. Our friends found a half full keg of wine. I had my two cups already and you better hurry if you don't want to miss out. They'll drink the rest without you."

The guards waste no time in leaving. The greasy one produces a whetstone and begins sharpening his short sword. Sebastian coughs lightly in order to gain the brigand's attention.

"However are you feeling, good sir?" Sebastian inquires innocently.

"Why would you ask me that?" responds the greasy-haired guard.

"I am sorry. I just want to see how you are feeling. You are the one that took the black-bladed knife from a Witch of Endorr, are you not?"

"Again, why do you ask that?" He is beginning to become irritated.

"Well, that blade is cursed. It was given to the girl properly but you took it from her improperly. Now I know you were ordered to do so by Master Plumbum, so there is probably a curse upon him as well."

"I don't believe you," snaps the bandit.

"Oh, that doesn't matter in the least. The curse will still work without your belief. I am sure of it."

"If what you say is true, what do you think the curse could be?"

A sly, slight smile grows on the face of Sebastian Wolfram. "I imagine it would be a subtle curse. Something you would not even be aware of at first. I have heard of curses that cause headaches that never stop. Or, perhaps, a man goes blind, slowly. Or all of his hair would fall out, and possibly other body parts. Who knows? But the fact is you took a cursed blade from one of the Witches of Endorr. And now your leader sits with it in his belt. No, I would not want to be him."

"Girl," directs the guard. "Remove this curse now!"

Mairin shakes her head. "I did not place the curse upon you. The dark blade did. I can do nothing."

"Liar," the guard says unconvincingly and wrinkles his forehead. "I'm going to see if there is any wine left."

The greasy-haired one is soon out of sight and the three are left alone. Talon studies their surroundings. The sun will set soon.

Talon says, "There is something not quite right about this place."

Mairin shakes her head. "I agree. You have a propensity for understatement. All those rat bones all over the place. They have been picked clean. I dread the coming night." Sebastian struggles against his ropes. "Well, these rapscallions are none too bright but they tie ropes well."

"Oh, I don't know about that." Talon brings his hands in front of him and removes the remnant of rope from around his wrist. Before Sebastian and Mairin can react, Tamarix appears from behind his master. The girl kneels and starts to pet the animal.

Sebastian cautions the two, "Talon, pretend you are still tied to the stake. Let them drink all their wine and let us see what the night brings. Perhaps we can use this to our advantage."

The two reluctantly agree. Talon says softly, "Thank you, Tamarix. But hide now."

Within moments they lose sight of the cat.

***

Just after the last rays of the sun fall below the horizon, Talon asks,

"Did anyone notice that? It was subtle, but it felt like a...wave of foreboding swept across the encampment.'

"Yes, I sensed it, too," responds Mairin.

Sebastian looks around uneasily. "There was something, all right, but I do not know what."

The revelers can be heard still. The captives recognize the unmistakable crunch of rat bones again and a slow moving, unsteady guard enters. He looks at his charges and sits. He has obviously had far too much to drink.

The first moon of the night starts to rise in the darkening sky, shedding its pale light across the plains of Endorr.

All under the canopy sense that something is terribly amiss. The ground begins vibrating under their feet. To their astonishment, they see that wherever rodents' bones had been ground into the soil, they sprout like seeds in the earth and swollen, sharp thorny bushes start to spring up at an accelerated pace.

All stare fascinated at this otherworldly spectacle. The brambles grow and twist and branch to a height of over four feet. Their impossible growth slows but does not stop entirely. Dark flowers and wicked, barbed-tipped thorns blossom. The cry of wolves echoes throughout the camp.

Those under the canopy become aware of an irritating buzzing. The short, stocky, smelly bandit staggers toward them, flies following. "What did you do, witch?" He steps closer. "How did you do this? You know, I never had a witch before." He grabs the girl by her hair, pulling her head back. He places his open, slobbering mouth over hers and tears at her clothes.

Talon's blood roars in his ears. An enraged, mad look comes over his face and a feral growl escapes his lips. He leaps up and delivers a devastating kick to the smelly man's belly. A whoosh of air is expelled by the falling, stinking assailant. Before he can rise and defend himself, Talon picks up a rock and slams it into the side of the man's head again and again, knocking him bloody and senseless.

Marin, wide-eyed, stares in disbelief.

The other bandit draws a short sword and rushes the half-elf.

Sebastian throws out his legs and trips the hapless guard. Talon uses the same rock, with the same results. While Mairin unties Mr. Wolfram, she asks, "What shall we do with them?" staring in dismay at the sprawled bodies.

Without hesitation, Talon snarls, "Let them be food for the rats...or the wolves."

Sebastian quips, "I doubt if the wolves would come near the malodorous one."

Talon says, "More for the rats."

"In any event, the die has been cast. Let us make good our escape while there is time."

"Not without my bow."

"I do not know if it is worth the risk, my young half-elf."

Talon insists, "It is worth it to me. Take Mairin to safety. I must recover my belongings."

The girl shakes her head and clasps his arm. "I'm coming with you, Talon."

Sebastian sighs in frustration. "If that's the case, we should all stay together." He surveys the terrain. "Maybe these thorn things will provide us some cover."

The sounds of revelry have been replaced by the sounds of terror and panic. Frantic shouts echo throughout the camp. "Rats! They are everywhere!"

More brambles start to grow faster now and chaos engulfs the camp. The trio moves with caution, using the growing thorn bushes as cover.

Sebastian whispers, "Girl, here is your ring back." He then places his medallion on his neck. "This is for good luck. And, Talon, take your cat-eye pendant."

They come upon the marauders who are using torches and swords to repel the mass of ravenous rats.

A defender yells hysterically, "Look! One of the witch's guards comes to wreak vengeance upon us."

From out of one of the caves staggers an unearthly sight. A tattered-garbed man with gaping gaps of skin missing from his frame lumbers toward them. He wields a chipped axe. The terrifying figure is shot squarely in the chest with an arrow, but shows no effects. Some of the bandits flee in panic. A brigand trips and falls backwards against one of the thorn bushes. He is impaled by a hundred barbed-tipped thorns. Feeble, jerking movements twitch from the broken body.

The bramble bush starts to grow again and glistening, dark blossoms bloom.

Talon whispers, "I see our weapons. They are just behind Plumbum, who is commanding his underlings. You two stay here."

With stealth that only an elf can execute, he makes his way undetected toward the captured weapons. Talon hesitates, and takes in everything before him. Fat rats scurry everywhere and dark-feathered birds squawk and circle above. The strange bramble bushes continue to grow uncontrolled. The unearthly human still swings his axe. Brigands shout and fight.

Talon slips unseen toward his goal, but is soon stopped in his tracks. A charred, colossal skeleton enters the chaos. It ignores everything around it and lurches directly to the now-empty wine keg. The burnt-out, giant's skeleton shows its irritation by mightily heaving the wooden keg at Brent Plumbum. It bashes him squarely in his face, knocking him back against one of the twisting thorn bushes.

Brent cannot move, and his body starts to shrivel. The unnatural brambles grow to twice their size and an inordinate amount of shimmering, black roses blossom and barbed-tipped thorns sprout wildly. Talon leaps over rats, dashes forward, and gathers the stolen belongings.

The men are defending themselves furiously, and neither notice nor care about the half-elf.

Talon returns to his friends. "This is our best chance. Run!"

Mairin frantically shouts above the din, "Where?"

Sebastian responds, "Away from here!"

Chapter 32

Before Mikal can act, Master Foxhill steps between Aden and Sir Rusel. "Now listen here. This is my library and my home and I will not tolerate violence of any type within these walls. Unless I am mistaken, I thought we were all on the same side."

Mikal stands next to the head librarian. "Aden, put down that staff. This has been a long and trying night. We need to get some sleep, not quarrel amongst ourselves."

Derrick expounds, "The library will be open in a few hours. I have a concealed back area that can serve as bed chambers."

They agree and are soon lying down to rest. The dwarf has been left snoring on one of the couches in front.

Mikal thanks the librarian for his hospitality. "I am in your debt but I must ask yet another favor of you."

Derrick smiles. "With the adventure you have given me this night, I am the one who owes. Anything at all. Just ask."

"My group and I are short on time. If you can rouse us just before noon, we will be on our way."

Derrick nods. "I wish I could accompany you, but I cannot," he sighs wistfully. "Just before noon then. I will have food and fresh water waiting for you. Get whatever rest you can."

***

Sir Rusel gently wakens Mikal.

The White Wizard questions the warrior, "Did you get any sleep?"

The knight shakes his head. "I have had enough sleep to last me many lifetimes."

"Where's the dwarf?" Aden asks.

As if on cue, Kairn stumbles into the room, drunk on sleep. The young boy follows and says, "Master Foxhill told me not to wake Kairn. He was a curiosity to our patrons. Some seemed to be fascinated

189

by him but I think others were irritated by his loud snoring. Well, he's mostly awake and my guess is that he's hungry."

Without saying a word, the dwarf noisily begins stuffing his face with the food that had been laid out on the table before him.

Derrick enters. "I see everyone's awake. If I may be so bold, Master Mikal, what are your plans for the day?"

"You know we must travel to the lake east of here."

The librarian smiles. "Yes, I thought so. I have a map." He unfolds a parchment and spreads it out on the table near the dwarf's food. "The lake Hydrargyrum means liquid silver. It is said that when the moons are full, its reflection looks like silver. If you take this path," he points, "you will find it fairly direct, but off the main road. You may take the map with you if you so desire."

Mikal thanks the master librarian. "We bid you farewell. We must be going. Your service has been invaluable." He bows.

Derek waves off any thanks. "All I ask is that sometime in the future please return to relate your story to me. And give my best to Talon. I hope he is safe."

"As do I."

***

Mikal cradles Majam in his arms as he leads the group through the city streets. As they approach the final gate, Mikal spies Marion Vetta on a balcony. She gives the wizard a slight nod, which he returns.

They exit the City of Stonegrove and turn east. Mikal explains to Sir Rusel the quest on which he has sent Talon. "I am concerned. I thought he would be back by now."

Sir Rusel responds, "Talon is a fine warrior and I have faith he will succeed in his assignment and we shall see him soon."

Mikal nods. "I hope you are right, my friend." He is vague when asked about Brian Quickhands. "Not everyone needs to hear about his fate, if you know what I mean." He glances at Aden.

Now it is Sir Rusel's turn to nod.

The day is bright and welcoming and the group makes excellent time. They stop to rest, and the ancient Knight asks if he might see the librarian's map. After studying the well detailed chart, Sir Rusel points to a narrow river.

"This is where I must go. It's not far off our path and it looks like it flows into the lake."

"Then that is where we shall go," responds the White Wizard.

Before sundown, they make camp next to the river. Sir Rusel studies the flow of water. "This should do just fine. The water is not deep. Please, we must gather some large rocks and lay them in the river and over them place firewood." Everyone looks puzzled. "I will explain after we prepare the way."

They roll boulders they find just off the shore into the river. As directed, the large rocks rest just above the surface of the water. Then they pile wood gathered from the nearby forest upon the rocks.

Sir Rusel inspects their work. "Yes, I think this will be just fine. Now I must wait for the sun to set so I can take my leave."

Aden asks with a raised eyebrow, "Why did you have us build this? And where do you think you're going?"

The ancient knight looks to Mikal. "After I was a Paladin for year and a day, I traveled to a…different place to capture and train my warhorse. She was magnificent. Bold on the battlefield. I lost her on one of the last encounters of the Wizard Wars."

"So, are you creating doorway to this different place?" questions Mikal.

"Yes, I am. I shall travel and enter an unpopulated land. There is some humanoid life, like fairies and such."

Aden chimes in, "There must be dwarves then, I take it."

The Paladin ignores the statement. "The grass is greener and softer and the water somehow tastes better. Always cool and refreshing. Trees large and strong. But the animals are something different. Smarter, faster than any animals here. But the horses are the most impressive. They love the water and are excellent swimmers. Their manes and tails are always thick and full. You can tell by looking in their eyes that they understand their importance in nature and how they fit in. It is as if nature rejoices and all revel in it. Humans are only allowed to visit. They are not allowed to remain. Majam would feel at home there."

"Sir Paladin, our time is short," the White Wizard reminds him gently.

Rusel, with a faraway look in his eyes, continues. "That's another thing about this place. Time is different. When I was first here, I thought weeks had gone by, but when I returned, just a few days had passed here." He refocuses on Mikal. "When I return, I shall look for you near the lake. If I cannot find you, I shall ride toward Stonegrove then onward to the valley." He looks at the fading sun. "Oh, I see my time draws near. I ask all of you to keep secret what you are about to see." He looks at Aden. "Even with the knowledge you possess you could not pass. One must be a consecrated Paladin to travel to this land. Light the firewood now."

Aden complies, and soon tall flames engulf the wood just above the waterline. The Paladin explains, "You see, Mikal, all four elements must come together at just the right time. Then the door will be opened."

Aden asks, "What are you going to do?"

"Watch." The ancient one stands tall and breathes deeply. He murmurs inaudible, arcane words. Then he runs and leaps through the flame. This is followed by a loud splash. Moments later, a dripping, chagrinned Sir Rusel walks ashore.

The Red Wizard snips, "Back so soon?"

"Are you all right?" asks Mikal.

A red-faced Sir Rusel lowers his head. "I forgot one of the elements. I must be getting old."

He bends down and picks up some earth in both hands. "Goodbye again, my friends. I will see you soon."

He mumbles the words again, inhales deeply, and leaps into the flame a second time. No splash is heard.

Aden wades into the river. "I cannot see him. Do you think what he told us is true?"

The White Wizard laughs.

"Apparently. Now we rest, for we leave at first light."

Chapter 33

They break camp at dawn. Later in the morning, they come upon a small fishing village on the lake. Majam is excited by the many odors in the air. Mikal inquires about renting a small boat.

"What do you want it for? You don't look like no fisherman to me," suspiciously asks an older man sitting on a rickety dock.

"I would like to take it to the small island in the middle of the lake."

The weathered man spits and laughs. "The only island in the middle of the lake is made of mist. You can get to it but you can't step on it."

"Nevertheless, I still would like to rent one of your small boats."

"You got coin, Red?"

"How much is required?" responds Mikal.

"Ten silver deposit and I give you five back when you return the boat."

Aden steps forward. "Too much. Six silver now and you return three."

The lake sailor chuckles, "Eight now, four on the return."

"Acceptable, you old fart."

Aden tentatively shakes the man's hand who says, "I'll have her trim in a few minutes."

The three step off the dock onto the shore. Mikal says, "You two will have to stay here. Only Majam and I can go."

The dwarf protests, "Aye shud go with yew if few are go wing un derg round."

"Thank you, my friend, but I believe just my cat and I should go."

Majam meows and stares above the three. The Red Wizard points. "Look, an owl circles above. I believe it's looking to land."

Mikal holds out his arm and, to the amazement of all, the night bird lands lightly on Mikal's forearm. There is a colorful ribbon in the bird's beak. The owl releases it and the colorful cloth starts to gently fall.

The dwarf snatches it from the air. "Ooh, itt iz sew be yew tea full. Itt chain jez cull er in the son lite."

"It doesn't take much to amuse you, does it, dwarf?"

Aden looks closely at the bird's left leg. "What do we have here?" He answers his own question, "It is a message." He carefully removes it and unrolls the narrow parchment. He reads aloud, *"Dear Mikal. I pray you receive this in time. Remember to stay on the path. Tell the last Guardian whom you encounter that Sir Rusel Ironwood fights in my name. Then show him my colors. I dispatched a mutual friend days ago. I hope he finds you soon.*

Evalon."

As soon as the message is read, the owl takes flight. It swoops over the water and snatches a fish and is soon out of sight. Aden quips, "The dwarf must have scared it. It seemed to be in quite the rush."

"As am I," laughs Mikal.

He lowers himself and his cat into a small rowboat. He asks the old man at the dock, "In which direction will I find the mist?"

"Oh, just row straight out. You'll probably see it sooner than later." He spits into the water and chuckles, "Good luck…it looks like you'll need it. Take good care of my boat."

***

"Well, Majam, it has been many years since I have rowed a boat. Please take the bow and direct me. We are looking for the mist and the island it conceals."

After a less than auspicious start, the White Wizard learns to control the small vessel rather well. Majam meows and conveys to her master *there is mist ahead.* He holds the course and soon he and the small dinghy are encompassed in a strange, gray cloud. He slows but continues to row.

"Do you see any land, Majam?"

No, but I smell dirt and stone.

Suddenly, Mikal feels the bottom of the boat scraping land. He looks over his shoulder but all he can see is the thick haze.

His cat sniffs the air. *We are here. You can carry me to shore.*

"How far is it?" pleads Mikal. "All I can imagine is this infernal vapor and hear the water lapping against the boat."

The wizard grabs his staff of light and his faithful cat and jumps from the bow. Surprisingly, the water is only ankle-deep. Unfortunately, after taking several steps, the waters still covers only his feet.

"I was expecting dry land by now. Majam, can you see anything?"

No, but the odor of stone is growing stronger.

Mikal is relieved when he finally reaches dry, solid footing.

The wizard takes a few more tentative steps. Then, astonishingly, like he has walked through a portal, a stone tower appears before him. It is bathed in dazzling sunlight. Through Majam's eyes, the wizard scans the tower before him. All the stones are different in shape and size. There are no windows that he can discern. His sight is drawn to the top of the rocky edifice. He knows what he seeks is waiting for him atop the tower.

"No. I have been warned about taking the comfortable path and must resist the temptation."

His cat leaps to the ground and sits before an iron, reinforced door built into the structure. Mikal attempts to open it, but it only creaks and does not budge. He tries a second effort and the door opens slightly. He gathers himself, and on the third effort, the heavy, creaking barrier moves just enough for him to squeeze past.

He allows his staff to shed light on his surroundings. Before him appears a winding, well-carved set of stairs leading upward. It is as if this inanimate object is inviting him to climb. Mikal finds that that his right leg has placed itself on the first step. With some effort, the wizard pulls himself away from the alluring staircase.

"I must stay focused. Majam, we are looking for a trap door. It may be concealed. Can you find it for me?"

The cat prances out of Mikal's limited sight. He follows her mewing, and finds her under the spiraling stairway sitting, her tail swishing back-and-forth. He lowers his staff of light and sees a trap door partially covered with straw directly beneath Majam. Attached is a thick, metal ring. The wizard twists the ring and pulls the door which reveals a downward opening. Mikal's red hair billows as a swirling breeze escapes the gaping, black hole in the ground.

"After you, my fearless cat."

Majam hesitates. "Well, what are you waiting for? I guess you want me to go first." He sighs. "Very well."

Before Mikal can lower his foot onto the first step, he senses the stairs upward beckoning him. "This is most strange… but I know what I must do and I shall."

With a concerted effort, he steps gingerly down onto the spiraling stairwell. His cat stays close at his side. Using Majam's superior sight, he cautiously makes his descent.

The walls are made from the same stone as the tower above. Every so often, some of the stones glisten as if they have had water seeping upon them. The White Wizard continues his spiral descent over countless stone steps. When he thought the steps would never end, they do. An impressive stone arch looms before him. He crosses the archway and enters a mammoth cavern.

Mikal is startled to hear rhythmic breathing. Just a few feet away, lying on an impressive, flat stone is a raggedy-clad man who appears to be sleeping…maybe even dreaming. He is on his back one moment and his side the next.

Mikal notices that one arm is definitely longer than the other and one leg is far more muscular than its counterpart. One side of this man's head looks swollen while the other is of normal size. One eye socket is deeply set while the other bulges outward. The most peculiar thing is that dust and broken cobwebs cover both man and rock.

"What is this poor, misshapen man doing here?"

Majam meows and Mikal clears his throat and says, "Excuse me, sir."

The malformed man sits up and brushes off the dust and cobwebs. He gives a long look to the White Wizard and his cat. "Oh, I am sorry. I must have dozed off for a moment. So you brought a cat, I see. No harm in that. I must ask, what is it you seek?"

Mikal bows. "To whom do I have the pleasure of addressing?"

The strange man grins widely, showing teeth missing on one side of his smile but not on the other. "No one's asked me that before. My name is Natrium. Some say that I am salt of the earth. Now that I have answered your question, what about mine?"

The White Wizard hesitates. "I am seeking enchanted armor for a challenge of combat."

A girlish giggle escapes from the raggedy man. "Well, I assume it's not for you. So you come on someone else's behalf. That could be good or bad, depending on the circumstances." The bizarre creature clears his throat. "Do you have any water? I am extremely thirsty."

Mikal offers his water skin. The eccentric one grabs it and drains it completely. "That was refreshing. Do you have more?"

Mikal shakes his head. The man continues, "You passed the first test by just getting here. Enchanted armor, you say? Listen to me. Travel this cobblestone path. It will vary quite a bit, but when you reach the fork in the road, go left." He scratches the clean-shaven side of his chin. "You know, it's been a long time since anyone has come to travel the stone path. You will be tested in many ways. You must stay on the path until you are no longer able."

The misshapen man spins and wobbles and sticks his tongue out at Majam. "Good luck, whoever you are."

"So, I am safe as long as I stay on the path?" Mikal queries.

"I don't guarantee anything." The peculiar man twitters. "I do not know anywhere that you would be truly safe. Maybe the grave. If you step off the trail, your quest ends there."

The wizard thanks the malformed man and starts down the road, smiling slyly. The odd man shouts, "The same rules apply to your pet."

Mikal's smile fades, his one advantage lost.

With Majam leading, he travels down the cobblestone. The road narrows and, not far ahead, Mikal is taken aback when he sees a huge spider obstructing the way. It appears to be wiping off its fangs with its two front legs.

"Well, my cat, what do you propose we do now?"

What do you mean?

"There is a large, vicious spider barring our way."

Majam sits. *Why don't you just step over it or go around?*

"But I cannot. It covers the entire road."

It does not. I agree it is a big spider, but even I can step over it.

The wizard was using his cat's sight, but now he enters her mind and sees what she sees.

"You are right, my fine, furry friend. The spider is no bigger than my fist. Certainly a large spider, but not the one I saw in my mind. Let us continue."

As they approach, the arachnid scurries off.

"Well, that wasn't so bad," Mikal thinks aloud. The cobblestones rise slightly as the two adventurers crest a small hill. Below them they see something glisten. On both sides of the cobble road are mounds of gold and other precious stones, rubies, and sapphires all giving off a rich light of their own. The wizard knows that even with his staff these precious objects would be just out of reach. He has never had a strong desire for precious gems, but he admits he is overwhelmed by the sight. He and his friends and even his school would want for nothing with this unbelievable cache.

Then he beholds a rare sight. The gold coins move unexpectedly and the huge head of a serpent rises above the sea of coins.

Mikal shakes his head and laughs. "Even if I could overcome this guardian, I could never carry off half the loot. I would probably hurt my back. No, Majam this is not for us. Let us continue."

The next area they chance upon is comprised of weapons. Swords and spears of all kinds, bows and special arrows that could take down giants glint in the fire light of the surrounding braziers. Like the riches before, Mikal has never been interested in weapons. Even his untrained eye, however, can tell that these are magnificent.

"Sir Rusel will need a new sword."

Among the splendid weaponry stands a warrior made of iron.

"Is that a statue?" Mikal asks aloud.

As if on cue, the iron eyes open.

Mikal says hastily, "Again, Majam, let us keep going forward."

Unexpectedly, the cobblestones under his boots become larger, sharper, and hot to the touch. The path is flanked with mounds of sand. Beads of perspiration roll down the wizard's face.

"I am confused. What allure is this offering?"

The cat prances gingerly on the sizzling stones. She looks up and leaps into Mikal's arms.

"Yes, you are thirsty as I am. But we have no water: I gave it away."

Around the next corner he hears the unmistakable sound of water splashing. Then he sees a wonderful, pristine waterfall pouring over an immense rock and splashing into a pool of refreshing water.

"Now I know, Majam, what it wants us to do. Water can be more precious than all the gold and gems or weapons in the world. Hurry, let us be gone from this."

They travel some distance before reaching the next area. Mikal can feel the approaching attraction. Torches flare to reveal a room with three sides and no roof but the cavern's ceiling. The room is filled with fantastic, magical items of all kinds. There are wands, mystic rings, and staffs imbued with powerful spells. There are medallions for protection and others that enhance magical ability.

"Dear cat, there is no doubt that just a few of these items would make me the most powerful wizard in the land. I alone could defeat the ebony, Evil One. I could protect the land forever. I would not even need to imperil Sir Rusel."

Majam meows and paws her master's leg. She catches his attention and directs him to look upward. Mikal spies a sleek, tall, alabaster pillar. Upon it sits a small, red dragon no larger than a common lizard. It is eyeing the wizard.

"If that dragon is the guardian, I could take whatever I wanted, for I feel no threat from it."

Majam enters her master's consciousness. *Please, look again, not only with my sight but with my mind as well.* Mikal lifts his gaze a second time. Now the sleek, alabaster pillar is thick and wide. It branches out at the top. An enormous, red dragon lurks upon it.

"Those deadly, dark eyes and razor-sharp teeth could devour both of us, Majam, in one snap of its jaws."

I would prefer not to be eaten just yet. We must be gone from here.

"I thank you, my friend, and I concur. Let us move along."

When Mikal looks back over his shoulder, he believes the dragon looks disappointed and hungry.

A short time later, the cobble path narrows until it becomes only a foot wide. The wizard looks ahead, and before him sees a rickety, wooden bridge at least forty feet long. Below the bridge, darkness fills the chasm.

"I believe we can traverse this. Here, I will hold you in my arms and use my staff as a balancing pole." The wizard starts out upon this strange structure. After but a few steps, the bridge start to vibrate. A deep voice echoes from beneath.

"Who walks upon my bridge? And what will you give me for passage?"

"I am Mikal Novastar and my pet Majam."

"What have you to offer?"

"I have a sizable amount of silver. You may have it all."

"I am a troll. I live under a bridge. What need have I of silver?"

Beads of sweat appear on Mikal's brow. He unclasps his father's cloak and shows it to the troll.

"This is an enchanted, traveling cloak. You may have it. It is dear to me, but my need is great."

"I am a troll. I live under a bridge. What need have I of a traveling cloak?"

Mikal's mind races.

"I offer you this onyx ring and a pendant from the School of the Three Moons. They are very valuable."

"I am a troll. I live under a bridge. What need have I of a ring and pendant?"

Mikal grits his teeth and takes a deep breath.

"I offer you a staff of light." He holds it out in both hands." Surely, you cannot refuse this!"

"I am a troll. I live under a bridge. What need have I of a staff of light?"

Mikal's voice trembles and he pleads, "I have nothing else of value. Please, you have to reconsider. I must cross your bridge and succeed in my quest. The fate of the entire land hinges on what I do. I beg you."

The troll's expression does not change. His eyes fix on Majam.

"A pet? Explain."

"A pet is…a treasured animal friend that offers companionship to its owner."

"Then you have identified the toll for passage."

A panicked expression crosses Mikal's face and he retreats from the bridge, clutching Majam protectively.

Mikal whispers to his cat, "Do you have any suggestions?"

Offer me.

Horrified at the thought, Mikal answers through clenched teeth, "Completely unacceptable. How could you even suggest it?"

I have explored the troll's mind. It is highly suggestible.

"And…?"

Offer him what he desires. He has been alone for so very long. Help me give him an illusion that will comfort him and satisfy his demand."

Majam leaps from Mikal's arms and searches the path and finds a soft, green, moss-covered rock.

Give him this

"What?"

Can you not enchant this stone so that it mirrors me?

"Easily."

Do so. I will place the chimera in his consciousness and he will believe, for he desires to. The easiest wish to believe is what one wishes to believe.

Majam jumps in Mikal's arms and disappears under his cloak. The wizard turns his back on the troll and picks up the rock. He touches his staff to it and intones, "Change and animate."

The rock becomes Majam's double, and purrs contentedly. Mikal faces the troll and says, "As you wish."

The troll reaches up and tenderly accepts the rock, a look of sheer joy and what might pass for a smile crosses his face. Eyes brimming with tears, he settles back and affectionately begins to stroke his purring, pet rock.

***

After satisfying the troll under the bridge, the cobble road widens to its usual width. They do not travel far before they come upon the fork in the road mentioned by the crooked man. As instructed, the two stay to the left. They come to another area in this subterranean cavern. On both sides of the path are bookshelves filled with old, arcane volumes of books. From Mikal's vantage point, he can make out some of the titles, but recognizes only a few. He can tell by their odor and appearance that they are ancient texts and ponders the wonders they could reveal.

Majam meows. She is sitting on the road and next to her is a book. The wizard hesitates then picks it up, taking care not to step off the path.

"I sense no guardian here. I wonder if opening this book will awaken it. Yes, Majam, I will not open this until we leave this place. Lead the way, my faithful friend."

They travel for some time without encountering any more enchanted areas. Mikal begins to wonder if he took the correct path. He hears vibrations in the air. Drumbeats, not loud but definite. He somehow feels that he is near his goal. As within the weapons area, braziers flare to life, sending firelight everywhere.

"Could this be the end of my quest?"

On display are myriad suits of armor. They are made of classic leather and iron and even steel. There are others made from material the wizard does not recognize. He passes a suit that must have been made from nothing but dragon scales.

"Impressive in every way."

An old, full gray-bearded dwarf appears from behind one of the suits of armor, holding a polishing rag in his right hand.

"Good day to you, sir, if it is day. One never knows in this infernal place. With the sound of the drums, I knew someone was approaching."

"Uh, good day to you, sir. I, uh…"

"Spit it out, man. What is it?"

"Pardon me for asking, but, uh, you are a dwarf, are you not?"

"How very observant of you."

"It's just that I know a dwarf and he…"

"Really, sir, you are beginning to tax me. How may I assist you?"

Mikal bows to the wizened dwarf. Only then does he notice that he has left the cobblestone path.

"I come seeking armor for a warrior to wear in a challenge by combat."

The ancient one chuckles. "Why, you have come to the right place. We have armor of every kind, the best in all the land, if I may say so myself."

"Did you make all these?" questions Mikal.

"Only a few. Most were brought here for safe-keeping. I mostly clean and polish them. I enjoyed it for many years, but, I must admit, it's become rather tiresome."

The wizard shakes his head. "There are so many and I am not sure about the size."

The dwarf waves his hand. "Do not worry about that. All these suits of armor have enchantments on them that allow them to vary their size to accommodate the wearer."

"Thank you for that knowledge, but I still do not know which one to choose. The warrior will have to face an opponent that projects an aura of fear. Do you have anything that can combat that?"

The full-bearded dwarf looks hard and long at the White Wizard. "I believe I have what you seek."

He shows Mikal a suit of armor that is set apart from the others. It possesses an emerald green sheen to it.

"This is exceptionally made, notice the fine craftsmanship. Oddly, it only has one additional enchantment upon it: its wearer will know no fear. Yes, I believe this is what you desire," says the dwarf.

"I must trust you, for I know very little of this trade. What must I do to obtain it?" The old dwarf shakes his head. "Now, that might present a problem. You must speak to the Guardian. He makes all the final decisions. I do not think he will like it, but I stand by my recommendation."

"Where can I find this guardian?" Mikal asks.

"Come, I shall show you the way."

The bearded dwarf escorts him to a small knoll. On top of it stands an immense iron, throne-like chair. There someone sits, but shadows obscure the wizard's view.

"Oh, Randolph, this gentleman is interested in one of the suits of armor." He beckons Mikal to step forward. "I am finished here and will now take my leave."

Mikal is taken aback when a massive, muscular man rises from the iron chair. He stands eight feet tall and carries a six foot, stone, double-bladed axe. It looks like it could crush a lion in one blow. But the most astounding feature is the head. It is that of a bull. Mikal has read about these creatures, but he thought they had vanished from the land long ago. Surprising him further, the Minotaur, like the dwarf, speaks with excellent diction and with a resonant voice.

"What is your name, traveler, and where are you from?"

The wizard bows. "My name is Mikal Novastar from the great City of Addis and this is my cat Majam."

"Nice cat. I must ask you, do you seek the armor for yourself or for another?"

The White Wizard replies, "For another."

The huge Minotaur bows his head. "That is good. You have just passed another test. What armor interests you?"

"It is one set apart from the others. It has a green hue to its metal. The good dwarf told me it has an enchantment against fear."

The great creature hesitates. "That is a dangerous suit of armor you have requested. Do you understand all the ramifications of that enchantment? The warrior will have no fear of anything, including committing crimes and other unspeakable acts. It will fear no one and nothing. For whom do you seek the armor, Mikal Novastar from the great city of Addicts."

"Uh, that's Addis. The man who must wear this armor is Sir Rusel Ironwood."

The mammoth Minotaur raises his great stone axe. "I know this name. He is not worthy to claim this armor. It would be disastrous. Leave now with your life."

"Wait," shouts the White Wizard. "I am to tell you that he fights in the name of the Lady Evalon."

The creature hesitates. Mikal reveals the ribbon he was given.

"These are her colors which he will wear in combat."

Mikal is shocked. The Minotaur lowers its deadly axe and bends to one knee. "If the lady wills it, the armor is yours."

A blinding flash of light encompasses the area and...the White Wizard finds himself atop the stone tower. Next to him is his cat and a set of armor with a shimmering green hue.

Chapter 34

Sir Rusel lands on solid ground. He rolls and regains his footing. He stops, takes a deep breath, and declares triumphantly, "I am here."

He takes in his surroundings. It is early morning. "I am sorry that I missed the dawn, for every sunrise here is special." He smiles. "I feel young again."

The Paladin sprints across a vibrant, green field filled with soft, tall grass. He chuckles, then breaks into a hearty laugh. He falls to his knees. "The door opened for me! I am a man reborn!"

The knight composes himself. "Now, to the matter at hand. I must find a fast, flowing river. The horses of this land gather to water."

As Sir Rusel walks through the tall fields of grass, he plucks the longest stalks and starts to twist and bind them into twine. "I will need a small rope in order to ride."

He travels over long, gradual hills, taking in everything his senses can detect. The sound of the wind and birds in the air exhilarates him. He savors the softness of each step he takes and the scent of the grass and flowers. The dazzling colors inspire him. He crests a pleasant hill, and before him sees the river he requires. He runs to the bank of this surging water and bends down and drinks deeply.

"I think I could live just on water alone here. Surely, this splendid river will show me the way to fulfill my quest."

Sir Rusel Ironwood walks like a young man, following the flow. A fish with multicolored scales leaps into the air and back into the life-giving waters. The Paladin encounters more trees along the bank. They are filled with birds and small rodents, all squawking and chirping.

The knight stops. "I revel in the music of life."

He hears the sound of splashing ahead, and approaches curiously. He sits on a boulder by the river's edge and stares at a most wondrous site. A small herd of magnificent horses known as the Raauh gather around the river. There are six. Some are full-grown while others are just foals. All are primarily white, but one of the older stallions has other colors mixed in; a touch of golden brown and bright beige. All have thick, graceful manes and tails that flow and bound as they gallop and leap. Four of them are in the water simply enjoying themselves. The knight wishes he had some apples. Then he remembers that one of the trees he passed was a apple tree. He cautiously stands and backs silently away. Once out of sight, he starts to run. In no time at all, he picks an armful of apples and happily returns to the river.

The Raauh are nowhere to be seen. He is disappointed but soon finds their tracks in the soft grass and follows their hoof prints for some time. They lead him to a secluded glen where the horses are grazing contently. He deliberately approaches and offers the apples he has picked. The youngest colt is the first to accept the gift. The others follow, and soon are munching on the red, luscious fruit.

One apple remains, so Rusel takes part in the feast. He stands apart from the Raauh at first, but over the next few hours each horse gets close enough so that he can pat and stroke their backs. The glorious sun starts to set as Sir Rusel stares transfixed at the picturesque site. The Paladin beds down for the night with the horses not far away.

***

He is awakened by the sound of the young colts running and playing and neighing. He marvels at the glorious sunrise and he feels it will be a good day. Soon the horses are off, and he follows eagerly.

After a short time, he realizes their direction and returns to the river. He sheds his chain mail and boots and dives into the cooling, rippling water. When the horses come close, he playfully splashes them. They are confused at first but the younger ones come over time and time again. He can tell they enjoy it.

The stallion snorts and the small herd leave the revitalizing water. They move to a bright area and begin to sun themselves. Master Ironwood carefully approaches one of the older Raauh. The magnificent creature studies the man with the bright, blue eyes.

Rusel pats and gently strokes the back of this resplendent equine. The horse is skittish at first, but settles down and begins to enjoy it.

The man starts to brush out mats in the mane. One by one, the others approach and he brushes and pats them down as well.

A distant howl is heard, and the horses are off in an instant and are gone from site. Sir Rusel ponders what he should do. Only now does he become aware of his hunger. He spends the next hour or so fishing with his bare hands in the flowing river. After some time, he does meet success and captures two colorful trout.

He builds a fire, scales the fish, and feasts. He regains his clothes and heads back to the secluded glen. Just before the fall of the sun, the herd returns. They all snicker and come close enough so that Sir Rusel can give them quick brushing, using a handful of stiff grass plucked from the field.

They sleep peacefully the second night.

***

A pleasant rain falls just before dawn, and, with the rising of the sun, ceases.

The knight approaches the herd. "Hear me, Raauh. My need is great or I would not ask this of you. The land I come from has evil festering in it. I have been chosen to combat a dark creature who rides a formidable steed. He is an abomination. I know I am not worthy, but I ask would any of you carry me to battle? I'll return you to this land as soon as I am able, if we succeed, of course."

The herd stands frozen for many minutes. The youngest colt strides and leaps and rears up on his hind legs. It lowers his head before the ancient Paladin.

The warrior returns the bow. "I am sorry but I cannot allow you to come. You are too young, but know you have the heart of a champion." The colt seems insulted and sulks back to the others.

"I thank you, though. You honor me."

The small group slowly turns as one and leave the glen. Sir Rusel runs in a different direction. He finds the apple tree and again fills his rucksack. He returns to the river and is relieved to see that the Raauh have returned.

He watches the horses frolicking, but does not enter into the sport.

Eventually the Raauh leave the water and start to sun themselves on the bank. Master Ironwood offers each an apple, which is eagerly accepted.

"Please, bear with me. I thank you for letting me spend this time with you, but my need is great and I must return to my home."

The knight looks for rocks and firewood to place in the river. Unexpectedly, he feels a nudge on his shoulder. He turns, and before him stands the full-grown mare. Her knowing, emerald eyes look deeply into his. She lowers her great head and Sir Rusel Ironwood bows ever so low.

With a tear in his eye, he manages, "I'm forever in your debt."

He pats and brushes her snow white coat and straightens her impressive mane. He returns to the river bank and places boulders in the river. He gathers large pieces of firewood and positions them on the rocks and sets them ablaze.

He turns to the great equine. "I ask you to trust me and carry me through the fire." He grabs soil in his left hand and expertly vaults onto his mount. The great horse hesitates, and backs up a few strides.

"Now, run and leap!"

Rusel points to the flame. The impressive horse understands, neighs, rears up on her hind legs, and gallops fearlessly toward the portal. She bounds high into the air while the Paladin recites the incantation to return him to his land.

They travel through fire and are gone.

Chapter 35

Talon looks around. "I wish we were not out in the open like this."

"I agree." Sebastian nods. "But if I may make a suggestion?"

"Please."

"We should travel at a steady pace. Any abrupt change of movement often catches the eye of a predator."

They agree, and set a deliberate cadence.

Mairin grabs Talon's arm, a concerned look on her face. "Talon, my father was going to that dreadful place from which we just escaped."

The half-elf nods. "Yes, that was the information we received, but Tamarix sensed nothing of him there. I believe he is safe."

"I desperately want to believe you," Mairin responds, holding his arm tighter.

"My best recommendation is to return to Stonegrove, his last known location. I know people there and I have made some friends."

Sebastian points east. "If the City of Stonegrove is our destination, I believe we should go this way."

They travel through most of the evening, only hearing night birds and howls of wolves in the distance. They are exhausted when they come upon the camp they had made a day earlier.

Talon shakes his head. "We have little water and no food. I suggest we get some rest and then scale the valley wall. There is water above and I can hunt."

"I agree," says Sebastian, "An hour respite, and we begin our assent."

Talon looks to his cat. "Tamarix, guard."

The Elven cat sniffs the air and leisurely circles the makeshift camp. Mairin falls fast asleep. The half-elf relaxes and tries to meditate on the waning stars above. Sebastian Wolfram watches them both. A half an hour later, Tamarix returns and demands Talon's attention.

He awakens Mairin and whispers, "Quiet, there is danger."

Sebastian moves closer to the two. "I know something is not right. I believe there are creatures out there stalking us."

The half-elf readies his bow. "By the way Tamarix is acting, he may have sensed a wererat."

Sebastian holds his pointed nose high. "There is more than one and the cat is correct: wererats."

Talon's bow starts to glow faintly.

"You stay here, Talon, and guard the girl. I will try to outflank them. Oh, and please, try not to hit me with an arrow in the darkness."

Sebastian Wolfram moves away without making a sound.

"Mairin, stay low. I will let them come to us. They may be surprised that my cat and I can match their night vision."

Minutes pass and the night is still. Tamarix's ears perk up and he stares in a fixed direction. The half-elf archer readies an arrow and follows his cat's line of sight. Talon's enchanted bow glows with greater intensity. The young archer eyes a target.

He lets his arrow fly: a lethal hit. Two more humanoid rats spring up and charge Talon and Mairin's location. The half-elf releases four more deadly darts, each scoring devastating wounds. Mairin looks over her shoulder and screams. The Elven cat is at her side and hisses menacingly. Talon turns and readies another arrow, but somehow this wererat is already upon them.

The wizard's daughter points and flings a light spell at the creature's eyes. Tamarix leaps on this rodent creature, biting and clawing. Talon takes aim and is careful not to strike his cat. The mystical arrow bores into the creature's heart, killing it instantly.

Everything stops and becomes unnaturally quiet, save for Mairin's ragged breathing. Talon hears a commotion that he believes is a struggle.

"Do you think it's Sebastian, Mairin? Do you think he needs our help?" He looks to his cat. "Tamarix, search for Sebastian Wolfram."

The loyal feline sets off, sniffing the ground. Within a surprisingly short amount of time, Sebastian returns, closely followed by the cat. He surveys the area.

"I see you have been busy this night. You are, indeed, a deadly archer."

The teenaged girl asks, "Are you injured? What happened to you?"

"Oh, I encountered only one of those lowly creatures. I believe he was the leader of this failed escapade. Their main group seemed to be stalking you two. May I ask why?"

Talon unstrings his bow. "I will explain later. You said you believe you encountered the leader? You seem no worse for it."

The white-haired man smiles. "This is not my first encounter with these large vermin. When my opponent saw his underlings getting cut down, he started to shy away. Most of these rats are cowards and..."

Talon interrupts, "I thought only magic or silver could harm them."

"Yes, that is generally correct, but this one did not know what I possess. Like I said, I confronted him and he ran. I believe the path that leads up the valley wall is now safe to scale. Let us take advantage of this now."

Midway through their assent, Talon presses Sebastian, "Did you talk your way out of a confrontation with wererat leader?"

"Oh no, my dear boy. I threatened him with my sword and knife. Like I said before, when he saw his minions die, doubt grew inside him. I showed no fear, and he simply fled."

Mairin asks, "So you've had some experience with these creatures?"

"If you must know, yes I have. I have traveled many places. I have spent time in the City of Umbra, a strange, interesting, and dangerous place. I have been to the borderlands, where there is only rock and sand. The people there are harder than the terrain," the white-haired man snickers. "I have even spent time in the City of Addis, a pleasant place to visit. I have been to anywhere and everywhere where there are coins to be made and challenges to be met."

They continue on the switchback trails. By late morning, they crest the top of the cliff and find a cluster of trees and a small creek flowing with fresh water.

Talon announces, "I will hunt. I won't be gone for long. You two should wait here."

Sebastian nods his head. "I find that most agreeable. We shall fill our water skins."

Talon and his cat leave immediately. The white-haired man with the pointed nose asks, "Young lady, when we were captured you used healing spells. You must have been trained in that art. Where was this, may I ask?"

Mairin looks to Sebastian. "Yes, I have had formal training... but where exactly I would rather not say."

Master Wolfram smiles. "Let me guess then. Definitely not Stonegrove. Perhaps from the School of the Three Moons in the great City of Addis, hmm? Am I correct?"

The young girl does not respond. Sebastian's smile widens.

Talon enters the camp holding two small pheasants. "This is not very much, but it should be enough to get us to our destination."

As they pluck and clean their late breakfast, Sebastian inquires, "Now would be a good time to explain to me why you attract wererats."

The half-elf takes a slow, long, deep breath. "Weeks ago my traveling companions and I encountered, how should I put this...a superior breed? They were much larger and even more vicious than any I have encountered and had grandiose schemes of conquest and domination. One escaped and swore vengeance upon us. Ever since then they have been on my trail, and no doubt, my friends' as well."

"A strange tale, indeed." The white-haired man brushes back his hair. "What did you do to them to have them pursue you so doggedly?"

Talon shrugs his shoulders, "Well, we did kill two of them and, like I said, one was unlike any other. Add to that, we foiled their designs."

Sebastian presses the issue. "What do you believe their designs were?"

The half-elf answers, "I'm not sure, but I believe they were being directed by some other powerful, maleficent creature."

Mairin interrupts, "The birds are done, let us eat."

***

Talon and his cat lead the group through high brush and lightly wooded areas. "I believe this is the most direct route to the main road."

Less than two hours later, Tamarix stops and sounds a warning. The half-elf and his cat stop abruptly. "We are very close to the main road and I hear some sort of ruckus ahead."

"Lower your voice," Sebastian directs. "I hear it also."

The small group advances cautiously through a clump of thin trees. They spy a wagon being driven by two merchants. It is being held up by three bandits. Mairin pleads, "We must do something."

Sebastian turns toward the girl. "This does not concern us and it will be over soon. We are safe here."

"It's not right. Help them, please," Mairin protests.

Master Wolfram shakes his head. "Young elf, arm your bow. You are my backup, although I doubt if I shall need it. Remain here."

Sebastian Wolfram strides onto the road. With his hands held slightly out and apart, he walks purposely toward the confrontation. One of the crooks notices his approach. Sebastian brushes his back his white hair and holds his pointy chin up in the air. He does not slow until he catches the leader's eye.

The leather-clad robber turns his sword to the white-haired man. "Who are you and what do you want?"

Sebastian slows but continues his approach. "I am here to assist. My name is not important."

The bandit is confused. "We don't need any help and we're not going to share our loot with anyone."

Sebastian snickers. "You misunderstand my intent. I was looking at you but I was addressing them." He point to the merchants.

"Wha...?"

Sebastian is upon the bandits' leader and, in a seemingly impossible maneuver, draws his knife and pivots around to the thief's back. He holds his deadly blade to the criminal's exposed neck.

"Drop the sword." It clangs immediately to the rocky ground.

The white-haired man slyly smiles. "You other two, let me explain myself. I have a Elven archer positioned in those trees. He has one of you as his target. Which one it is, is beyond me. If you believe me, I recommend highly that you leave now and avoid the arrow. If you do not, I guarantee at least one of you will die."

Seconds later, the clamor of metal falls to the hard earth, and the two would-be bandits are out of sight. Sebastian lowers his knife and slashes the back of his captive's hand, severing tendons.

"You will never be able to grip a sword or knife again. Now hurry and join your friends, you embarrassing little man."

Talon and Mairin step out onto the main road and join Sebastian. The two merchants are confused by the whole situation. A heavyset, balding one stutters, "Th-thank you, sir. May I ask who are you?"

Sebastian bows slightly. "I, sir? I am your rescuer and deliverer and these are my two associates, a half-elf archer and a teenage girl. We are bound for the City of Stonegrove."

The older merchant nods quizzically at the acknowledgments. "I would offer you coin, sir, but we have very little. It is all tied up in what we carry. Our casks are filled with fine wine and our crates carry tasty, vine-ripened dates. I can offer you some of these."

The white-haired man hesitates. "In all likelihood, I just saved your lives." He looks to Talon and Mairin. "But if you tell me you have no coin, I must believe you. I will gladly accept some wine and dates."

The merchants produce two bottles of wine and a small container of fruit. "I thank you again, and coincidently, our destination is the same. But as you can see, there is little room in our wagon. Find us in the City of Stonegrove and we will see that you are properly rewarded."

They rattle their reins and the mules start to pull their heavy load. They are soon out of sight.

Mairin inquires, "You didn't give them our names. Why?"

Sebastian turns. "Oh, I thought we are keeping secrets. I did not see the need. You do know those two had much coin with them and there was room on their wagon. If we meet them in the city, I would wager that they would not even acknowledge us. I've seen their kind often. They are avaricious and they also feared us. At the very least, the wine seems acceptable. Let us share some dates."

Chapter 36

Mikal kneels and closely inspects the newly acquired suit of armor. The late afternoon sun reflects off its well-forged, glistening metal. He looks for his cat and finds her curled up inside the metal helm of the enchanted mail.

"Well, you look cozy in there, but we must be off. It is odd, though, that when we first arrived on this obscure island, I was convinced that what I sought lay at the top of this tower. And now I am here with the object of my search. Could it all have been an illusion and the suit of armor was here all along? Oh well, something to ponder. Let us descend these stairs. I hope that enchanted metal is not too weighty."

It is a slow and difficult descent which includes many rests, the clanging of armor against the walls, and steps that echo throughout the tower.

"Pray tell me that this is the last step, Majam."

With some effort, Mikal struggles from the tower. He rests the armor on the stony ground. "I must pause for a moment, and then I shall drag it to the boat. I wish you could help me, Majam."

The cat does not respond for she is staring transfixed at a strangely familiar sight.

"Oh, I don't think that feline can help you, as magnificent as she is, but maybe I can be of service."

The White Wizard turns and his jaw drops. Before him stands an impressive man wearing a flowing, gray cloak. He sports long, gray hair held back tightly with a strip of leather. He has an angular face with deep lifelines etched into it. His eyes are also gray. Mikal recognizes the soft smile and the rough, granite arm. Here, with his arms akimbo, stands Ebon Usher, the Stone Mage.

He touches the tower's surface with a massive hand. "Good stonework. The rocks enjoy being part of this structure. It's been here for some time."

Mikal finds his voice and manages, "How did you get here?"

Ebon smiles. "Did you not receive the note? The Lady sent me. She thought you may need some assistance. So here I am. You sure made a lot of noise descending those stairs. If nothing else, may I help you with your new, fashionable clothes?"

"You heard me? And you did not think to offer assistance?"

The Stone Mage shrugs his shoulders and smiles broadly. "Oh, I considered it but thought some physical labor would be good for you."

Mikal shakes his head. "Ever since I left the School of the Three Moons, even breathing seems to me like physical labor."

The wizards laugh.

"I see your cat is doing very well. The Lady Evalon insisted that I ask about her. She enjoyed your cat very much when you last visited her."

Ebon Usher effortlessly picks up the enchanted armor. They walk to the boat with Majam fidgeting in Mikal's arms.

"She does not seem to care much for water."

The Stone Mage chuckles, "Few cats do," and carefully places the green-hued armor in the small craft.

Mikal inquires, "Where is your vessel?"

Ebon points west. "Not far from here. I made mine. It's actually a raft, but it served me well."

Mikal asks sheepishly, "Will you row us back?"

Master Usher nods. "I shall try, but may I remind you," he reveals his stone arm, "that my left arm is far stronger than my right."

The White Wizard is still fascinated with this man. His left arm, all the way to the shoulder, is made of rock. Mikal remembers that his friend will eventually turn completely to stone, and not only does he accept this, but welcomes it. To be an avatar of stone is his greatest desire.

They disembark and set a zigzag course through the swirling, purple haze. It is quite some time before Ebon rows a direct course. As they emerge from the curtain of mist, Mikal directs his cat to the bow. He enters her mind.

"Are you able to direct us back, Majam?"

The impressive feline holds her pink nose up in the air, a bit insulted, and looks to the right. The White Wizard directs the Stone Mage in the direction indicated.

"Oh, Mikal Novastar, I almost forgot. The Lady told me that she received important information concerning that thief you travel with… Blunderhands or whatever, that he no longer is in servitude to that character, Bass Molar. I do not know the circumstances of his dismissal or his current location, but she assured me that she will pass on any information to you as she receives it."

Mikal smiles. "That is excellent news. I hope he fares well. With any luck, I will see him and Talon soon."

By sundown they return to the small fishing village. A young boy throws them a rope and secures the other end to a wooden post. The weathered, old man sits on the dock. "Well, I see you made it and you brought a passenger and cargo back with you. I should charge more for that." He spits and laughs lightly.

The cat is the first off the boat. She bounds onto the dock and scampers to dry land, where she sits and waits. Mikal settles with the owner of the small boat and he and Ebon follow the wooden pier to the shore. Not far inland, they spot a small fire and, warming himself by it, stands the Red Wizard. He rises when he sees Mikal arrive.

The White Wizard says, "Aden, may I present to you Ebon Usher. As incredible as it may seem, he is what is known as a Stone Mage. Ebon, I present to you Aden Ferrum, a Red Wizard from the City of Umbra."

They exchange simple bows.

The Red Wizard looks to Mikal. "How is it that you attract such odd and exotic people and creatures?"

Mikal laughs. "You should include yourself in that category."

Aden ignores the barb. "So, I see that you were successful in your quest and you did find some peculiar armor. There is a green color to it. Is it covered with moss or slime of some sort?"

Ebon shakes his head and answers, "No, I believe it has to do with the enchantment upon it."

The White Wizard concurs and asks, "Tell me, where is Kairn?"

"I do not know for sure, but I believe he's gone native. He's been helping them…" he points in the direction of the small fishing village. "Assisting with their nets, helping the blacksmith, and eating an extraordinary amount of fish."

Mikal smiles. "I hope Sir Rusel has been successful. We will stay the night and leave early in the morning."

A short time later, the dwarf appears, carrying an armload of fish. "Wheel ete gould two knight."

"Kairn, meet Ebon Usher, a Stone Mage. Ebon, this Kairn Lanthanide Kavon." The dwarf drops the fish and stares agape at Ebon's left, stone arm. He steps forward and touches the appendage.

"Eye lie kit."

Mikal interjects, "We should prepare our meal."

***

The village awakens before dawn. The fishermen set out in their fishing vessels with the hope of filling their cargo holds.

The adventurers rise and what little fish is left over from last night is quickly eaten. The dwarf and Ebon Usher start to break camp.

Unexpectedly, two elders approach Mikal, one with a severe limp.

The older of the two asks, "May we have a word with you?"

Aden quips, "Can I hold you to that? A word.

Mikal ignores the Red Wizard. "Yes, certainly. I hope we have done nothing objectionable."

"No, no, not at all. Let me introduce myself: I am Jonah and this is my cousin Ahab. He suffered a severe fishing accident some time ago."

"I am sorry to hear that," Mikal responds.

"It's of no matter now. I would like to inquire about your dwarf."

The White Wizard shakes his head. "Excuse me…my what?"

"You see, we are shorthanded and our would-be blacksmith skills are… limited. Your dwarf seems to enjoy fish. We would like to buy him."

"What? I am no slaver."

"Forgive us, we would like to buy your servant then."

"He is not my servant. He is a free man. Look at him: what do you see?"

The two turn toward Kairn and hesitate "We see a dwarf, not exactly a man. Besides, he's even missing an arm."

The White Wizard lowers his voice and speaks very slowly, "We shall be leaving now." He considers. "I may ask him if he chooses to stay but it will be his decision, not mine."

The elders bow. "Thank you for considering our proposal. You understand, we do have coin."

"Leave," Mikal growls.

Aden asks, "What was that all about?"

"They thought we owned Kairn and they wanted to buy him."

The Red Wizard laughs, "They must have very low standards in this part of the land."

Mikal is not amused.

He directs everyone to pack up and declares, "I wish to leave as soon as possible. Majam, show us the way to Stonegrove."

The cat knows that her master is fuming, and she sets a quick pace.

Chapter 37

Aden steps next to Ebon Usher. "That is an interesting left arm you have there." The Stone mage nods. Aden continues, "Tell me, just what kind of magic does a Stone Mage possess? No, let me guess. You speak to rocks."

Ebon looks to Aden who says, "Oh my, I believe you can. What do they say back? Are they *hard* to get to know?"

Aden laughs. Ebon Usher abruptly stops and places his left hand heavily on the Red Wizard's shoulder. "All of these stones and rocks and pebbles and gravel have been here longer than any man. Their knowledge is beyond anything that can enter into your hard head." He starts ever so slightly to squeeze Aden's left shoulder. "And remember: rock is stronger than bone."

The Stone Mage releases the bruised shoulder and quickly catches up with Mikal and Majam. Everyone can hear Kairn snickering.

***

Mikal, speaking to no one in particular, muses, "I believe we are nearing the City of Stonegrove."

Majam stops and, with her tail held high, looks to the east. Mikal enters her mind. *He was successful.*

The Wizard sees a lone rider mounted upon an impressive, white charger, gliding over a green meadow. Sir Rusel Ironwood's mount skids to a halt. "Hail, Mikal Novastar from the great City of Addis and his companions! I see you have been successful also."

He leaps from his newly-acquired steed and bows. "Let me show you this fine animal." The White Wizard watches the great creature's head lower toward his cat. For some moments the two animals look fixedly at one another. Mikal effortlessly slips into the mind of his cat. *She is a fine horse with a courageous heart but is fearful of what is to come. She wants to return home as soon as possible. The Paladin has chosen wisely.* As an afterthought *I like her.*

The contact is broken and the horse holds her head high once again. All take turns greeting the magnificent mare.

Mikal, still scratching behind the horse's ear, says, "Sir Rusel, this is the man who is in charge of your enchanted armor. He is Ebon Usher, a Stone Mage. Ebon, this is Sir Rusel Ironwood, our champion. He is to face the Ebony Knight."

The two strong men bow and clasp hands. "Well met," they say in unison.

The White Wizard smiles. "Let us continue to the city."

Aden points ahead. "I see the walls of Stonegrove."

Sir Rusel abruptly stops and faces Mikal. "I cannot take my horse into the city. It would not be right, for she knows only of the wilds. I shall make camp by the river." He points in the distance. "There is a small group of trees that will offer us shelter. Also, I would like to make a request. Could someone bring a brush so I could give my mare a proper rubdown? She deserves so much more, and if I am to ride into battle, I must have a saddle. Are any of you experienced riders?"

The Red Wizard steps forward. "I could ride before I could walk, and I appreciate your impressive steed."

"Thank you, Aden. I believe a light saddle would suffice. I do not want her to be burdened with heavy, leather, combat gear."

"I concur. I will procure for you a proper brush and a fine saddle."

"One more thing," Sir Rusel asks, "if you can find a ripe, red apple or two, I think she would enjoy that."

"I shall be at your camp within two hours, if my… master allows."

Mikal smiles and nods his head.

The White Wizard, the Red Wizard, Ebon Usher, and the one-armed dwarf watch Sir Rusel ride away. As they cross a bridge to enter the city, their pace slows considerably. There are more guards at the gate than usual and they are asking questions and inspecting goods. Despite a few questioning looks, Mikal and his companions pass unimpeded through the gate and into the city.

Aden asks, "Where are we going now?"

Mikal, holding his cat in his arms, replies, "I believe the most advantageous place would be the Yellow Toad Inn."

Aden nods. "And by the time we get there, I wonder how many of your friends and enemies will know our location."

The White Wizard does not laugh.

They wind their way through the city streets. Mikal tries to orient himself to his surroundings. The people who pass by take little notice. Through his cat's eyes, he extends his sight.

"Is it my imagination, or is that person staring at me or at someone in our group?"

He notices an extremely tall female wearing a sheer veil that obscures what appears to be smooth, bronze skin. Her exotic eyes follow their group.

Abruptly, a young rider rears to a stop. "Hail, Mikal!"

Majam raises her head and Mikal recognizes the Baron's son, Robert Craig.

"Hail, good Sir," Mikal responds.

The Baron's son dismounts expertly. "I must thank you for that wondrous night, hunting and slaying foul creatures. Could anyone ask for more?"

Mikal smiles but does not respond.

"I do not see Talon."

"He is not with us currently, but I hope he will return soon. You know Aden and Kairn, and this is Ebon Usher."

They exchange slight bows.

Robert Craig asks, "Where are you going and how can I be of assistance?"

Aden steps forward. "Our destination is the Yellow Toad Inn. Tell me where I can purchase a well-made saddle and reins."

The Baroness' son hesitates. "We have some fine saddles at our stable. They are slightly worn but finely crafted."

After Aden describes what is needed, Robert Craig deftly swings himself up on the back of his horse. "I shall deliver the saddle and accouterments in less than an hour to the inn. Fare-thee-well." He lightly spurs his horse and is off.

***

Mikal, Aden, Ebon Usher, and the one-armed dwarf enter the Yellow Toad Inn. The innkeeper greets them warmly. "Welcome, Mikal and companions."

The White Wizard smiles. "It is good to see you again, my friend. We would like a room, and I insist that I pay for it."

"No, no, not necessary." The innkeeper holds up his hands. "When you last left, not one, but two impressive ladies instructed me that they would pay all your expenses upon your return. May I recommend the loft? It is spacious and has two beds and I can provide a third."

Aden raises an eyebrow. "Not one, but two impressive ladies?"

A blushing Mikal accepts the kind offer.

"I'll send fresh food and water up presently."

The proprietor directs the group to the aforementioned quarters. Upon entry, Aden opens the one window and scans the surroundings. "It would be difficult to enter through this portal and it provides an excellent view."

Along with the two beds, the room has a wooden table with three chairs and a large trunk to stow gear. Within minutes, there is a knock on the door and the innkeeper's wife enters carrying a large tray with clear water and fresh food. She greets everyone with a smile and lovingly pets Majam's head.

"I have not forgotten about you, my feline beauty. I'll bring you some fresh milk." Majam purrs contentedly and the portly woman leaves the room. Mikal starts to pace and lines crease his forehead. "I thought there would be some word on Talon and my daughter by now. I am beginning to worry."

Aden suggest, "Why don't you ask that night person, what is her name?"

"Marion Vetta?"

"Yes. That's it. Would she not have contacts?"

The White Wizard nods. "You may be right, but I do not know how to contact her. She has always found me."

Aden states the obvious, "Well then, I suggest we wait."

Upon finishing the food and drink, a knock is heard at the door. The innkeeper opens it enough for his head to appear. "Excuse me, sirs, but there is a young noble lad in the main hall who claims that he has the items that you asked him to procure."

The four descend the stairs and enter the main hall. Robert Craig, and two servants carrying the requested items, stands grinning with his arms opened wide.

"What do you think?"

Aden carefully inspects the gear. "You are correct. These are made with craftsmanship and attention to detail. They are not up to my standards, of course, but I believe they will suffice." He faces Mikal. "With your permission, my master, I shall deliver them to Sir Rusel."

Mikal nods. Ebon Usher surprises the White Wizard with a request of his own. "I, too, would like to present the enchanted armor to Sir Rusel to see if it is adequate. He must ride fully regaled so that his wonderful mount becomes accustomed to the added weight."

Mikal hesitates. "Yes, the two of you together would have a greater chance of success. Kairn and I will wait here. I hope I soon receive good news. Good luck, gentlemen."

Chapter 38

Aden Ferrum and Ebon Usher arrive at Sir Rusel's simple camp.

The Paladin stands as the Red Wizard and the Stone Mage dismount and display the goods. "Let me see what you have brought." He inspects the commodities. "This is a fine saddle…and two brushes. I thank you. I have endeavored to explain to Snow…my name for my horse…about the saddle, the bit, the bridal and the reins. I believe she understands, for she is quite perceptive. But first I must treat her to a proper brushing." Ebon explains why he brought the armor. "The horse and rider must adjust to the unaccustomed weight together."

"I agree. But first, I must orient her to the saddle and gear only. Inform Mikal that I will be at the designated area one day before the combat."

Aden joins the Paladin in brushing the fabulous steed. "I believe the White Wizard expects us to travel together."

Sir Rusel hesitates. "You may be correct, but I won't have it." He scans the horizon. "I remember this area. There is a secluded glen not far from here. I shall go there and meditate and prepare myself mentally for the impending engagement. Thank you, my friends. Leave now."

The Stone Mage says, "I almost forgot. I have the two apples you requested; one for your mount and one for you." He tosses the fruit and Sir Rusel expertly catches one in each hand.

"They look very tasty. I thank you again."

After the two wizards leave, the Paladin saddles his suddenly skittish horse and mounts the animal. He tentatively prods Snow to a slow canter. After several strides, the magnificent mount accepts the unaccustomed items upon her and soon horse and rider furiously race the wind. They gallop through a river and the white steed relishes the splashing as she crosses the flowing water. Her strides grow faster and stronger, her splendid mane flowing. Sir Rusel's eyes water with the wind and both man and animal lose all sense of time and become one.

It is early evening before they return to the makeshift camp, not exhausted but exhilarated. The Paladin removes the saddle and gives Snow a loving brushing and offers an eagerly accepted apple.

He tearfully manages, "You are magnificent. Tomorrow I shall don armor and we shall go to a special place."

***

The Paladin suffers a difficult night, sleep filled with bewildering dreams. He awakens often and the nightmares linger. A number of times he checks on his beautiful horse and reassures her that all is well.

He tries to will away the feeling of foreboding growing inside him.

Just after dawn, he awakens with a start. It takes a moment to orientate himself. He draws a deep breath and exhales slowly. "I am Paladin," he reminds himself. "I need to focus on the task ahead."

He wades into the river until the water becomes deep and warm. He is surprised to find his marvelous mare joining him in the calming river. He successfully captures a fish and has a satisfying breakfast while his steed grazes in the tall, golden grass. He meticulously dons the suit of armor and tightly fastens the black, leather straps.

He saddles Snow, mounts, and places the enchanted helm on his head. The two easily forge the river and travel until they come across an obscure, seldom-used path that leads to a narrow switchback trail up a short cliff. They conquer the difficult, ancient way, and soon a small, level area lies before them.

In its center, Sir Rusel sees an unnatural, large, flat rock. It reminds him of an ancient altar where sacrifices might have been offered. To the right of this formation is a deep impression set in the stone wall of the cliff that offers protection from the elements. On the other side of the boulder/altar is a spring bubbling forth, leaving a clear, small pool of water. It overflows and sends a narrow stream down the face of the cliff.

"We rest here," he tells his mare. "There's some grass still growing and plenty of water."

After seeing to his horse, he places the enchanted armor on the stone altar. He explains to himself, "I must remember my friends...my fellow Paladin. I will honor their names and memories. But I am forgetting more and more. Perhaps I have trod this land for too long." He walks over to Snow and strokes her luxurious mane. "I know, I know. One of my primary goals is to return you to your land as soon as possible. You miss your family. It is difficult for me to even remember mine."

Taking his broken-tipped sword in his right hand, Sir Rusel assumes a fighting stance. He goes through a set motion of swordplay and tries to remember killing blows that he had delivered in former battles, and attacks he had successfully defended. He relives dangerous dances from the distant past. This goes on for hours. When he is satisfied that he has done all to prepare mentally, he walks to the cool, bubbling spring and drinks. He splashes the refreshing water over his body. He closes his eyes and enters a meditative state. His breathing is steady, his body relaxed. He extends his senses far. His eyes flutter open.

"He is out there, and not far away. I know his destination."

Sir Rusel dons his armor and saddles his mount. He leads the horse down the switchback trail. He stops and looks into his charger's eyes. "I may be able to do what I had only hoped I could do this very night."

He mounts the mare and rides with purpose and determination. The sun has set and his progress is slow but his direction is true. He enters a dank swamp and spies the Dark Harold sharpening a vicious sword.

Sir Rusel Ironwood draws his weapon. "You! Foul creature, let us end this now." He charges.

Chapter 39

"Excuse me, Master Mikal, but there are three women here to see you."

The White Wizard stands and says, "Three, you say?" The dwarf smiles lopsidedly. "Please, by all means, allow them entry."

The first to enter is not a woman at all, but a blond, powerfully built man who scrutinizes the room with vigilant eyes.

Three stately women appear in the doorway and step inside. There is Madam Burnshire, the Baroness Elizabeth Stannum, and a third Mikal does not recognize. She is of average height with black hair just starting to show a hint of gray. Her skin is smooth and her eyes have a sparkle to them. There is something…enchanting about her.

Madam Burnshire says, "Mikal Novastar, I present to you Josephine Regan. She has the ear of the Duke and deals with the physical, social, and mental issues inside his court."

The intriguing woman offers her hand. Mikal gently takes it in his own… and time seems to stop. Vivid images flash through his mind. He sees pages of a book that is not a book at all. This woman has been a White Wizard for some time and does not allow her age to show. The healing arts are her specialty. As the White Wizard gleans information about the sister, he knows also that she has received knowledge about him. It all happens in an instant. They finish a simple handshake.

"Lizabetha," she asks, "May we please sit?"

Mikal, finding his voice, mutters, "Where are my manners? Please. I shall fetch some tea for us… it is quite flavorsome."

Madam Burnshire, with wave of her hand, interjects, "Allow me." She motions toward her personal guard. "Arnold, would you be so kind as to ask the innkeeper for some tea? You may remain on the first floor. Go, now."

The headmistress' eyes linger as he leaves.

She looks to Kairn. The dwarf stands and, with an exaggerated wave of his good arm, he bows low. "Isle gowan keype the bee gwon

229

cump panny."

Mikal addresses the Baroness. "Your daughter is very brave. She helped to cure me and she was secure when I left her just days ago."

"I thank you for those kind words. I am concerned about her."

"As are we all," Madam Burnshire mutters. She looks to Mikal. "If you have not heard, it appears that Brian Quickhands is now a free man and has left the City of Umbra. Hopefully, he will return soon."

Mikal nods. "Yes, I did receive that welcomed information and am looking forward to that day. No doubt he will have a story or two to tell."

Josephine addresses the White Wizard. "I have some confusing news." Just then a knock on the door interrupts the enigmatic woman and the innkeeper's wife enters carrying a tray full of hot tea and a saucer of milk. She smiles, leaves the tray, and closes the door behind her. They take a moment to thoughtfully sip their tea.

"You are correct, Mikal Novastar," Josephine says. "It is quite delicious." She deliberately puts down her cup. "I have information on a mutual friend. It seems that Amadeus Whitestone's farm was burned to ashes."

"Oh, please don't…"

Josephine holds up her hand. "Inexplicitly, all the livestock were found accounted for and roaming the grounds. There were no bodies."

Mikal stands shakily. "I sent Talon to take my daughter there. I thought she would be safe."

"We also received information from the School of Three Moons. A half-elf kidnapped a student from the school days ago. They have sent out search parties and a reward has been posted for the student's return."

The White Wizard ponders the information as he starts to pace back-and-forth. "Well, it would appear that Talon was successful in locating my daughter."

Madam Burnshire asks, "Where do you think he would have taken her?"

Mikal thinks for a moment. "Maybe to the small town of Ulna. Yes, I believe he might have taken her there."

The Baroness speaks, "If you provide directions, I shall send two investigators to see if that is so."

Mikal responds, "I thank you. I recommend you have your riders stop at the library. Master Librarian Derrick Foxhill will provide them a map to Ulna."

Josephine Regan requests, "Mikal, please sit down. You are making all of us nervous." Mikal complies. "Now for another matter. The three of us have our own contacts and, how shall I say this…abilities. We sense something of great import on the near horizon. Do you know of what we speak?"

The White Wizard nods. 'Yes, I believe I do. You sense the presence of a Dark Knight. I have summoned Sir Rusel Ironwood, a Paladin of old, to be my champion. He is to face the Ebony One in single, mortal combat."

Madame Burnshire asks, "They both agreed to this?"

"Yes. And two nights hence they will engage in the Valley of Endorr. I procured an enchanted suit of armor for our champion and he has acquired a fine charger to ride into battle. We must find him a suitable sword or somehow fuse his broken-tipped weapon."

No one speaks for some time. The Baroness softly asks, "And what if your champion should lose?"

Again a long silence. Mikal shakes his head. "He must win. But I am forced to admit, I have thought about this possibility. However grim things are now, I believe they could grow far worse. The Dark Harold is being directed to do what he does by an evil that surpasses even his own. It seems his servitude might soon be over, however, and this may free him to spread wanton destruction and fear at his own desire. No, the Paladin must not fail. The confrontation occurs in two days and I shall leave tomorrow morning. I will be there to bear witness. I have been aided by the Lady Evalon."

The three regal women are surprised by this admission. Mistress Josephine speaks, "We all have heard of the lady, an Earth Mother, but we have had no actual dealings with her." She pauses. "You are blessed, Mikal Novastar."

The White Wizard smiles. "I am not sure if I would have chosen that word exactly, but your presence here is a blessing to me. I am in your debt."

Madame Burnshire rises. "Again I say, you are truly a hero. If there is anything you need or desire, you have but to ask."

Mikal nods. "We shall take our leave. Farewell for now."

Chapter 40

The Dark Harold has no time to mount. Sir Rusel charges and slashes his sword downward with speed, but little power. *It would not be proper to attack him when he is ill prepared.* The blow easily deflects off the dark armor. The Paladin pulls up and turns his horse around and waits for his adversary to mount and gird himself. The Knight combatants hesitate to take measure of each other. Then they charge with abandon.

At the last instant, Sir Rusel directs his steed slightly away from his opponent. The dark-clad knight swings his sword, but to no avail. The snow-white mare circles her opponent. The Dark Knight raises a double-bladed axe and crashes it down on the Paladin's shield, which cracks. Sir Rusel rides in closer and exchanges quick blows, then backs away. He leans forward and whispers in the ear of his magnificent mare, "One more time should show me his syle. Off we go!"

The ancient Paladin is shocked to see the Shadow Knight spur his glistening, midnight mount forward with a vengeance. Sir Rusel holds his shield high. The heavy axe hammers into it, and the Paladin feels the blow to his very bones. Then, maliciously, the ebony mount rears and viciously bites the white steed's vulnerable ear.

Sir Rusel swipes at the mouth of the foul creature. As the raging horse's front legs return to the ground, a bony hoof tears into the chest of the white steed. The dark leg continues downward and produces a glancing blow on the cannon bone of the foreleg. Sir Rusel is not immediately aware of these wounds.

"He has won this round and I've seen enough. Let us be gone."

After retreating a safe distance, the Paladin detects a flaw in his mount's gait. He pulls her into a tight circle and looks down and is shocked to see a crimson-colored fluid spattered across her chest.

"No!" he yells.

The Dark Herald is mounting another charge. The ancient Paladin refuses combat. "Let us see if you can outdistance them even in your wounded state."

The green-hued clad knight gains a short lead, but cannot build upon it. "I pray the wound is not serious but you are still bleeding and he is still pursuing."

Like a bright dawn, an idea springs forth inside Sir Rusel and he directs his mount left. Shortly, he advances toward a swiftly flowing river. He does not slow and they gallop into the flowing water. Halfway across, the river deepens and the horse must swim. Sir Rusel knows her love of water may be his best chance at survival this night. They cross the deepest part until he feels his mount's hooves on watery ground. They struggle, but finally achieve the safety of the far side.

He turns to his pursuer. The Ebony Knight is kicking hard into the flanks of his dark steed who resists this water and its current. Despite persistent, vicious spurring, the horse does not pursue.

The Paladin frantically dismounts and inspects Snow's wounds. They are not life-threatening but his horse has lost much blood. He tears a strip of cloth from his garment and places it directly on the bleeding gash. He holds it there for many minutes. The abrasion on the leg appears to be a bruise rather than a cut.

He speaks calmingly to his horse. "I am so sorry about this. I should have been more careful. It does look like the bleeding has slowed greatly. Here I shall lead the way. We must find Mikal Novastar and he will heal you."

Chapter 41

Talon observes, "There are many travelers on the road to Stonegrove this day." He looks ahead. "There it is, the Phalanges River. We must cross it to enter the city."

They wait in line on the long, stone bridge that leads to one of the twin main gates of the city. Their progress slows to a crawl. Talon looks over the crowd. "They are searching and questioning everyone."

Sebastian scans the scene around them. He sees merchants of all kind, simple travelers, and peasants that make up this patchwork caravan.

The half-elf tells Mairin, "There is a legend of the building of this city and of two star-crossed lovers."

Mairin responds, "I do remember reading something about that. Tell me, do you think the stories are true?"

Talon looks into her eyes. "I know them to be true."

The girl holds the half-elf's gaze. They are interrupted by a commotion behind them. Mairin comments, "It looks like those two hooded men moved up in the line before their time. That's not right."

Sebastian Wolfram looks hard at the two hooded men. "No, it is not right. Stay close."

Time passes as they inch their way toward the shadow of the looming gate. Unfortunately, they find themselves behind a large wagon overloaded with exotic items. A number of guards take their time and thoroughly inspect the contents. The wagon is eventually allowed to pass and lumbers through the grand, stone arch.

"When we gain entry to Stonegrove, what is to be our destination?" Sebastian asks.

Talon shrugs his shoulders. "My best guest would be the Yellow Toad Inn."

Mairin interrupts, "Do you smell that? There must be a seller of cheese on the other side of the gate. The aroma is pleasantly pungent."

Talon agrees and scoops up his cat. A husky and obviously bored sentry approaches them. "State your name and business." Uncharacteristically, Sebastian steps back and says nothing.

"I am Talon of the Deep Woods. This is Sebastian Wolfram, a traveler, and my friend Mairin."

"State your business. Where are you going?"

The half-elf decides to use the same strategy that Mikal used on their first visit here. "We are to see Madam Burnshire, the headmistress of the School of the Red Salamander."

The guard looks hard at Talon. "I know who she is, but I don't know what she would be doing with the likes of you. Here, the three of you stand over by the wall and wait. You there, watch them."

Mairin takes Talons hand into hers. Talon has never felt anything like this before.

A young guard approaches and assumes a pugnacious stance before them. Two small wagons are next to pass. Mairin observes, "That is odd. I did not see those two hooded men go by."

She turns, but Sebastian is gone. An old wagon appears and abruptly careens into a number of gatekeepers. Talon drops his cat as one of the cloaked men brandishes a curved knife and coldly slays one of the guards. The other assailant catches the young girl's eye and charges. Sebastian returns, knocks down the charging attacker, wields a knife of his own, and dispatches him expertly.

The other hooded figure now has a deadly blade in each hand. He and Sebastian square off and take the measure of each other as Talon and Mairin try to run. They hear Sebastian saying something about how his opponents are incompetent, greedy fools. Guards, merchants, and beasts of burden are crowded under the shadow of the stone arch.

Enigmatically, a blinding flash of light explodes, temporarily blinding everyone. Sebastian Wolfram is the first to regain his vision and finds himself standing over a second dead assailant. He looks about and can neither see nor can he find any trace of Talon, Mairin, or the cat.

He can only smell the pungent odor of cheese.

Chapter 42

Shortly after the three imperial women leave Mikal's room, Aden Ferrum, Kairn, and Ebon Usher enter. The Red Wizard shakes his head. "Tell me, Mikal, what power do you possess over women that three would come to your room in a rundown inn? This is not how it is done in the City of Umbra, or any other proper city. And I suppose it's a waste of time to ask you why they were here?"

The White Wizard smiles. "They came of their own volition. And if you must know, we exchanged information."

The Stone Mage waits a moment to see if the two are finished. "Well, let me share this. Sir Rusel was very pleased with our gifts and said he would meet us in the Valley of Endorr. There were things for him to do and he said for us not to worry."

Mikal shakes his head. "I was hoping we would go there together. But legend has it, the Paladins of old often meditate before major battles. We must trust him, but I am uncomfortable with it. Now Kairn, I believe I know the answers to these questions but I want to make sure. As a blacksmith have you worked with swords?"

The dwarf steps forward and looks drolly at Mikal. "Eye yamma fine ear blak smith with won narm than annie hue minn with to. It's innar blood. Ike kan forge annie sord bet ter, har der, shar purr." He then spits on the floor.

The White Wizard laughs. "That's good enough for me. Aden, I ask your pardon, but again I must leave nothing to chance. Is your flame hot enough to melt steel?"

Aden holds up his iron staff. "You know the answer to that."

Mikal nods. "There are a few things for us left to do now, but I would like to get some rest and have a good meal. We should leave before dawn for the Valley of Endorr."

***

The rest of the day passes uneventfully, but Aden Ferrum does leave twice for short periods of time and offers no explanation. The group shares an evening meal, but Mikal does not eat much, though the dwarf makes up for what he does not. Darkness fills their loft. The Stone Mage and the dwarf seem content sleeping on the floor. Aden has one of the beds and Mikal and his cat share the other.

The White Wizard has a restless night, waking often to stare out the second-floor window. With his cat by his side, he senses strange things are afoot, but he knows not what. A half hour before dawn, a knock is heard at the door and the innkeeper and his wife bring in breakfast, which includes fresh cream for Majam. They finish their morning meal in silence. After gathering their belongings, they meet the couple on the first floor and Mikal thanks both of them.

The innkeeper winks. "There are people waiting for you outside."

Just before the morning light cracks the horizon, the group walks out the back of the Yellow Toad Inn. They find four saddled horses waiting for them. Surprisingly, the Baron's elder daughter, Mary Rae Stannum, along with three attendants, is there to present them.

"Good morning. A gift from our stables. To make your travels faster and easier." Aden scrutinizes one of the fine-looking stallions. He examines the bridle and saddle. "Yes, he will do. You do owe me a horse, do you not, Master?"

Standing in the morning shadows is Marion Vetta and in a quiet voice asks, "Mikal, may I have a word with you?"

The White Wizard steps from the group and is engulfed in the morning shadows. "I have strange news for you. We believe your room was watched all night by a shadowy character we detected. But every time we tried to apprehend this sly rogue he slipped away. Also, this night we have received many odd reports. Rats were seen scurrying from the city by the score. Some undesirables tried to slip away undetected. Others, how shall I say this, we believe dangerous suspects, have not been seen recently. I just thought you should know."

He nods, still holding his cat in his arms. "I thank you, and I will think about what you have told me."

"I wish you good luck, Mikal Novastar from the great City of

Addis. If you leave by the eastern gate, there will be no questions asked."

Aden and Mikal easily mount their horses. Ebon hesitates but is soon upon his mount as well. Kairn needs assistance from one of the young baroness' attendants. Majam rests on the saddle just in front of her master. The horses canter to the eastern gate and pass through the great stone arch unhindered. They cross the River Phalanges and ride hard for the next two hours. Mikal holds up his right arm and yells to lessen the pace.

Aden pulls abreast of the White Wizard. "We have made good time so far. Maybe we should walk our horses for a while."

Mikal agrees and the four dismount. They eat bits of food and drink water on the way. At a small creek they let the horses have their fill. They mount up, helping the dwarf first. They regain their quick pace and by the afternoon they come to the top of the cliff wall and look down on the Valley of Endorr. They make their descent without incident.

Mikal surveys his surroundings. "I think we have earned a slight respite. Let us rest the horses and have a bite to eat."

Majam bounds from the saddle and starts to search the area. The group, by happenstance, is at the exact spot where Mairin, Sebastian, Talon, and his cat had camped just days prior.

Majam knows.

The magnificent cat enters her master's mind. *They have been here recently.*

"Who?"

Talon, your daughter, and a scent I do not recognize.

"How long ago?"

That is difficult to tell…within the last two days.

"In which direction were they traveling?"

Up the valley cliff south.

"This is good news, but also confusing."

The White Wizard shares the information with his companions. "Ebon Usher, I would ask you to return to the City of Stonegrove and see if you can find any information about my daughter and Talon.

Look here," Mikal points, "upon your return travel west across the valley floor. I am sure we will notice your arrival."

The Stone Mage accepts the request, mounts his horse, and takes the trail up the cliff.

Mikal ponders his current situation. "Majam, I believe we should wait here for a bit. The reason why, I know not."

His cat starts to clean one of her paws. Aden asks, "What are we waiting for? I say we continue."

Mikal, still scanning the valley floor, insists, "I wish to wait here. We shall leave when I choose."

Aden shakes his head. "You know, you remain a mystery to me still."

He walks over to his horse and starts to brush him. Kairn idly pokes at a cactus with his knife. The White Wizard closes his eyes, his cat beside him. "Someone unknown will soon find us." He pauses. "Something is amiss with Sir Rusel, although we shall see him soon enough. Majam, why do I see some things clearly but the condition of my daughter and Talon and the approaching confrontation is closed to my sight?"

Mikal gasps involuntarily and his eyes open wide. "Oh my, before sundown this valley will be teeming with creatures great and small, benevolent and malevolent."

The White Wizard's trance is broken by a yelp. Mikal looks about. Aden shakes his head and sneers, "Our handy dwarf has poked himself with a cactus needle."

Chapter 43

Sometime later, the three mount their steeds. Mikal takes point, with his cat sitting in the saddle just in front of him. They canter in silence across the valley floor. Aden can sense that the White Wizard is deeply musing upon the present and the near future. The Red Wizard again notices many different flocks of birds flying hither and thither, and wonders.

They advance toward a tall pile of rocks and turn left toward the Witches of Endorr's cave. Aden asks, "Do you think they will be expecting us?"

Mikal responds, "They will be waiting."

A guard appears among the rocks and waves them forward, saying, "Sister Aurum is waiting for you above. I'll take the horses."

The three dismount and Mikal hands the reins to the sentry.

"Expect one or two more riders."

The man nods. "I'll be on the lookout."

Sister Aurum greets them at the opening to the cavern. "Welcome. Follow me." She stops and takes Mikal's sleeve and addresses Aden and Kairn. "I must speak to Mikal privately. You two may continue, and you will find food and drink waiting for you."

With impatient steps, she leads the White Wizard to a small but well-kempt room. "Here, have some tea. We both must relax and gather what peace we can. Events that have been set in motion are coming to fruition, but for good or ill I do not know. I am becoming frustrated."

Mikal nods. "I know what you feel. Much of our futures will be determined in the next few hours."

"Mikal, let me tell you about a dream I had this morning. I saw a multitude of people atop a high hill. Suddenly, they all roll down one side of the hill into tall, green grass, laughing delightfully. But there is a second half to the dream. I saw the same hill with a multitude of people who fell to the other side, but I could not see their outcome. I raced to the top and peered over. To my horror, they had crashed upon steep and sharp, rocky cliffs. Only a few survived."

The White Wizard hesitates. "I pray for green grass and laughter."

They share a smile and are interrupted by a knock on the door. A servant enters and announces, "A horse and two riders have arrived."

"Escort them to me at once."

The two riders are immediately brought to the room. Leading the way is Ebon Usher followed by a white-haired man with a pointy nose.

Ebon explains, "Just after I arrived at the main road, this gentleman flagged me down and told me a strange story that I think you should hear."

The white-haired man steps forward, eyes wide, and takes full measure of the Wizard. "My name is Sebastian Wolfram. Do I have the honor of addressing Mikal Novastar?"

The White Wizard looks to Sister Aurum but says nothing. The stranger continues, "I have been traveling with a half-elf named Talon and a teenaged girl named Mairin."

Mikal blurts out, "Where are they now?"

"That is difficult to say. We tried to enter the City of Stonegrove yesterday afternoon. There was a backup on the bridge. Then there was a commotion. Criminals most foul tried to accost your daughter. As I fought them, there was a blinding light...and the two youths vanished."

Mikal stiffens and demands, "What do you mean, they vanished?"

Sebastian thoughtfully rubs his chin and smoothes back his white hair. "I mean just that. I consider myself a superior tracker, but there was absolutely no trace of them. I searched and lingered in the area for some time. The last thing that was said to me by Talon was 'the Yellow Toad Inn.' I found its location and waited nearby, hoping that either one would show, but neither did. Mikal Novastar, I was not the only one watching that night. I saw you and your companions leave in the early morning. I followed the best I could, but you did travel fast."

The White Wizard asks, "How long were you with them?"

Sebastian explains how they met, how they were captured on the plains of Endorr, and how they escaped. Mikal thanks Sebastian and asks Ebon Usher to escort the white-haired man to be introduced to rest of the group.

After they depart, Sister Aurum asks, "Do you believe him?"

Mikal thinks for a moment. "Yes, I believe I do... but there is something about him of which I am suspicious. Now, let me ask you a question, Sister. Does your sight reveal anything about my daughter and my friend Talon?"

The witch closes her eyes and meditates for a moment. "They are both alive and currently not in immediate danger. More than that, I cannot say."

"Well, that will have to suffice." The White Wizard shakes his head. "There are too many things to think about and to worry about. Let us join our companions."

***

They meet in a cavernous room. Ebon Usher stares fascinated at the cave wall. He moves his stone hand up and down the rock face. Speaking to no one in general, he mutters, "I do not know why more people do not live in a place like this. These rocks have witnessed much over the long years."

Most of the occupants are eating or drinking or carrying on conversations. A guard enters and reports. "Young Monica and Catherine are escorting a warrior here, leading a large, white horse."

Sister Aurum points. "You three, bring buckets of water and brushes. Mikal, would you would be so kind as to come with me? The rest of you please remain here."

The young witch sets a hurried pace as they leave the cave and walk the short path. There they find Sir Rusel kneeling, inspecting his charger's wounds. Monica and Catherine bring fresh hay.

The White Wizard addresses the knight. "I was hoping you would have been here earlier."

The Paladin stands, ignoring the statement. "Will you please help her?"

Sister Aurum gently inspects the horse's ear, chest, and the bruise on her shin. "Do not worry, Sir Rusel, these wounds are easily treated."

Mikal asks, "How did this happen?"

The Paladin lowers his gaze and takes a deep breath. "I found the dim Knight and met him in combat."

"What!" exclaims Mikal.

"I was seeking any edge I could find for our upcoming duel. I saw and experienced his fighting style and I believe I can counter it."

The White Wizard shakes his head. "That was a foolish and dangerous thing to do. What caused these wounds on your steed?"

"It was that foul, dark mount he rides. He bit and kicked Snow. We broke off the attack and crossed a swiftly flowing river. The Shadowy Knight's horse would not follow. You should have seen Snow, Mikal, even with her injuries, she carried me across. She was magnificent."

Sister Aurum interrupts, "You are fortunate, Sir Rusel. Now let me see about this ear."

The horse lowers her head for the young, healing witch who recites a prayer and places a soft kiss on the injury. Within moments, the wound improves. The White Wizard holds his staff of light in front of the bloody chest. He mutters inaudible words as his staff glows gently and this wound is healed. He repeats the process over the shin contusion. The three Witches arrive, carrying water and brushes, and start to wash and clean the horse.

"Now, Rusel, let us go up the path so you can get some rest." Mikal asks Sister Aurum, "Do you have a forge somewhere in your network of caves?"

The young witch nods. "Yes, we do. I am told that it is well built."

Mikal turns to Sir Rusel. "Please, tell me that you have the broken tip to your sword."

The Paladin removes a leather strap from around his neck, the tip tied to it. "I have carried this with me for so long."

"Well, with the craftsmanship of the dwarf and the fire of the Red Wizard, we should be able to repair your sword within an hour."

Sir Rusel bows his head and softly says, "I thank you and am forever in your debt." The three enter the common room. The White

Wizard directs Sir Rusel. "Please, give your sword and tip to Kairn. Aden, will you supply the flame necessary to repair this weapon?"

The Red Wizard stands. "I look forward to it."

"Sister Aurum, would you get someone to show them to the forge?"

"Yes, Sister Argentum will escort them. Good luck, gentlemen."

"I shall join you shortly to assess your progress," Mikal adds.

The White Wizard now looks to Ebon Usher. "Good Sir, our Paladin's shield is fractured. Can you repair it somehow?"

The Stone Mage inspects the convex piece of armor. "Yes, I believe I can. There has been something I have wanted to try for some time. I will need to go to the room with the forge." He leaves with a deep, throaty vibrations sound as he rubs his stone hand across the metal shield.

Sister Aurum addresses Mikal. "In three hours, dusk will be upon us."

***

The Stone Mage enters a large, carved out room with a high ceiling. He witnesses the dwarf closely inspecting the broken sword and tip. A servant is working the bellows that stokes the fire.

Kairn looks to Aden. "This izza fine lee kraf tid ain chent sord. Sum uv the mett tills that ar blendid ar diffy cult two eye denty fie. The blade haz deaffen knit lee ben made buy dwarves."

The Red Wizard shakes his head. "I am not interested in your sword lore. Let me fire the blade and tip and be done with it."

Kairn yells, "Not sew fast. This must bee dun with skillin pre sij un."

Aden laughs. "Are you sure the White Wizard chose you for your skill and precision?"

The dwarf growls and stares hard at the Red Wizard. Kairn takes a deep breath and focuses on the task at hand. He lowers the sword into the flame, slowly turning the blade. He then takes a heavy iron tong, grabs the tip, and places that also in the blazing inferno and waits.

"Yew their, stow ker, the fur niss sizs hottie nuff. When eye die

245

rect ewe, grab the sordin play sit on thee anne vill."

Kairn nods and the servant takes the weapon and hurriedly complies. The dwarf, with hammer in hand, starts to rhythmically pound the metal blade. He stops for a moment, and then continues.

Aden observes, "It is not hot enough."

Kairn nods in agreement. "Back away," directs the Red Wizard and points his iron staff directly at the sword. It flares, and engulfs the Paladin's blade. He maintains his red-hot fire for some time. Abruptly, he shuts down his flame and pulls his staff away.

"Now strike, dwarf!"

Kairn steps in closer, the forge radiating heat. The dwarf resumes his rhythmic pounding. He directs the servant to turn the blade over. Again and again the heavy hammer slams into the ancient weapon. Kairn stops and inspects the Paladin's sword. He looks toward the Red Wizard. "The blayd diz stilt two hard two werk. Yore flay miz knot hottie nuff."

Aden Ferrum steps close and confronts the dwarf. "It cannot be my flame; it must be your inferior Dwarven skill."

Kairn drops his hammer and slams his fist into Aden Ferrum's jaw, knocking him down. "Let me speek slow lee two yew so that ewe will under stand. Yew may shamy and riddie cule me, but knot my Dwarven hair a tidge."

Aden, sitting on the ground, shakes off the punch. "My, my. That was an almost human response about time, for a one-armed dwarf."

The White Wizard appears with his cat. "What has happened here?"

Ebon Usher explains the situation. Mikal steps close to the radiating heat of the forge. He stares at the sword and its broken tip. People speak, but he does not hear. His staff of light whispers to his mind. He stares at the glowing, metal blade, and the white of his eyes start to swirl. He lowers his staff and murmurs ancient Dwarven words. The staff flares to life. First a red flame, then a blue. The White Wizard continues to concentrate as the flame erupts to pure white. All back away, save the White Wizard, because of the waves of oppressive heat. The blade and the tip of the sword start to produce their own dazzling light. Mikal does not stop, but recites another ancient spell as he deliberately moves his flaming staff up and down the fragmented steel. The heat continues to rise. He repeats the words and procedure again and again, louder each time. Majam screams alarmingly as Sister Aurum bursts into the heated room.

The young witch shouts, "Do something! He is losing himself in a dangerous spell."

Aden Ferrum runs through the searing heat and knocks the White Wizard down, breaking the enchantment. Kairn grabs his hammer and seizes the moment. He starts to pound on the now malleable metal. With sweat pouring forth, he maneuvers the tip onto the blade and they instantly fuse together. He grabs the sword's heated handle and douses it in water from a nearby barrel. Steam and an impossibly loud hiss fill the room. Moments later, Kairn grabs and raises the weapon high.

"Now, this iz a sord that ken kill thee Ebon knee Nite!"

Sister Aurum runs to Mikal. "Are you hurt?"

Aden helps the White Wizard to his feet. Mikal's face and hands look as if they are badly sunburned. "I do not believe I am. After I saw the blade was hot enough to work, another spell entered my mind and I placed it into the sword. I will explain the enchantment to Sir Rusel when it is time."

A rhythmic, deep vibration fills the room. The Stone Mage stuns everyone by walking up to the heated forge and placing his stone arm into the glowing embers. He continues his resonant vibrations and scoops up some molten rocks and places them on the Paladin's splintered shield. They cool and form a stony, pitted covering over the metal.

Ebon Usher smiles. "It is harder than the day it was made. I do not think that Shadowy Knight will like the feel of his weapon ricocheting against it."

Mikal, in a soft voice, says, "Let us present these enchanted items to Sir Rusel." They find the ancient Paladin in the main common room. He is attended to by two alluring witches, though he does not seem to have any interest in their impressive charms. They have just finished outfitting Sir Rusel's newly polished armor.

Sister Aurum gains the warrior's attention. "Your time draws near. I present to you your shield, restored by Ebon Usher."

The Stone Mage steps forward. "Your shield is now a combination of metal and stone. May it protect you from all harm."

Kairn proudly steps to the fore. "Hear iz your sord, fourged and reap aired buy Dwarven skill. It is the fine nest blayd eye have ever scene."

The dwarf bows and presents the sword to the ancient Paladin. The White Wizard speaks and all listen. "I have placed an enchantment on that blade. Every time you strike your opponent's armor, it will heat up. But I must caution you, if the blade gets too hot you will also feel it through your gauntlet."

"I will refuse to feel it," Sir Rusel responds.

Chapter 44

Mikal Novastar and Sister Aurum lead a long procession from the cave, which includes everyone, save the Stone Mage and Kairn. Before them stands Snow, saddle and bridal looking very much like her name.

The ageless Paladin thanks the sisters. "You have done a most wonderful job. She looks beautiful." He lovingly strokes Snow's long neck.

Sister Aurum steps forward. "Sir Rusel, you are to champion the colors of Lady Evalon." She ties a multicolored ribbon around his right arm. She rises on her tip-toes. "A kiss for luck, my gallant warrior."

The Paladin blushes ever so slightly. "Mikal Novastar from the great City of Addis, I need words with you."

The White Wizard steps close to Sir Rusel. The Paladin whispers for some time in Mikal's ear as the White Wizard nods.

This time, Sir Rusel, walking his magnificent mare, leads the procession. As they move to the valley floor, they witness strange sights and sounds. There is a countless number of animals and unearthly creatures moving about.

Sebastian Wolfram exclaims, "I hear riders advancing."

Moments later, the Baron Stannum and his son thunder forth, leading a score of armored knights. They pull up in front of the solemn procession. The Baron bows. "I see I am not too late. We have the finest warriors representing all the noble houses from the City of Stonegrove. We are here to bear witness and to see that the rules of combat are followed."

Sister Aurum returns the bow. "You are most welcome."

They continue to cross the plain. Untold flocks of birds fill the air. A large black hawk swoops in front of Sir Rusel and his steed. A green-blue light surrounds the bird. It morphs into a beautiful, young lady with impossibly long, black hair.

"The Lady has sent me. Through my eyes she shall bear witness to this event."

Again Sister Aurum bows. "We are honored. Please join us."

***

Ebon Usher places his stone arm on the dwarf's shoulder. "I need you to do something for me. Get your hammer and fill a bucket with water. I shall return shortly. Hurry."

Kairn fulfills the Stone Mage's request. He is surprised when Ebon Usher returns carrying an ornately carved alabaster statue. "No questions now. Follow me."

The two soon overtake the slow march from the cave. Ebon then directs the dwarf to a nearby, secluded area. "Here, I notice, there is sand. Pour the water onto it."

The Stone Mage places the statue made of alabaster on the wet sand. "Now, Kairn, strike the statue with your hammer until I tell you to stop." The dwarf hesitates. "There is no time for questions, please just do it," Ebon commands.

As the dwarf pounds the statue, the Stone Mage holds out his arms and again produces a resonant, vibrating sound emanating from deep in his throat. Kairn can tell that an enchantment is being placed on the water, the sand, and the pummeled pieces of alabaster, but he does not know its nature.

Ebon Usher smiles. "That is enough. We must collect the sodden paste in the bucket. Hurry now." The bucket is soon filled to the brim. "I am sorry, my friend, but you must either run to catch the procession or find your horse to do so. Mine is near and I must go to the Paladin with all haste. Thank you and good luck."

The Stone Mage summons his horse, deftly mounts, and rides to meet his friends. The dwarf drops his hammer, grips his enchanted axe, and starts to run. "Isle ketchem!"

As Ebon Usher rides, he spies movement across the plain. Animals of all sizes are positioning themselves for the event. He arrives to see a large, black hawk transform itself into a beautiful, young lady. He dismounts, and joins the solemn procession next to the Red Wizard.

Sebastian Wolfram surveys the area and exclaims, "I am aware of many packs of wolves and there are bears of different types. Some of the larger animals I do not recognize. There is a multitude of rats and, among them, foul wererats. I see at least two giants, and there may be more. Not all of these creatures side with the Dark Knight. Some oppose him. Others are here to simply watch and witness the spectacle."

Sister Aurum stops and looks to the Paladin. "Our time draws near."

The Stone Mage, carrying the bucket, approaches Sir Rusel and his charger. "The enchantment I placed on your shield was successful, so I enhanced the spell to protect flesh." With his stone arm, he scoops up some of the enchanted paste and holds at arm's length. "Explain to your horse that this may feel uncomfortable, but it will not harm her in any way. On the contrary, it will shield her from that shadowy, unearthly creature."

Continuing the deep, throaty vibration, he smoothes the sandy, alabaster concoction over Snow's forelegs, chest, head, and ears, but before he can cover her long neck completely, the glistening, white paste is depleted.

The Stone Mage steps back and smiles. "The enchantment is temporary, but Snow is protected now as if she were wearing armor."

Sir Rusel bows. "My horse and I thank you for this."

The Paladin looks around, takes a deep breath, and expertly mounts this magnificent steed. Sister Aurum and Mikal Novastar raise their arms in unison and bestow a blessing upon the warrior and his charger.

The White Wizard looks long and hard at the age-old Paladin. "You are now prepared. Know this: we are all with you."

"Not so fast." Aden Ferrum strides forth. "Do you think I would let you ride into battle without a gift from the Red Wizards? Take a moment and explain to your horse what I am about to do. I shall encompass you in flame. It will neither harm nor warm you but you will be a sight to behold. So, let us see if we could turn the tables and throw some fear into that foul, bastard Knight."

The Red Wizard holds up his arm and staff, closes his eyes, and recites a spell. A small amount of flame jumps to the helmet of the warrior Paladin then, like water falling, it engulfs Sir Rusel. The expanding flame continues to cascade across the back of the mare, down her legs, and then reverses and surrounds her head.

Sir Rusel draws his now flaming sword and rides forth to meet this supreme challenge.

It is a sight to behold, the flaming horse and rider charging across the plain.

Chapter 45

Sir Rusel does not ride far before he encounters the Ebony Knight, who sits on his sable steed holding a barbed-tip sword in his right hand and a double-bladed axe in his left. The Paladin sees that his opponent has also had his armor polished recently.

In the background, the Knight and horse are supported by many of his minions: two Witch Ravens, each with long, drooling smiles; the undead ever so slowly swaying back and forth; rats by the thousands and other crawling, biting, and stinging creatures scuttle across the rocky ground. There are wererats with glowing, red eyes and slithering tails; dark-feathered and foul birds fill the air above. They seem to all smirk with confidence, but upon the approach of the fiery apparition, they gasp and take steps back, all save the Dark Harold.

Mikal and Sister Aurum stride forward, leading their group for a better view of the imminent battle. Aden Ferrum surveys their moving procession as creatures increase their number. A large, proud pack of wolves trot alongside them, their mannerism showing no aggressive tendencies…yet. A huge, black bear lumbers along on their opposite flank. A small herd of horses join them. Colorful flocks of birds fly above with their numbers growing as they move closer to the deadly arena. Aden has no idea from whence they came.

The two mounted warriors take measure of each other. Their focus is so intense that they lose sight of all that is happening around them. Their world exists of two warriors and their steeds alone. Sir Rusel leans forward and whispers into his Snow's ear, then leans back and sits tall in his saddle.

He points his flaming sword accusingly toward the Dark Knight and declares, "You have committed murderous and unspeakable deeds against life and the land. This night you will reap what you have sown!"

He kicks his horse and charges his deadly opponent. The Shadowy Knight shows no fear, but when the blazing Paladin closes in, the black steed shies away from the fiery sight. For just a moment, the Black Knight loses control of his stallion. Sir Rusel rides by and brings his enchanted blade down upon the dim helm of his opponent. The Dark Harold swings his sword but to no effect, since his opponent is out of reach. Sir Rusel reins in his horse, turns, and charges for a second time. The deadly Knight brings his barbed-tipped sword down on the Paladin's rock-reinforced shield. Sir Rusel swings his sword low, striking the onyx armor under the arm of the foul Knight. The blow glances off. The Paladin is convinced he saw his weapon flash red.

The two implacable warriors gather themselves and charge. As their mounts collide, Snow's stony front cuts ever so slightly into the stallion's muscular chest, but the war horse does not back down. Equine and warrior lock into a deadly, spiral dance. The dark-hued knight slams his sword onto the Paladin's shield.

The horses join the lethal drama, biting and gnashing each other. Sir Rusel scores two more hits high on the seemingly impenetrable armor. Because of their positions and close quarters, the Dark Harold cannot use his massive axe effectively, though he continues to pound the Paladin's defenses with his barbed-tipped sword.

As they separate, the dual-weaponed warrior slams his double-bladed axe against Sir Rusel's shield. The spectators cover their ears to protect themselves from the loud, irritating, scraping sound that the weapons produce. The Paladin feels the blow deep in his bones. They separate, and continue in a deliberate, deadly circle, each looking for an opening to strike. A simultaneous charge, and horses and riders collide with a thunderous impact. The horses raise their heads and scream, as the riders twist and turn them into position. As the distance shrinks between them, the Dark Harold swings both his weapons with an indefatigable force. The Paladin's shield holds, but his arm is bruised and battered as the blows continue to rain down upon him.

Sir Rusel's blade glows brightly and continuously, and now, when he scores a hit on his opponent's armor, it leaves a deep singe mark.

In the distance, a storm gathers but few notice. Dark clouds and a low, distant, rolling thunder is heard on the darkening horizon. Onto the arena of death, leaps a wererat. It hesitates, then takes a clumsy, swinging lunge at the white horse's flanks.

Sebastian Wolfram grabs the Red Wizard's shoulder and points. "Do something quick! This could change the whole outcome of the struggle."

Aden Ferrum raises his staff, takes aim, and releases two solidified flame arrows toward the wererat. Both score devastating hits and burst into flame upon contact. With its fur ablaze, the foul creature collapses to the ground. Unconcerned with his fallen subordinate, the Nefarious Knight charges his opponent again, trampling the hapless creature beneath sharpened hooves. Sir Rusel repels the attack.

The Paladin's encompassing flame starts to dwindle but his sword stays aglow. Sir Rusel alters his tactics and rushes his opponent, but at the last moment directs his horse to swerve to the right. At the last instant, he scores a hit on his opponent's helmet then continues to ride away. He repeats this attack several times and each time his enemy fails in his attempts to retaliate. The Shadowy Knight starts to show frustration and, worse, his mount cannot match Snow's speed.

Sir Rusel continues this onslaught strategy: strike and ride. The foul Knight is expending much effort with little effect. But on the next charge, he anticipates correctly, and the ebony stallion slams into the side of the white mare. She is stunned and struggles to maintain her footing. Her hind legs buckle for just a moment, causing the Paladin to fall heavily to the ground. He rolls, gathers his wits, and stands, readying himself for the next charge. The Black Knight circles his downed opponent and senses the tide has turned in his favor. He brutally boots his stallion, charges, and pummels the Paladin's shield with his massive double-bladed axe. The sound is shrill and agonizing.

He turns and brings his deadly weapon down with merciless force, but again, the shield holds. Sir Rusel feels these blows deep within him and his arm grows weary. He swings his sword, but to no avail. The dim stallion rides past unscathed. The Ebony Knight again circles, his aura of fear strong and expanding. Even his own minions are affected and start to shy away.

Sister Aurum and Mikal Novastar conjure enchantments against the growing dread. The Dark Deadly Knight holds his weapons high as vapor billows from his stallion's nostrils. He intends to trample his seemingly defeated opponent under menacing, heavy hooves.

Sir Rusel plants his feet and readies himself for the onslaught. At the last instant, his magnificent mare charges and crashes into the side of the horse and rider. Both collapse to the rocky ground. Sir Rusel's foe uses his sword as a crutch to lift himself up. The Paladin seizes the moment and bashes his glowing weapon into the barbed-tipped blade of his opponent which holds but for a moment then breaks in two. The Shadow Knight loses his balance and falls to one knee, but manages to swing his axe in sweeping arc.

Sir Rusel steps back to evade its blow. This gives the Shadowy Knight the opportunity to rise to his feet. He drops his broken sword and grips his battle-axe with two massive hands. The black stallion regains its footing, as the two exhausted Knights pause and take the measure of the other once again. Their mounts circle in a deadly ballet, black and white, white and black.

The axe-wielding Knight rushes the Paladin and swings with lethal force. Exerting great effort, Sir Rusel raises his shield and sidesteps the attack. The Paladin continues to strike his dangerous opponent's helmet low, next to the right shoulder. The first drops of rain create a hissing sound as they land on Sir Rusel's glowing, red sword. The Ebony Knight presses his attack and pummels the Paladin's shield knowing he would be defenseless without it.

The Paladin's left arm is battered and bruised and his shield lowers slightly. He counters, and scores two more hits, low on the helm. The blows leave red scorch marks on his opponent's armor. The Paladin can feel the heat from his blade as it filters through his gauntlet and burns.

***

The two war horses rear and the shadow stallion kicks the white mare on the forelegs but her stony enchantment deflects the sharp hooves. The dark horse continues his attack and, with two quick strides, tears at the left hip of the snow-white horse. The wound draws blood but the white mare will not be outdone. She turns and bites the back hip of her opponent. The crimson blood glistens off his ebony coat.

With a painful leap, the stallion starts to run in an orbital path around the two combating Knights, closely pursued by the white mare. The ground is becoming soft and wet. The rain hisses as it pelts the combatants' armor. Unexpectedly, the dark, pernicious horse skids to a halt, raises its haunches, and delivers a powerful double kick to his pursuer. The mare takes two blows to her chest. Again, her stony enchantment prevents serious injury, but it knocks her off balance and she collapses to the ground.

The indomitable steed rushes his downed opponent, leaps, and kicks with his forelegs. The mare rolls and gains her footing, but not before sustaining two more wounds to her right hip. She gallops to gain distance between her and her tormentor. She then pivots, eyes her pursuer, flares her nostrils, and charges headlong into the dark steed. The two equines collide again. Snow's rocky exterior slices into the flesh of the Ebony Knight's horse. Both creatures lose balance and crash heavily to the ground. The mare is first to regain her footing. She presses her advantage, rears, and tears deep lacerations into one of the forelegs of the sable horse. The crackle of lightening and the sound of thunder scream with the coal black equine.

***

To the Shadow Knight, this battle he wages is a test of strength, which he knows is to his advantage. His opponent's defenses are weakening and will soon collapse. He is convinced that victory is inevitable. To the Paladin, it is a test of will and determination. Advantage: Sir Rusel.

"I cannot and will not succumb to my adversary," Rusel says through clenched teeth.

After several deep breaths, the grinning, confident, axe-wielding Knight advances. The Paladin struggles to hold his shield high. Again the massive double-bladed axe crashes down upon it. Sir Rusel staggers for just a moment, but retaliates with two quick strikes to the helmet.

It glows red.

Sir Rusel winces in pain as his sword flares to cobalt blue. The sizzling of the rain upon his weapon imitates a multitude of angry, hissing serpents. The Paladin steps back, hesitates, then valiantly attacks and scores two more striking, burning hits, then deftly steps away. The huge Knight swings his axe to no avail. Sir Rusel again engages and brings his glowing, blue sword down upon the dark helmet, causing it to glow more brightly. The Knight delivers only a glancing blow off the Paladin's shield. Sir Rusel keeps moving in a slow ring around his opponent. The Paladin attempts a feint but the Evil Knight does not respond.

Thunder fills the air for all to hear, save the two Knights. The Ebony One roars diabolically and charges and before Sir Rusel can bring his shield high, he swings his double-bladed axe and scores a deep, devastating blow into the Paladin's left shoulder. Sir Rusel continues to block out his pain. He counter-attacks, swinging his sword to his enemy's helmet, and continues to bear down against his opponent's armor. The Paladin cries out as his sword flares to an intense white-hot and slices through the searing metal armor of his opponent. The smell of burning flesh fills the air.

The Black Knight panics and releases his grip on his weapon. It remains embedded in Sir Rusel's shoulder. Reacting to the burning pain in his neck, the Dark Herald tries to remove the white-hot sword protruding from his flesh. His gauntlets and hands melt around the intense, flaming sword. With a look of utter disbelief, the Ebony Knight sinks to his knees, jarring the burning weapon from Sir Rusel's blistered grasp.

Chapter 46

Everything stops. Only rain whispers through the silence.

Not far from the battle, the Stone Mage lowers himself to the ground and slams his left, stone arm deep into the earth. He hesitates, and then stands tall.

He hurriedly addresses Mikal. "Wizard, move our people back now. The rocks and stones are going to open, scream, and rend."

The White Wizard hesitates. Majam meows a warning. Mikal feels a slight vibration under his feet and he understands. Just before the storm's full fury hits, he gives the command for the others to retreat.

He turns with his cat and runs toward Sir Rusel. He is followed by Ebon Usher and Aden Ferrum. Before they can reach the mortally wounded Paladin, the earth starts to tremble. Many stumble. The Stone Mage grabs Mikal as the Red Wizard falls. The vibrations lessen and the three continue. Mikal is the first to reach the now kneeling Sir Rusel. Blood gushes from around the axe that is deep inside him. His charred right hand hangs loosely from his arm.

The White Wizard puts his arms around the grievously wounded Paladin and lightly kisses his cheek. In a panic, he starts to recite a healing spell.

Sir Rusel's eyelids flutter open. "Is Snow alive? Mikal, your promise."

The Stone Mage turns and yells, "Take him away from here at once, or we are all lost."

Mikal and Aden pick up the fallen Paladin and start to carry him away. They struggle as the entire valley ground convulses violently and the rocky soil in front of Ebon Usher rends open and chaos erupts. He watches as the Ebony Knight's body tumbles down the newly formed chasm. The long fissure in the ground separates the Stone Mage from the White Mare. She frantically turns her head to the right then left, torn by indecision.

The Dark Herald's minions are in total panic. The magnificent mare flares her nostrils, takes three strides, and leaps the yawning abyss. She gallops and soon reaches Sir Rusel. Mikal turns and sees the Stone Mage staring transfixed at the jagged opening in the ground. The White Wizard yells, but to no avail. The ground shakes again. The unearthly fracture opens wider, taking in its stony maw all things near. Through Majam's eyes Mikal sees the legs of the black stallion as they disappear from sight.

Aden Ferrum shouts, "We must remove the axe!"

The White Wizard nods and lowers his staff. Aden struggles to remove the destructive weapon from the Paladin's ruined shoulder.

Instantly Mikal's staff flares to life as he places it on the hemorrhaging, gaping wound. It cauterizes the flesh.

"Hurry, now, help me place him on his horse," Mikal orders. With much effort they succeed.

The White Wizard points. "Take him to Sister Aurum."

The storm swells but the earthquakes subside. Finding himself alone, Mikal picks up Majam and turns to search for Ebon Usher. He takes only a few steps, and he spies the Dark Herald's multitude of minions in full stampede coming directly toward him.

Through Majam's eyes, he is shocked to see wild Dorsi, the large, aggressive, female, buffalo-like animals from the Plains of Peristalsis, charging across the valley floor. Hordes of rats squish beneath the wild Dorsi's hooves. He hears a ravenous roar from two huge, black bears as they tear into bewildered wererats. Myriad flocks of birds seek shelter from the storm only to plummet to the ground due to the weight of soaked feathers. Mikal places his cat in his traveling cloak.

The White Wizard conjures a protective sphere around them. At first, many of the wild creatures shy from the glowing white light. One obese Dorsi breaks through, however, and clips Mikal's arm and spins him around. Then another charging wild beast strikes the Wizard and slams him heavily to the ground. The last thing Mikal hears before losing consciousness is the sound of howling wolves.

Chapter 47

Two armored knights from the City of Stonegrove search the Valley of Endorr. The taller of the two holds a torch in one hand and a sword in the other. His brother-in-arms probes the air in front of him with a long, pointed spear.

"Ahh! I slammed my toe on this accursed rock. Lower the torch so I can see where I'm going."

The taller one observes, "Well, at least it stopped raining, but the thick clouds obscure any light from above. Do you think he still lives?"

"I do not know. Doubtful. He could've fallen in one of the newly formed openings in the earth. He could have been trampled or even eaten by some foul creature." He takes a tentative step. "Watch where you walk. There are dead birds everywhere."

"I think he may still be alive. I've heard that wizards are tough to kill." He cocks his head. "Wait. Did you hear that?"

"Yes, I did. What do you suppose it is?"

"It came from that direction." He points to his left with his long spear. "Look, something is glowing on the ground."

The two armored knights approach cautiously. There is a soft, white light steadily pulsating ahead.

They continue toward it. "Is that the wizard we seek lying on the ground?"

"It's hard to be sure. You said you've seen him before in the city?"

"Yes, he walked right by me during the wererat incident. But that was during the day and he was walking. He looks different on the ground and it is so dark."

"Look. That large, black creature next to the body...is it a rat?"

The creature meows loudly. Mikal's staff of light lies across his body. Its white glow wanes and waxes, matching the wizard's breathing. Guarding him from further harm stands his large, black cat Majam.

The knights hesitate. "I thought you said he had a white cat. That creature is as black as this night."

"See if he still lives."

The knight puts down his spear and, under the watchful eye of the black cat, he places his left hand on the wizard's shoulder.

"Mikal Novastar, we have been sent by Baron Stannum and Sister Aurum to find and return you to their care."

The wizard's eyes painfully open.

"Can you walk?"

Mikal struggles to sit up. "My head…how it aches." Running his left hand through his red hair, he discovers a sizable lump on the back of his head.

"Here, Master Wizard. Let me help you." The knight carefully lifts Mikal to his feet.

"The world is swimming about me. There, hand me my staff to steady me.

***

The journey back to the witches' cavern is slow and includes many stops for rest. It is well past midnight when the three reach the Witches of Endorr's cave. At its entrance stands Sister Aurum and Baron Stannum.

"We were all so worried," says the young witch, her brow furrowing.

"My head is throbbing and my stomach is uneasy. How fares Sir Rusel? Tell me true."

"First you must sit," directs Sister Aurum. "Let me look at that head of yours. I shall have tea for you presently. It will alleviate your pain and stomach distress." She gently probes the pulsating lump on the back of Mikal's head. The wizard winces even with her gentle touch. She starts to softly hum and then recites a healing spell specially designed for head injuries. An even younger witch enters, carrying a tray upon which rests a cup of steaming tea.

"You have yet to speak of Sir Rusel," Mikal persists.

"We will take you to him presently. But for now, at least taste the tea, please." After taking his second sip, the wizard identifies a strong mint flavor. There is a second taste which he does not recognize.

Mikal, a bit impatiently, declares, "I am pleased to say that my stomach feels better and my head pain has lessened. Now, will you take me to see Sir Rusel?"

With his staff in his left hand, a cup of tea in his right, he is escorted to one of the healing chambers.

"I must prepare you, Mikal. His condition is grave. We have done as much as is possible for him. He drifts in and out of consciousness. He asks about Snow often. We explain to him that she is being treated and should fully recover, and it does seem to bring him some comfort. At times he is delirious and talks to people who are not there."

"Oh, really? Perchance, has he mentioned names?"

Sister Aurum hesitates. "I believe he spoke of a Sir Thoren and, what was the other? I believe it was Sir Balin."

"Curious." Mikal takes another sip of his tea. "I believe those two names are associated with the Paladins from the Wizard Wars of long ago."

Baron Stannum adds, "Yes, I believe you are right. I knew I had heard those names before."

Sister Aurum lightly knocks on a large, green door and opens it. The White Wizard follows his cat inside. In the center of a large room lies Sir Rusel on a featherbed. Placed in front of the footboard is his enchanted rock-encrusted, iron shield. Majam leaps to the foot of the bed. Mikal stares at the unmoving Paladin. A white, linen sheet is draped over him and two healing sisters attend him. One focuses on his mangled shoulder while the other wipes his brow with a cool towel. Two splendidly arrayed knights stand at the head and the foot of the wooden bed.

"These are Honor Guards. It is the least I can do for this brave warrior," explains the Baron. Mikal notices Aden Ferrum and Kairn also in attendance, but set back. The White Wizard puts down his cup of tea and hands his staff to Sister Aurum.

He approaches Sir Rusel, kneels at his side, and whispers close to the Paladin's ear, "Sir Rusel, it is I, Mikal Novastar."

Moments pass. The Paladin's eyes flutter open and focus on the wizard. He tries to smile through broken teeth. "Remember your promise."

Mikal nods. "It will be fulfilled, I swear."

"I wish I had my sword, but my hands do not seem to work well."

Mikal smiles. "You left your sword where it belongs, on the battlefield in your enemy's neck. You have brought honor to yourself, to all Paladins, and to the Land. We are in your debt. I thank you, my friend."

Sir Rusel's eyes roll back and he slips into unconsciousness once again.

The White Wizard stands and asks "Is there nothing we can do for him?"

The Red Wizard steps forward. "Look at him. Even if somehow you could save him, with that ruined shoulder, you would have to take his arm. Look at his hand. There's nothing left of it but a charred husk. A warrior who cannot wield a sword is not a warrior who would wish to live."

Mikal strokes his soft beard. "I hear and understand, Aden, but I still do not want him to die. It is foolish of me, I know but..."

The Baron interrupts, "I side with Master Ferrum."

Sister Aurum looks the White Wizard in the eye. "I wish there was something I could do but it is beyond me."

"Release him to travel and meet his Brothers-in-Arms," says Baron Stannum.

Soon after, Sir Rusel, the fallen Paladin, dies.

Chapter 48

It is mid-morning when the Witches of Endorr start to solemnly file out of their cavern. They are followed by twenty knights in highly polished armor. The last two carry the prepared and cleansed body of Sir Rusel on a pallet supported by their shoulders. Next walks Mikal Novastar and Sister Aurum, closely followed by Aden Ferrum and Kairn. The end of this column consists of coven's servants and guards. No one chooses to stay behind.

The Paladin's body is reverently laid on a newly-constructed litter pulled by the magnificent mare Snow. The Knights mount their steeds. The Baron leads the solemn procession.

Sister Aurum whispers to Mikal, "You fell fast asleep soon after the passing of the Paladin. I gave instructions to the Baron to lead us to the far side of the Valley. There is a small, fast-flowing river which I believe will satisfy your needs."

The wizard nods. "Yes, before I woke this morning I saw this place in my dreams. It will do nicely."

They move in a straight column for some time. Mikal becomes aware of small flocks of colorful birds that fly and swoop and then alight on the pallet, as if paying respect to the Paladin. Some distance off to the right, a huge, black bear shadows the somber march. Other small animals appear and watch intently as the funeral moves across the valley floor.

Noon passes and they do not stop. Again, Sister Aurum turns and speaks softly to the wizard. "Mikal, if you have not noticed, Ebon Usher is lost. We could not find his body anywhere."

Mikal shakes his head slightly. "If the Stone Mage does not want to be found, no one will find him. I am confident he is still alive."

"Another bit of odd news. That white-haired man Sebastian is also missing, though there were two separate sightings of him after the battle. Both reports had him alive but covered with cuts and bruises.

Again, no trace of a body has been found."

The wizard strokes his beard. "That is indeed curious. Let me ponder this news."

For another hour they travel. Different birds come and go, visiting the fallen warrior or even spending time perched on the back of the white horse.

Everyone is dumbfounded when the Baron breaks into song. A young knight with a full, resonant voice joins in the somber, warrior song. Mikal has never heard it before, but it seems very ancient and fitting for the occasion.

The Baron signals and the procession halts. He then directs four knights to find wood and construct a funeral pyre. Soon all is prepared.

With great care, the body of Sir Rusel is lifted and laid to his resting place. A large, black hawk swoops to the ground and morphs into a beautiful, young girl with impossibly long, black hair. Mikal and she acknowledge each other. All the Sisters of Endorr form a circle and raise their hands high to bless the body of the fallen Paladin. They begin singing a hymn that is not a dirge, but a song of thanks, then lower their hands and heads and pause a moment to say their private goodbyes. They then depart.

Sister Aurum and Mikal step forward. The young witch speaks. "No man could be more valiant than Sir Rusel. He gave up his life so that we might have a better one. Henceforth, in our coven, his name will live forever and will be spoken with great reverence."

The White Wizard waits for a moment. "When my need was greatest, Sir Rusel was there. This warrior always wanted to help and protect others. When he was asked to defend the land and face a fearful foe, he did not hesitate. He was honored to be chosen. He won his final battle because he would not allow himself to be defeated. The stakes were too high. I am honored to have met this man. Goodbye, my friend, I miss you sorely."

Mikal lowers his gaze. He is eventually escorted back to the others by Sister Aurum. The twenty armored knights march in unison and form a ring around the Paladin's pyre. Aden Ferrum steps forth and holds his iron staff high. An intense flame erupts from its tip and instantly ignites the dry wood. Even the Knights are forced to take steps back. An inferno of fire surrounds the fallen Paladin. For a moment, it seems like the dancing flame refuses to touch the dead warrior.

The White Wizard's eyes start to swirl and he sees two, seemingly endless columns of phantom warriors regaled in splendid, ancient armor. The flame erupts and now engulfs the fallen Paladin's body. Mikal cannot believe what he sees. Ghostlike, Sir Rusel sits up, unscathed by the burning conflagration. He steps down from the burning wood. Another ghostlike apparition approaches. He presents to Sir Rusel an immaculate, shining sword and shield. The phantom warriors fall to one knee and bow their heads. Sir Rusel accepts the sword and shield and walks among his fallen brethren.

Without thought, the White Wizard taps his staff of light on the ground. It reveals for all that wish to see Sir Rusel escorted away by his brothers-in-arms.

Chapter 49

For some time no one says anything. Eventually, food and drink are brought forth. Most recount and discuss the last twelve hours. The Baron spends time with his daughter. It is mid-afternoon when he approaches the wizard and the witch.

"Master Mikal Novastar, I should return to the city presently, if you think it is safe."

The White Wizard nods. "I sense no evil left in this valley."

"Then would you care to join us?"

"Thank you, Baron, but I must leave tomorrow morning for there is a promise I must fulfill. I am eager to return, though. I am overly concerned about my daughter and my friend Talon. I wonder if you would make inquiries about them."

The Baron bows. "It will be done as soon as I return. Do not worry, we will find them."

Sister Aurum takes the Baron's hand. "We all thank you. Your knights have been most gallant."

"And you are most kind. Please watch over my daughter."

"I shall. Worry not. Your daughter will return in a few months. I have seen it."

The Baron nods and mounts his horse. "Oh, I almost forgot. The young knight with the strong voice has an uncle who is a much respected bard in the City of Stonegrove. We shall relate to him what has transpired here. I daresay the 'Ballad of Sir Rusel Ironwood' will be celebrated across the land."

The Baron prods his horse and leads his twenty knights across the valley floor.

The young witch turns to Mikal. "I have been wondering what your plan is for Snow?"

"I promised Sir Rusel that no matter the outcome, I would see her safely returned to her land. I believe I can accomplish this. We shall prepare the portal then wait for sundown."

The wizard turns to the witch. "Tell me, do you plan to remain at your cavern?"

"I believe so, at least for the present."

"I hope you can reestablish your coven."

"We will. The Valley's curse has been broken and has started its re-growth. Our numbers will increase with it. I have seen it." A frown crosses her face. "Master Mikal, I still find it curious and frustrating that I can see so little of your future or your daughter's. She and Talon are hidden from me. I know you will face the Ebony Wizard, but know that you cannot defeat him alone. Beyond that, I see nothing."

Aden Ferrum interrupts the two. "Excuse me, should we not start to prepare the way of Snow's return?"

Mikal measures the sun in the sky. "I believe you are correct. Let us begin."

They gather large rocks and place them into the river near the bank. Then they gather firewood which they place upon the stones. The witches, their guards, and servants watch with interest.

The White Wizard leads the white horse within a few strides of the stones and firewood. He bends down, grabs wet earth, and paints two black marks on the mare's chest.

"Now, Aden."

The Red Wizard ignites the firewood. Mikal, standing next to the white horse, recites the words that Sir Rusel had imparted to him.

"It is time," and he slaps the horse's flank. She responds with a neigh, but does not approach the water and fire.

"Again," directs Aden.

With greater force, Mikal cuffs the large horse's behind, and yells, "Go, home awaits you."

But the horse will not move. The Red Wizard looks to the sun. "Our time grows short."

Majam meows loudly. Snow lowers her head and turns to the right. The White Wizard's eyes start to swirl. To his amazement, he spies the ghost of Sir Rusel adorned with exceptional armor. A new sword is at his side. He silently strides forward and gently kisses the magnificent mare. She lowers herself to the ground. The reinstated Paladin mounts his white steed. She rises and holds her head high. Sir Rusel nods goodbye to the wizard and his cat. With two strides and a leap, they are gone.

Mikal hears a question from one of the servants. "I wonder where she went."

The White Wizard whispers, "The horse and rider have gone home."

"Rider?"

Majam, who is lying on a sun-warmed boulder licking her front right paw, is instantly on her feet, poised as if to pounce. She glares at the man. His eyes turn blank, his jaw slack.

You saw what I had my Master see.

Satisfied, she resumes licking her front right paw.

One of the guards wades into the river. "I heard no splash."

Aden laughs. "Because there was none. We sent the horse home."

After the excitement dies down, all decide to spend the night camped under the stars by the river. A pleasant, uneventful evening ensues.

On the morn, they return to the witches' dwelling. After gathering some supplies Kairn, Aden, and Mikal mount their horses that they received in the City of Stonegrove.

"Well, this is goodbye for now, Mikal," says Sister Aurum. "I pray that you are soon reunited with your daughter and Talon. I wish you a safe journey. Do you have everything?"

Mikal searches the many concealed pockets of his traveling robe. His fingers brush the contour of the ancient text he found in the tunnels under the silver lake. He frowns and begins to frantically check his others pockets.

"What is it?" asks Sister Aurum.

The White Wizard looks at the young head-witch. "This does not bode well. My black blade is missing. I cannot have lost it. Someone has stolen it! But who and for what purpose is another mystery I must solve; and soon."

"I have every confidence that you will," says the young head-witch.

"Bass turds," says the one-armed dwarf.

ADDENDUM

In the first draft of our book, the following dialogue took place in the early pages between Mikal and his mentor Wizard Whitestone. We edited it out because it occurred to us that if it remained some readers might think that they needed to read our first novel The Way of the Wandering Wizard in order to enjoy this one, and that is not the case. Here it is in its entirety.

"Mikal, tell me, did you ever imagine all the things that happened after you walked by my farm those many weeks ago? You made new friends: Talon the half-elf, poor Brian Quickhands, Fox and Hawk. You had run-ins with the Macrophage and were later befriended by them. From what I understand, you may have even influenced the way they view the world. Impressive.

"And the Stone Mage you encountered, Ebon Usher. I believe I might have gone to school with him. It was so very long ago. If I remember correctly, it was he and three others who were always asking different questions in class: what if… could you… is it ethical? They exasperated many of the professors at the School of the Three Moons, I can assure you.

"Then, just before they were to be graduated, they all just slipped away into the night. Rumors circulated for weeks, but no one knew where they had gone. You have said that Ebon lost track of the others. I wonder what became of them. He is slowly turning into stone and has accepted his fate? Truly remarkable.

"Meeting the Dragon Em-Le must have been fascinating. You even performed a quest in her name. How I envy you. She sounds like an extremely intriguing creature, very intelligent. And you are correct that she experiences the world differently than we. I would love someday to meet her.

"But I'm most envious of Evalon the Earth Princess. I've heard stories about her for some time and I believe she is a harbinger of hope, a powerful force for good. I have a strong conviction that you will meet her again. In fact, I believe she will play a significant role in your future.

"And who could forget Jocomund, and Sir Grey, and Penelope, and... listen to me babble. I have become a foolish old man."

"Never. Not if you live another hundred years."

They continue in silence.

Mikal eventually says, "I am concerned about what has become of Brian Quickhands."

"Do you fear for his life?"

"Not necessarily. I do worry about his livelihood, however. A thief without fingers is a poor thief indeed."

"But why would Bass Molar wish to lessen Brian Guinness' profitable talents? In any event, I do have informants in the city of Umbra and hope to be hearing from them soon. With any luck, what they have to report will ease your mind."

Mikal is far from convinced.